Past Praise for Mary Connealy

"Enough twists to keep Connealy's fans on the edge of their seats. Readers will be captivated from the first page to the last."

Publishers Weekly on *Toward the Dawn*

"With a vivid setting, compelling characters, and a suspenseful, thought-provoking story, this book will please fans of inspirational historical romance."

Booklist on *Chasing the Horizon*

"Connealy's lively writing keeps the reader fully engaged. A sure bet for readers who enjoy books by such inspirational western authors as Amanda Cabot and Tracie Peterson."

Booklist starred review on *The Laws of Attraction*

"Connealy kicks off the WYOMING SUNRISE series with a spirited, suspenseful romance . . . a richly detailed adventure that captivates till the end."

Publishers Weekly on *Forged in Love*

"The first in Connealy's WYOMING SUNRISE series offers strong female characters and a richly developed historical backdrop."

Booklist on *Forged in Love*

Whispers of Fortune

Books by Mary Connealy

THE KINCAID BRIDES
Out of Control
In Too Deep
Over the Edge

TROUBLE IN TEXAS
Swept Away
Fired Up
Stuck Together

WILD AT HEART
Tried and True
Now and Forever
Fire and Ice

THE CIMARRON LEGACY
No Way Up
Long Time Gone
Too Far Down

HIGH SIERRA SWEETHEARTS
The Accidental Guardian
The Reluctant Warrior
The Unexpected Champion

BRIDES OF HOPE MOUNTAIN
Aiming for Love
Woman of Sunlight
Her Secret Song

BROTHERS IN ARMS
Braced for Love
A Man with a Past
Love on the Range

THE LUMBER BARON'S DAUGHTERS
The Element of Love
Inventions of the Heart
A Model of Devotion

WYOMING SUNRISE
Forged in Love
The Laws of Attraction
Marshaling Her Heart

A WESTERN LIGHT
Chasing the Horizon
Toward the Dawn
Into the Sunset

GOLDEN STATE TREASURE
Whispers of Fortune

The Boden Birthright:
A CIMARRON LEGACY Novella
(All for Love *Collection*)

Meeting Her Match: A MATCH
MADE IN TEXAS Novella

Runaway Bride: A KINCAID BRIDES
and TROUBLE IN TEXAS Novella
(With This Ring? *Collection*)

The Tangled Ties That Bind:
A KINCAID BRIDES Novella
(Hearts Entwined *Collection*)

GOLDEN STATE TREASURE · 1

Whispers of Fortune

MARY CONNEALY

BETHANY HOUSE

a division of Baker Publishing Group
Minneapolis, Minnesota

Published by Bethany House Publishers
Minneapolis, Minnesota
BethanyHouse.com

Bethany House Publishers is a division of
Baker Publishing Group, Grand Rapids, Michigan

Printed in the United States of America

Library of Congress Cataloging-in-Publication Data
Names: Connealy, Mary, author.
Title: Whispers of fortune / Mary Connealy.
Description: Minneapolis, Minnesota : Bethany House, a division of Baker
    Publishing Group, 2025. | Series: Golden State Treasure ; 1
Identifiers: LCCN 2024017589 | ISBN 9780764244391 (paperback) | ISBN
    9780764244506 (casebound) | ISBN 9781493448883 (ebook)
Subjects: LCGFT: Christian fiction. | Novels.
Classification: LCC PS3603.O544 W54 2025 | DDC 813/.6—dc23/eng/20240429
LC record available at https://lccn.loc.gov/2024017589

Scripture quotations are from the King James Version of the Bible.

This is a work of fiction. Names, characters, incidents, and dialogues are products of the author's imagination and are not to be construed as real. Any resemblance to actual events or persons, living or dead, is entirely coincidental.

Cover design by Dan Thornberg, Design Source Creative Services
Cover image of man by Miguel Sobreira / Arcangel

Baker Publishing Group publications use paper produced from sustainable forestry practices and postconsumer waste whenever possible.

25 26 27 28 29 30 31   7 6 5 4 3 2 1

To my cowboy husband

You're retired now, but you'll always
be a cowboy at heart.

ONE

June 1874

A fist slamming against the door startled Beth Ellen Hart. She shrieked and dropped the china bowl she was washing, which shattered on the floor.

"Get out here! I want answers!" a man's voice shouted. He sounded furious.

Gretel came running into the room. They exchanged frightened looks.

Ellie grabbed the gun Zane kept on the top shelf of the kitchen cupboard.

The shouting and slamming went on as Ellie marched to the kitchen door, determined to drive off whoever was assaulting her house. That was her favorite bowl!

"Wait!" Gretel rushed to her side, snatched up the Winchester 73 rifle from over the back door and stepped to the side. "Stay out of my line of fire."

Ellie nodded, then shoved back the latch on the door and jerked it open. The stranger's fist, which had been aiming at the door, missed hitting her in the nose by inches. She ducked out of the way so swiftly she fell over backward. Her gun went sailing.

A cracking sound from behind her was Gretel cocking Zane's Winchester.

The man stepped into the kitchen and reached down for Ellie.

"*Zuruckbleiben du, schmutzig schurke,*" she said.

He opened his mouth, probably to shout some more, then clamped his jaw shut. Gretel tended to lapse into German under stress, and that drew his attention—that and the rifle pointed at his chest. He straightened away from Ellie and stared at Gretel.

Ellie scrambled to her feet, ran for the gun she'd dropped, and aimed it again at the man, who stood there looking addled. She was well away from Gretel, so they had him at the point of a triangle.

Ellie had no idea what Gretel had said but could guess and added her own warning. "Get off my land."

The man was not overly tall, five-foot-nine or so, with dark curly hair under an odd, round hat with a narrow brim. He wore a dusty suit of clothes that looked to be many years old. Clean-shaven with blue eyes that shot lightning at her.

He saw the guns and didn't attack if that was his plan.

"Where are my brothers?" He was still mad, snapping at them, face taut and fists clenched. But he stayed put. "I'm not leaving here without them."

That was when Josh stepped up behind the man. "Do I need to send for the sheriff?"

It was a bluff. The sheriff would be unable to get to their ranch for about an hour, and that was if they sent a man for Dorada Rio, the closest town to their northern California ranch, on a galloping horse, found the sheriff immediately and rode straight back at full speed. And Ellie wasn't about to hold this man at gunpoint for that long.

"Talk, mister," Ellie said. "What do you mean barging into my house like this?"

"He punched Ellie, Josh. Knocked her to the floor." Gretel's hands trembled on the heavy rifle.

Josh shoved the man forward. "Sit down."

He took the gun from Gretel and pointed the barrel toward the floor. "You punched my sister?"

"I don't want to sit down. And no, I did *not* punch your sister. I was knocking on the door. She pulled it open and was in the way. I—"

"You're not going to tell me that my sister hit you right in your fist with her face, are you?" Josh said it as if he were the very voice of doom.

"I did not hit her—I would *never* hit a woman. She ducked and stumbled back and fell." The man's blue eyes shifted to Ellie. "Tell him I didn't hit you."

Ellie enjoyed a very sweet moment letting him sweat as he looked between her and her tall, blond Viking of a brother. She had the same Nordic coloring as him but was built with finer lines, thank heaven. But truth was truth. She didn't need to add reasons to think ill of the man. He was awful enough.

"He was pounding on the door when I opened it." She looked at Josh and caught a spark of humor in his eyes. "His fist came right at me with no intent to punch me. I ducked and fell just like he said. He never touched me."

"Give me my brothers now, and I'll be glad to get off your stinking land. We're leaving California and heading home to New York."

They all turned back to the disheveled, antagonistic man.

Ellie had some notion of what he might mean, yet it galled

her to cooperate. "What are your brothers' names? And don't think we're going to let some stranger come riding in here and leave with our boys."

"*Our* boys?" The man's eyes narrowed. "They're *my* boys. My brothers' names are Thayne and Lochlan Mac—"

"MacKenzie?" Ellie's heart sped up. She rested a hand on her heart. "Those boys are your brothers?"

"They're here then?" His breath whooshed out, and he bent forward as if he might collapse. "I'm Brody MacKenzie. You took my brothers off the streets of San Francisco. I'm here to take them back with me."

Ellie lowered her gun and stared at Mr. Brody MacKenzie. "I'm Beth Ellen Hart. I go by Ellie. This is my brother, Josh, and the woman who aimed that rifle at you is Gretel Steinmeyer."

"We have over two dozen children here at our school," Josh said, setting the rifle back on the pegs over the door. "Every one of them orphans. If those boys are your brothers, then why were they living on the streets?"

"And hungry," Ellie added, hands propped on her hips. "Wearing nothing but rags."

"Cold. Soaked through from the winter rain," Josh went on.

"Uneducated." Ellie glared at the man.

"Unwanted." Josh crossed his arms tight over his chest.

"Unloved, even by their brother," Ellie said. "That is, if you *are* their brother."

"I am their brother. They ran off—I've been searching for them."

She could see as much. The man wasn't a spitting image, but similar enough, especially similar to Thayne, even down to the Scottish brogue in the way he talked. "If you weren't

12

taking care of them before, how are we to believe you'll begin taking care of them now?"

Brody's shoulders sagged, and he sank into a chair at the kitchen table. He rubbed his hands over his face. "They're alive and well? Were they bad off when you found them?" Then his temper flared. "What are you doing with them, them and all the children you sweep up off the streets as if you think they're trash? Are you forcing them to work on your ranch? If they've signed anything, indentured papers and the like, I'll fight you in court. They're too young to sign—"

"Stop talking before you make a bigger fool of yourself than you already have." Josh stepped to the door and said to Ellie, "Let's take him out to see these boys we're forcing into labor." He jabbed a finger out the door. "But you're not riding off with them until you convince us they'll be safe with you this time. Because they sure as certain weren't safe with you before when they slipped by your notice and managed the journey alone all the way to California from New York. Lead the way, Ellie."

Ellie stepped up to look closer at Brody MacKenzie. She saw it in his eyes, a shine that could've been tears. Relief that he'd found them? He seemed to care about his brothers. At least right now he did. But Josh had the right of it, and she hardened her heart against feeling any sympathy for Brody. He was going to have to convince her before she let those two troublemaking scamps out of her sight.

———— ✦ ————

His brothers. It had to be them. He hoped and prayed and kept the tears from falling through sheer grit.

Brody followed the woman. Ellie Hart. She had on a pretty yellow calico dress that almost matched the yellow of her hair. He'd hardly looked around when he came riding in wild with fear, which he covered with anger.

"You know, this ranch is notorious in San Francisco for snatching up children and hauling them away, never to be heard from again."

The woman, Ellie, glanced back over her shoulder, then looked on past him. "We're notorious, Josh."

A faint chuckle sounded from behind Brody. "I can't wait to tell Zane he's known as a kidnapper and child-enslaver. That oughta make him mad."

"Michelle will calm him down, I expect."

Both of them laughed.

Brody listened to the back and forth at the same time he rounded the house, a nice-sized ranch house, and gazed past the huge barn to see sheds and more houses and a big whitewashed building two stories high. Every structure was well built. The houses had gardens out front with fences encircling modest yards. A prosperous ranch that almost looked like some of the small towns he'd visited.

Horses grazed in a corral. Chickens pecked at the ground behind a wire fence. He smelled hogs but didn't see them, but they could be behind any one of a dozen outbuildings. And spread out over miles of rolling grassland, he saw red cows with white faces, grazing and fat and contented.

But it was the big building that drew him.

Ellie must have noticed, though she seemed to be walking fast, her attention averted.

He, of course, was focused on the house and not paying the pretty blond woman with the sassy attitude any mind.

"Your brothers are most likely in class. Though they've been known to sneak off and not return until mealtime." This time she looked at him with a single arched brow.

"It's them all right. Those two are hard to keep ahead of. I shoulda known better than to go off to college. They were too much for Ma, and heaven knows Pa was no help."

That earned him a sharp look, but she didn't say why. Probably blamed him for abandoning them. Fair enough. He blamed himself.

Ellie reached the door and swung it open to complete silence.

It was a school. He could smell it. Chalk dust and books and, well, he couldn't say what else exactly. He just knew a school when he smelled one. They stepped into a wide hall lined with several doors in a row straight across from him and two sets of stairs leading to the left and the right.

"The upper floor has bedrooms. Several children in each room and bunk beds. We call it a dormitory. The boys on the right, the girls on the left. The upstairs are divided so there's no access between the two sides without coming down here. Most rooms are for three or four, but your brothers stay in a room where it's just the two of them. That's because we aren't full."

His brothers had always shared a room more fit for a closet, and when Brody was home, he slept in there with them. The two of them in a room big enough for four would be the finest place they'd ever stayed.

Ellie continued, "The children are in special individualized classes this time of day." She pointed to the door farthest to the right. "Morning is four grades divided up by age, the afternoon targeted to each child's skills. Thayne has shown an unusual gift for math and science. He focuses on that in his afternoon classes, with a few related subjects like physics and calculus."

Thayne, his impish sixteen-year-old brother, had a talent

for arithmetic? How had they gotten him to sit still long enough to find that out?

"And Lochlan is fascinated by geography. He's always studying maps and asking questions about the world at large."

Now, that sounded like Brody's fourteen-year-old brother. He was searching for MacKenzie's Treasure. He probably loved geography because reading a map might lead him to a gold mine, though it never had for their pa.

"We keep the rooms quiet, Brody." Ellie spoke softly as she reached for the doorknob to the right. "I'll go get your brothers and bring them out. My older sister, Annie, is their teacher for this session, which this late in the day will be special skills. Be very quiet. Annie believes that teaching the children to direct their own studies, work independently, and most of all control themselves are the main goals of a teacher."

She opened the door. Though Brody kept quiet, he was standing right there and saw Lochlan in plain view right in front of him.

Lochlan saw him. His eyes went wide. He leapt to his feet, screamed, and jumped a full foot off the floor. "Brody! Thayne, come quick—Brody's here!" He turned to the room and shouted, "My brother is here!"

Brody took one second to see the severely annoyed face of the teacher and winced, but only for a second because his brothers came charging at him, and he found himself overcome with happiness and relief.

His brothers' boots thundered across the floor. There was an eruption of talking and excited laughter from the schoolroom. Then they hit Brody so hard he'd've fallen if he hadn't staggered into Josh. Josh kept him from going down under the onslaught.

And then Brody held them. His brothers. Alive and well. "I found you! Thayne, Lochlan . . . thank God, thank God."

His brothers, now nearly full grown, were all right. And now Brody had another chance to do things right. Be a good big brother. Show these two he loved them and wanted to take care of them.

TWO

Annie came toward the back of the room.

Ellie flinched at the fire in her sister's eyes. Annie liked order and ran things very tightly in her class. Ellie envied her that skill, one she herself did not possess.

Right now, the whole class was a flurry of whispering, with students of all ages standing and craning their necks, trying to see what was going on. Not a single one of those ten boys was studying, and Annie would have her hands full getting their minds back on their work.

Every orphan child, or so Ellie believed, dreamed of finding his family. Dreamed that someone out there, a ma or a pa, maybe even a brother, might now be searching for them. It was a wild dream without much hope behind it, yet it had just come true for the MacKenzie boys.

They had sure enough disrupted class. But Ellie could hardly fault the boys for their excitement.

Then Annie reached the door, looked out at the hugging trio, and her expression softened.

Ellie said quietly, "That's Brody MacKenzie. He's been hunting his little brothers."

Nodding, but with the look Annie sometimes got when

her motherly sentiment was awakened, she smiled and then pulled the door shut.

Ellie wished her luck with getting the class to settle down.

Josh picked Brody's hat up off the floor, looked at it with disdain, then took charge of the MacKenzies. "Come on back to the house, and we'll figure out what to do with you."

Ellie bit back a smile. Her brother liked to take charge, maybe because he didn't get much chance to do so. When their oldest brother, Zane, was around, he ran things—so long as he could move fast enough that his wife, Michelle, didn't take over.

Annie Hart Lane was the oldest of the four Hart children. A widow and mother, she'd been on her own for several years before her husband was killed and she moved back home. No one could tell her what to do. Then came Josh, a mighty tall and tough former sailor who'd lived away from home for a long time and seen the world. It wasn't exactly easy being a little brother.

That left Ellie, the youngest of them. Out of pity for the poor guy, Ellie did her best to mind her big brother, but honestly it was only to make him happy. She didn't need anyone ordering her around.

The MacKenzies stopped hugging and started talking. Josh got them moving, but it was all stop-and-start with more talking and hugging interrupting their progress.

She caught snippets of the rapid talk. They were from New York, and she'd heard they were a fast-talking breed from back east.

"The journal told us California, but—"

"But then we jumped onto a train that was already rolling—"

"Real orphans could have found homes if you hadn't—"

"How's Pa?"

The three of them fell silent at Thayne's question.

Brody looked at both of them. "You knew he was sick when you left."

"Brown-bottle sick, not real sick." Lochlan continued toward the house, where Josh was steering them.

Lochlan's offhand quip about a brown bottle told Ellie a lot about their messed-up family situation.

"Pa died."

Thayne and Lochlan stumbled to a stop and turned to stare at Brody.

Thayne broke the silence first. "B-because we left him alone?"

Lochlan reached out and caught Brody's arm. "He was always yelling at us. Throwing us out of the house till we hardly lived there. We came home late at night to sleep. He didn't cook for us, nor for himself."

"We brought him a loaf of bread or whatever we could . . ." Thayne glanced at Ellie. "Uh, whatever we could find."

She was quite sure he meant whatever he could *steal*.

Thayne went on. "He swore he was done with the journal for good. He meant it this time."

"He always meant it," Brody said quietly.

"But this time," Lochlan said, sounding distraught, "he threw Grandpa's journal into the stove."

"He burned the journal?" Brody's brows arched nearly to his hairline. "He must've really meant it then."

"Stove wasn't lit." Lochlan shook his head in wonder, but at what? At his father throwing a journal away? Grandpa's journal? What was in it? Ellie had never seen a journal. "He'd never done that before. Anyway, I fished it out of the stove."

"He started screaming at us, Brody." Thayne sounded

grim as death. "He threw a chair at us. When it broke, he picked up a leg and threatened to use it on us. He as good as drove us out of the room and told us not to come back."

Elle had the sudden sick feeling that she and Josh shouldn't be listening to this. The MacKenzies were so caught up in their talk that they were saying things she suspected they'd rather not speak of in front of anyone else. The boys certainly hadn't spoken like this up until now.

They'd come along when Michelle had found them at the Child of God Mission, giving her a sad tale of living in San Francisco all their lives, with no home since their pa had run off and their ma had died. Two boys almost too old to count as orphans, especially Thayne. Plenty of sixteen-year-old boys were on their own, doing a man's work.

They ran off from the mission at least once a week, Sister Agatha had told Michelle. They had no change of clothes. Hungry and cold in the late spring. They'd been here two months now, midsummer in California, no mention of a brother or a father—who had clearly been alive when the boys left him.

No mention of anything about their past. And no sign of a journal. They were talking about it now. They clearly had it, but they'd been very sneaky. If they'd ever looked at it, it'd been done in secret.

That was exactly like them. Bright, hardworking scamps right down to the bone. Lochlan, the younger of the two, was the worst. But Thayne was always ready to throw in with whatever Lochlan cooked up.

They'd run away twice now and been gone two days the first time, then four the next. Both disappearances had thrown the whole ranch into chaos as search parties spread out looking for them. Both times they hadn't been found.

They'd come home voluntarily. Near as Ellie could tell because they'd gotten hungry.

They all reached the house and went inside.

"Can we have something to eat, Miss Ellie? We're starving." Lochlan often did the talking for the two. And they were always starving. But it was near the end of the school day, and Annie always saw that they got a snack.

"I've got chicken in the icebox, and you can have bread and jelly."

Lochlan leapt into the air, both arms high. "I love fried chicken. And can it be apple jelly please? Do you have any?"

Ellie looked at Brody over the tops of the boys' heads. Though it was as well Thayne was a bit ahead because he was as tall as Brody.

He rolled his eyes.

She said, "Growing boys." Then she got busy pulling out the chicken.

Josh came in a pace behind her and went straight to the coffeepot, which was simmering on the stove.

"Grab a seat. We need to talk." Josh grabbed the heavy pottery cups. "Coffee, Brody, or do you want milk? You're probably hungry."

"Coffee sounds good."

The MacKenzies sat with a great scraping of chairs.

"I'd take milk, please," Thayne said with decent manners.

"Me too. I want milk." Lochlan was always a little slower, but he came through when Ellie caught Brody glaring at him.

"Please." Lochlan grinned at his brother. "It's so great to see you, Brody. We gave up on you ever coming home."

"I hadn't had a letter the whole school year, and I wrote plenty."

Lochlan and Thayne exchanged a look. "Ma died early

last fall. She was the one who always wrote to you, I s'pose. Thayne and me got jobs."

"You quit going to school?" Brody sounded dismayed.

Ellie was busy getting out the butter and jelly from the icebox and pulling bread out of the clever roll-top bread box. She got things set on the table and did her best not to miss a word or a frown or even a shrug. She sat at the foot of the table, Josh at the head. Brody sat across from his brothers. It seemed she was learning more about these boys in a few minutes than she had for months.

The boys were clearing the table of food at top speed, to the point Ellie got herself a cup of coffee, refilled Josh's and Brody's cups and didn't even try to eat, for she was afraid she'd have to fight the boys for a single crumb.

"Let's get you boys packed up. It's a long hike to the nearest town, and I didn't bring extra horses. But you can ride double on the one I rented. I'll walk. If we head out now, we can be in town to—"

"You're not going anywhere," Ellie interrupted.

"We aren't letting the boys walk off into the night." Josh set his cup down with a loud click.

"What kind of brother are you?" Ellie rose from the table, glaring at Brody.

He got a mule-stubborn look in his eyes. Ellie had dealt with her brothers plenty of times, so she recognized it.

"I'm the kind who wants my family reunited. Thank you for taking care of them." He sounded stilted and not all that thankful. "I've got a job waiting for me in Boston. I made some promises, and I have to return. I was planning to get you boys and Ma and move there. Now we'll go without her." Sadness crept into Brody's voice. "I could have made all of your lives so much better. Now Ma won't get that."

23

He squared his shoulders and lifted his chin. "Once we're there, I'll get the boys settled into school, then go to work and support us all."

"You're not going anywhere."

Ellie figured, based on that mule look, that they'd have a fight on their hands keeping the MacKenzies here, but then Lochlan said, "We like it here, Brody. We want to stay."

Brody's mulish face melted into hurt as his head snapped around to look at his younger brother. "You don't want to go with me?"

Lochlan reached across the table and patted Brody clumsily on the hand as if trying to soften the rejection. He knocked his milk cup over, but it was empty now, and Josh caught it before it rolled onto the floor. "We'd be glad to get a visit from you now and then."

Brody seemed frozen, gaping at his brothers. Finally, almost as if he were breaking ice, he turned his neck unsteadily, looked at Ellie, and said quietly, "Is there somewhere I can talk to my brothers alone?"

—— ✧ ——

"This is your room?"

Lock smiled and sat on the bed so hard that he bounced. "Best room I've ever slept in, Brody."

Thayne dropped onto his back on the bed. Both were bunkbeds, and his brothers were on the bottom bunks. Ellie had said they sometimes slept three or four to a room, but several of the boys had grown out of school and left to get jobs. His brothers had a room to themselves. There was a single desk and chair. Brody took the chair, dragged it to the foot of the beds, and sat so he could face his cheerful brothers.

24

Lock lay down as if he were ready for a nap.

Brody heard thundering footsteps outside the door.

"School is out." Thayne folded his hands behind his head. "There's always food after class—besides breakfast, dinner, and supper. A snack after supper, too, if we want it. Bread and butter and milk. Sometimes cookies. But we've just eaten, so let's stay in here and talk awhile."

"Is this an orphanage?" Brody didn't quite understand what the Harts were up to.

"It's sort of an orphanage, I guess. It's honestly more like a boarding school. They work with several orphanages in San Francisco to give street kids a warm place to stay with plenty of food." Thayne added sheepishly, "I think they're mad at us a little for claiming to be orphans when we had a family."

"Tell us about Pa." Lock wanted to change the subject away from their lies, but Brody was sure they wanted to know what had happened back in New York.

"He was alive when I got home. I was frantic with worry for you two, but I had to stay and care for him. Then bury him."

Thayne flushed and moved his hands so they were clutched over his belly. "We couldn't stay, Brody. He wouldn't let us. He as good as drove us out of the place."

Lock swung his feet off the bed and sat up. The bunk overhead was just a bit low, so he had to lean forward to not conk himself in the head. He rested his forearms on his knees and clasped his hands together. "We could have gone back. He was drinking and out of his head. But he'd've passed out, and we could have gone back. We'd done it plenty of times before."

Brody hated thinking of how hard Pa had made the boys' lives.

"But by then we were good at living on the street." Thayne thudded his hands on his belly, slowly, steadily. "Finding food as best we could. We were alone after Ma died for a month or two, before Pa came back. So we'd been living like that for a while. We could find work sometimes, carrying packages and holding carriage horses for freighters. With the money you sent, we kept the rent paid and had enough food to survive. We knew you were coming home in the spring and thought we'd just hang on until you got there. We'd met some of the boys who lived on their own on the streets and teamed up with them."

"They taught us how to get by. Which diners tossed out food." Lock paused, looked at Brody too long, then shrugged and said, "How to pick pockets and steal a bit from street vendors and such places. Talking to them is how we found out about the orphan train, and we wanted to go west, see if we could make sense of Grandpa's journal."

Body's jaw tensed, but he didn't speak of the lies and thieving and the mad run to California. Didn't scold them. "I should have come home. I knew when Ma stopped writing, something had happened. But I was so close to done, and Ma always wanted me to finish. I sent money—"

"We got it, Brody, and it made the difference in keeping the room and getting by till Pa came home. Then he got it."

"And spent it on drinking." Brody rubbed his forehead.

Neither of them responded, but they didn't need to.

"Pa was alive when you got there?" Thayne asked.

"Yep, but barely," Brody said. "He could hardly get out of bed. I knew enough from my schooling that I figured he had pneumonia and was sure he didn't have long. I couldn't just leave him. I should have come after you right away. I did search for you and heard about the orphan train. You were on their list of children that had been sent west."

"We used our real names. But we didn't tell Pa or leave word anywhere. We didn't know how to do that. We figured if you got home and wondered about us, you might track us down."

"An orphan train? And you ran from it?"

"Sure, we had no interest in being adopted. We climbed off the train in Cheyenne, Wyoming. We were told if no one adopted us there, we'd have to go back to New York. The lady riding with us, Miss Tilda, was nice and real worried about how no one would adopt us." Lock shook his head. "We picked just the right moment and then slipped into the baggage car. And off we went. We hid from the conductors all the way to California. That's where the journal told us to go."

"That stupid journal."

Lock surged to his feet, lifted the mattress on the top bunk, and pulled out the journal. An old thing, leather-covered. Inside it were pages and pages of their grandfather's scrawled notes.

"We made it to San Francisco and heard . . ." Lock glanced at the door behind Brody and lowered his voice. "We heard about a family who takes in street kids, brings them to their ranch, teaches them and cares for them and helps them get a good start in life. And it was halfway across the state of California."

Lock shook the journal at Brody's face. "Real close to where Grandpa MacKenzie's journal says to go."

"That's where you ran off to the two times you disappeared? You're trying to follow the notes Grandpa left?"

Lock, his light brown eyes sparkling with excitement, nodded. Lock was the image of Pa, from his blond good looks to his restless, reckless heart.

Thayne, blue-eyed and dark-haired like Brody and Ma, was calmer but no less determined. They'd been raised on stories of the lost MacKenzie's Treasure.

"Did you talk to Pa? Did he try to throw you out, too, or did he just hate us?" Thayne, always more thoughtful than Lock, frowned until his brow furrowed. "Never could figure out why Pa took us in such dislike—he wasn't like that before."

"He wasn't thinking right. His mind was addled. He didn't seem to know who I was at first. He didn't throw me out, but then he didn't have the strength to do such a thing. Once I got home, he quit getting out of bed. As if now that he had help, there was no need for him to do a single thing for himself."

"We told him Ma died. Maybe that set him against us." Lock couldn't keep the grief out of his voice. Pa had always favored him over Brody and Thayne. To the extent Pa cared about anyone, he cared about Lock, probably because his youngest son listened to his tales of treasure with rapt attention.

As if Pa abandoning them, leaving his wife and sons to provide for the family, made him a great hero instead of absolutely worthless.

Brody didn't know what to say. His pa had been terrible when Brody got home. Furious and hateful toward his sons, Brody included. But it was all jumbled, and part of the time he was raging at Ma, who'd been dead for months.

Pa had been brought so low, he allowed himself to be cared for. He demanded that Brody buy him liquor, and Brody refused, which made the ranting worse. But even if he'd been so inclined, Brody had no money. With Pa to care for, he couldn't work. He'd borrowed money from the doctor, who'd given him a job on the promise that Brody would return and work the money off. Brody had been very careful with that bit of cash, kept a roof over their heads until Pa was dead and buried. He'd written to Dr. Tibbles in Boston that he'd be delayed, then set out to find his brothers.

"I want you boys to come away with me. I have to go back. Like I said before, I made promises. I owe a very kind doctor money. I gave my word I'd collect my family and be back. He knew it might take some time, but he had no idea I'd come from New York City to Boston by way of California. I've written to him and told him I might be delayed for a long time, but I would be back."

"Brody, no, we're the closest we've ever been to MacKenzie's Treasure."

He saw the mutinous expression on Lock's face. Thayne left off lying around, sat up, his chin jutted out in a stubborn scowl. "We're close. I know it."

"It's all just a dream, Thayne. Pa searched for years and never found a trace of the gold. And Grandpa's writing is strange, like he was confused—"

"Not confused, Brody. He was deliberately being secretive. He wrote down enough, but it's in a sort of code."

"No, Lock, it isn't. We've all read that book." Brody admitted to himself that he'd barely looked through it, and that was years ago. He believed the journal had ruined Ma's life and led to Brody's little sister Theresa's death. He'd always hated it. "It's nonsense. There are tales of gold hoards lost all over the Rocky Mountains. Not one of them is true. I have to go back, and you gotta go with me. I want you to stop living in Pa's feverish dreams."

"We want to stay here."

Brody rolled over Lock's protests. "You can go to school—"

"We're not—"

A firm knock on the door cut off Lock's angry refusal to cooperate.

"It's Ellie. Please join us in the house for the evening meal. It's ready in just a few minutes, and we'd like to talk more with you."

All three of them clamped their mouths shut. They didn't have to tell the whole world what was behind their foolish run across the country.

Lock tucked the journal back under his mattress. He moved so fast, Brody was sure he'd done it many times before.

Brody approved of not speaking of it because it was an embarrassment. But as for Lock and Thayne, he knew they didn't want anyone to know their secret.

Brody stood from his chair, which nearly blocked the door, then opened it to see that Ellie had changed from the earlier yellow calico to a better dress, bright blue with lace at her neck and wrists. The blue matched her eyes and made them shine.

"We appreciate that, Miss Hart." He wasn't sure what he'd called her earlier. Had he even said her name? He'd been so angry, then so relieved, it was all a bit muddled.

"Please, everyone in the house is named Hart. My name is Beth Ellen, but I prefer Ellie, and I'm trying to train my family to say it. Call me Ellie."

"And a lot of MacKenzies in here. Call me Brody." Brody caught himself smiling at her and wondered how long it'd been since a single moment in his life had inspired a smile.

Ellie stretched her neck to look around him. "Ready to eat, boys? It's a bit early, but Josh, Annie, and I feel we should have a nice long talk with all three of you and then decide what happens next."

There was nothing to decide. Brody was taking his brothers and leaving. So the talk wouldn't be long, and it probably wouldn't be nice.

His brothers pushed past him, as if they hadn't eaten since dawn, and they probably still had crumbs on their faces.

"It looks like the answer is yes, Ellie. Thank you." Brody pulled the door shut behind him and walked alongside Ellie toward the house.

The boys were flat-out running. When had they ever not been starving?

THREE

The meal was ready. There'd been chicken for lunch and plenty of it. Three extra men for a snack hadn't dented the supply.

Gretel had a mountain of mashed potatoes and creamy chicken gravy, while the garden had supplied them with peas and baby carrots and lettuce. There was corn bread instead of the usual biscuits or baked loaves, with molasses to pour over it. And Gretel had made three pies, which were just now coming out of the oven. She'd baked two to leave here, it seemed, because she made up a basket and took food away with her, along with two little children.

It appeared that the Harts cleaned up their own kitchen.

Brody didn't like to admit it, but he'd been starving more often than not for months. Paying the rent on their tiny apartment had taken almost everything he had.

The bit he had extra he'd spent sparingly, thinking of what it might take to find his brothers. As it was, he'd known the boys would head for California, using the journal as a guide. Beyond that, Brody didn't know much, and he had almost no money. He'd hidden in a few baggage cars, and after getting tossed from one by a heavy-fisted conductor, had ridden shotgun on three stagecoaches. That had been a nerve-racking job because he was no hand with a gun.

He'd had to stop in some little town just as he'd crossed into California because there was no stagecoach, and no way to sneak on the train. He'd found work at the general store, prying open wooden crates and stocking shelves. He'd carried heavy loads to wagons and sometimes carried things home for elderly ladies.

He'd been at it two weeks, with very little food, asking questions about his brothers before he knew two boys matching his brothers' descriptions had been seen around town, then headed out west. Finally, he scraped together the price of a train ticket to San Francisco. Every second of his trip west he'd been increasingly frantic about his missing brothers. Then in San Francisco, he'd been hunting high and low for his brothers until he'd found the Child of God Mission. And that pointed him right here.

In short, the growling of his stomach embarrassed him, and he tried to wait patiently while Josh said the mealtime prayer. Then Brody passed the food like a civilized man, even as he wanted to dive headfirst into the bowl of steaming whipped potatoes with the melting butter in its center.

Josh was at the head of the table just like when Brody had arrived. This time Ellie was on his left, with Annie at the end with her little girl Brody heard called Caroline. Brody sat directly across from Lock, while Ellie faced Thayne.

"We aren't going to be able to let you leave with the boys, Brody." Ellie said it quietly while Brody had his mouth full of potatoes.

That was no coincidence.

As he struggled to swallow, his brothers cheered.

"You can stay here with us, Brody," Lock said, almost

buzzing with excitement. "The school is always looking for teachers."

Finally, his mouth empty so he wouldn't choke, and hurt by his traitorous little brothers, he said, "I'm not a teacher. And you *are* leaving here with me."

"The thing is, Brody," Ellie began, "when we—"

"My brothers are *mine*. I am taking them away with me. You have no right and no authority to tell me no." His eyes zeroed in on Lock. "Nor do you." Brody went on. "We'll set up a home, and I'll—"

"We *do* have that right, Brody." Ellie glared at Josh, who seemed content to eat while his sister did the talking.

Annie had her young daughter, maybe four or five years old, and kept busy feeding her.

Brody decided, since Ellie was doing all the talking, that he'd just glare right at her. "You do not."

"We don't just sweep children up off the street as if we think they're trash, as you put it earlier. We work with an orphanage in San Francisco. They insist we sign papers, identify which children are coming, gain the agreement of those children, and that their names are properly registered. We're granted guardianship of the boys. In exchange we offer good food, shelter, education, and job training in a field that interests them. And we keep them safe because there are cruel people who abuse street children, and there are those who ignore them and treat them like they're a nuisance. We make sure they find kindness here and loving care. And although it's never happened before, we don't just let them go when someone, however deserving, asks for them. Not even a brother. A brother who somehow let them get all the way across the country without missing them. They've been here for two months, Brody. Where have you been?"

Brody knew that was true about the registry because it was how he'd found his brothers.

He was all set to start yelling, demanding, grabbing his brothers and running off. Instead, he felt ashamed. "What do you want me to do to prove I'm fit to take them?"

Ellie was braced for his anger, it seemed, for she almost toppled over when he responded rationally.

To keep up with the behavior, he started to eat again. He noticed his brothers were on their third piece of chicken, judging by the pile of bones.

Through a mouthful of chicken, Thayne said, "Be a teacher here, Brody. Or be a doctor."

Josh had a forkful of lettuce halfway to his mouth. Ellie was serving the boys more potatoes. Annie was wiping her daughter's chin. They all froze and turned to stare at him.

Ellie recovered from the freeze. "You're a doctor?"

Brody felt a strange squirm of embarrassment as they all stared at him. "That's where I was when the boys ran away. Pa was a drunk who threw them out of the house. Ma was dead, but I didn't know it. She hadn't written, but she was never regular about it. "I'd just graduated in May from Harvard Medical School. I went home to—"

"Harvard?" It was Annie's turn to squawk. "You're a graduate of Harvard Medical School? When you talked about setting up somewhere and working, you meant as a doctor?"

He wasn't sure just why they were all acting so strangely.

Josh cleared it up. "We've been trying to persuade a doctor to come and set up at the ranch since we started the school. We've even built a doctor's office and a small facility for patients. There are rooms upstairs—the three of you would fit comfortably in there. We have a lot of people here on the Two Harts Ranch. Ten of our cowhands are now married

35

men, some have children. That's besides the orphans and our family. Michelle has mentioned many times we should consider applying for status as a town and seeing if we could get a post office and bank. She single-handedly got a telegraph wire out here and got the rail line to come to Dorada Rio."

"I saw houses out back, but a town?"

"The Two Harts isn't like a usual ranch with a bunkhouse and a couple dozen cowhands," Ellie said. "Cowhands are often wanderers. We have encouraged our cowhands to think of the Two Harts as their home. We build houses for any of our hands that marry. We include their children in our schools. And we aren't just a ranch. We've got farmland, too. It takes a lot of help to keep it all running smoothly."

"Gretel and her family have children," said Annie. "Zane and Michelle are expecting a child. Right now, Michelle is the closest we've got to a doctor, and she'd tell you she's not close at all."

Ellie nodded. "Brody, say you'll stay. Stay here and be our doctor. You'd be an answer to our prayers. Anyway, you have to stay for a while, until we agree to let the boys leave with you. At least be a doctor for us until then."

"I-I don't know if—"

Thudding boots turned their attention to the back door. A fist hammered until the door rattled.

It reminded Brody a little of how he'd come here this afternoon.

"Someone, come quick. Sally Jo is having the baby."

Brody didn't even think. He just leapt to his feet and rushed to the door, even as Annie rose to open it. He beat her there, thrust the door open, and said to the frantic young man, "I'm a doctor. Lead the way."

He'd left his doctor bag on his rented horse. Where in the

world had it gone? Looking over his shoulder, he saw Annie busy with her child, and Josh, not even a remote possibility to help deliver a child. "Ellie, come with me. Josh, find my horse and bring my doctor bag."

Brody then ran after the footsteps that were tearing away into the night.

———— ✧ ————

Pete Trainor held the door open for Brody. "So you're a real doctor? What luck. Michelle has served as a midwife, but she's gone now."

Brody didn't ask him to lead the way. There was screaming, and it led him right to a woman in distress. He went to her side and took her hand. The hollering cut off, but he thought the contraction was ending so he didn't give himself too much credit.

"I just finished with medical school. I worked at a hospital in Boston back east and probably delivered two dozen babies. What's your name?" Brody had heard the name Sally Jo, but he wanted to treat her with kindness and respect.

"S-Sally Jo Trainor." Her forehead was soaked in sweat. She had dark blond hair that was pulled into a disheveled braid.

"Well, Mrs. Trainor, having a baby is one of the most noble things a woman can do. I'm here to help you, and I'm trained in all the most modern methods, but honestly, the baby will just come on its own. I'm just here to encourage you and take care of the details." He noticed a little boy as he peeked up over the edge of the bed, his eyes awash in tears. Probably scared to death by the commotion. "And what's your name, son?"

"I'm Jamie. My ma is having a baby, she said, but she's d-dying, isn't she?" The tears broke into wails of fear.

Brody looked at Ellie, who'd entered the room. "Why don't you go get my brothers? They can help keep Jamie from worrying. Then come on back in here." He darted a glance at her that, despite his calm demeanor, told her to hurry.

She must've read his expression or his mind or his tone, or maybe she was just scared because Ellie then dashed away.

Mr. Trainor rounded the bed and picked his son up. At first he clung to the bed as if he were being ripped from his mother's arms forever. Then in a sudden shift, he threw his arms around his father's neck and held on like ivy on a pine tree.

"Mr. Trainor, why don't you take Jamie on out." And fast, Brody hoped, because Sally Jo had started to tighten her grip on his hand, which meant another contraction was coming.

As Pete walked out, Brody shifted his attention to Sally Jo. "I can see that the labor pain is coming again. This time start breathing slow but hard as the pain increases. Don't fight it. It hurts because it's the hardest work you'll ever do."

He knew he had a soothing voice. One doctor he worked with called him a crooner, another called him a whisperer, as if with his voice he could reach past fears and pain to the patient's inner self and calm them.

"Now breathe, slow and calm. We're going to get through this real soon. It isn't going to take long at all."

He'd've probably said that anyway, but she had her second contraction fast after the first. He rested one of his hands with utmost gentleness on her stomach, rigid with the muscles from pushing the baby.

Sally Jo had her eyes fastened on him and never blinked. She breathed as he talked to her, encouraged her. She whimpered but didn't scream, not like before. The contraction went on for a long time. They were definitely near the end.

Finally, she relaxed.

"When did your pains start?" He felt blood circulating again in his fingers.

Blowing out a deep breath of relief, she managed a smile. "Probably the middle of the afternoon. They weren't bad, though, and Jamie took all day and night. I didn't want to go to bed right away, so I made supper and got us fed and hoped I could get Jamie to sleep before I had to settle in to birth the new one, but it's hard, Doc. Hard." Her voice grew louder. "It's not like last time. If I have pains like this all day and night—Doc, I can't bear the thought." Her face reddened as fear laced her voice.

"It's not going to last that long." He sure hoped anyway. "A second little one often comes much faster than the first. In fact, I think we'll have this baby here with us in an hour or so. Definitely not all day and night."

Her blue eyes went wide as if he'd begun singing an angel chorus. "Really?"

"Yes, really. I don't want to intrude on your modesty until Ellie . . . I mean, Miss Hart, comes back. A woman should be here with you." He tried to distract her for the next hour or so. "Michelle—that is, Mrs. Hart, your boss's wife—delivered the first baby?"

His effort to divert her attention ended when her hand tightened on his. Brody remained calm outwardly while inside he was urging Ellie to hurry. He needed some help. Judging by the speed of this latest contraction and the power of it, this baby was coming soon. He needed both hands free.

He was crooning to Sally Jo, using his free hand to press a cool, wet cloth on her forehead, encouraging her to breathe rather than scream. The contraction was done as Ellie came back in. She had his doctor bag, so Josh must've found it.

"Your brothers are here," Ellie said, trying, he thought, to match his soothing tone of voice. "Josh is in the front room with Pete and your son." Ellie took the cloth, all her moves easy and graceful.

"Doc, something is happening."

Brody did his best not to startle Sally Jo as he adjusted things and was just barely in time to deliver a plump, wriggling baby. With a smile, he said, "Miss Hart, can you find a pair of scissors in my doctor bag?"

"Michelle had me steril . . . uh, starry, I mean she had me soak them in boiling water."

Sally Jo jerked her head up, eyes riveted on the new baby, tears mixing with the rivulets of sweat pouring from her forehead.

Brody saw the basin of water beside the one he'd been using to soak the cloth. "Ellie, hand me the sterilized scissors, please."

Before Brody could give the little tyke a swat on the backside to get him breathing, a strong cry broke from the baby. Grinning, Brody met Sally Jo's eyes. "Your son has strong lungs. He's a healthy, good-sized boy."

He soon had the baby wrapped in a soft blanket Sally Jo had ready, and he rested the baby against her chest, then tended to the last part of delivering a baby. As he restored Sally Jo to modesty, a knock sounded at the door. A response to the crying by the fretful father.

Brody's eyes met Ellie's. They were awash in tears, and a smile beamed so bright it could've lit up the room.

"I'm going to let Papa in. Are you ready to introduce your son, Mrs. Trainor?"

Sally Jo took a quick swipe of her eyes with the blanket Ellie had pulled higher. The little boy was cradled in Sally Jo's left arm, close against her. She gave Brody a firm nod.

Brody stepped to the door, swung it open, and was nearly trampled by the worried and excited Mr. Trainor.

"It's a boy, Pete," Sally Jo said. "We have another son."

The dreamy joy in Sally Jo's words made Brody feel like an intruder. His eyes again met Ellie's, and he nodded toward the door. She smiled and followed him out of the room, closing the door behind her. The two of them paused, looked at each other and grinned.

"I've never helped bring a baby before," Ellie said. "You knew just what to do, and you kept her calm. Thank you for your help." She cleared her throat rather delicately and added, "We have five more pregnant women on this ranch. And about ten other children, besides the twenty-four orphans. About thirty cowhands, ten with wives, and the Hart family. We could really use your help. We can discuss your pay. You'd definitely earn money besides having a home provided. I'd like you to at least give it a try. You can see if working here suits you."

Brody knew how helping deliver a baby affected him. It was like being part of a miracle. He was always a bit awestruck, and he shouldn't make a decision when he was in such a state. But he couldn't resist the idea of having everything settled, being with his brothers again—who didn't want to leave anyway. But he couldn't do it. He'd made promises to Dr. Tibbles. The man had been so kind and generous, Brody couldn't betray his trust. Right now, though, at least until Ellie agreed to letting the boys go with him, he could stop his travels for a while.

He smiled, admiring her pretty pink cheeks, caused no doubt by all the excitement. Her bright blue eyes looked tear-washed by happiness. "I can stay for a while, but—"

Then he got hit with two tornadoes.

"Brody! Great! Thank you!" His little brothers, bursting in and shouting over each other, were thrilled that he'd agreed to stay.

It annoyed him some because the little scamps just wanted to run off and hunt treasure. Yet he was so glad they were alive and well, he wrapped his arms around them and held them, just held on tight to his family.

His eyes rose to meet Ellie's again. She was smiling at the happy little huddle of MacKenzie men, her hands folded at her waist.

FOUR

"It was full daylight when we went in there?" Brody looked up.

Ellie saw the starlit sky. "It didn't seem to take that long. She delivered the baby only minutes after we got here."

"We went in after supper, and time loses its meaning during a birth. And afterward there's still much that needs to be done."

"Let me show you to the doctor's office and your rooms above it—two bedrooms, a washroom with a bathtub and a shower, and a sitting room with a kitchen. The doctor's office is well set up." Ellie gestured toward what was nearly a street these days, with houses and a bunkhouse, Michelle's invention shed, barns and corrals, and the students' housing. "There's very little furniture upstairs. Kitchen table with two chairs. I'm not sure if there are pots and pans, dishes and such. And there's a bed in one of the bedrooms."

Ellie looked at the boys, tagging along behind them, whispering to each other. They seemed elated to be staying. Brody looked likewise, lit up from the inside by delivering little William Brody Trainor. Billy. They'd named their son after the man who'd delivered their baby. "Boys, you know where we set up the doctor's office?"

"Sure, we helped with the last of the building when we first got here."

"Would it be all right for you to stay in your regular rooms tonight? We can get bedsteads set up for you by tomorrow."

"Sure, Miss Hart." Thayne almost bounced with high spirits, and Ellie had to wonder if he could even sleep.

"We'll go on to bed now." Lock nearly slammed into Brody. "I'm so glad that you're here, Brody. I'd like to stay up all night just talking to you."

"Tomorrow is Saturday." Ellie hated to separate them. "You can spend the day together and eat in the house with us again until we get a few supplies laid in for you. Your brother should be free, unless he gets patients already." Ellie gave Brody a wide-eyed comical look. "We started right in working you, so no promises."

The boys gave Brody another hug, and tears burned in her eyes to see the long time they spent holding each other. Then the boys let go.

"I love you, boys. I'm so glad I found you and that you're well. I was so worried."

"I love you, too, Brody." Lock slapped him on the shoulder.

"Good night. We'll spend tomorrow catching up on each other's lives." Thayne headed for the schoolhouse.

The two were whispering and shoving at each other, laughing just like always, only maybe even more gleeful.

"This way, Brody." Ellie led him to the second building on the north side of their street of homes and businesses. They had a blacksmith now and a tinsmith. A farrier and a butcher shop. These things were common enough on a ranch, but with the way everything was laid out, it was starting to look like a small town.

A coyote howled in the distance, and an owl hooted in the night. Beyond that the only sound was a gentle breeze.

She reached the doctor's office. In the moonlight, a sign over the door that said *Doctor* was just barely visible. Brody reached past her to grab the knob and open the door. It struck Ellie as a very gentlemanly thing to do.

"You said you went to Harvard? In Boston?"

"Yes, and I grew up in New York City."

"I lived in San Francisco for a couple of years. My sister, Annie, is a widow, and her husband's brother and his family lived there. They took me in while I attended college. So I've lived in the city. But I like it out here better."

"It's different. So quiet."

Ellie went inside and found a lantern on a desk. She lit it. It struck her that being alone here with him wasn't proper. "The stairs are through that door. I-I guess I should let you explore on your own." She handed him the lantern.

He said, "I owe you an apology for the way I stormed in here earlier. I just . . . I've spent the whole trip out here worried sick about the boys. I imagined the worst. I'm sorry I shouted at you when you've been taking care of my brothers better than I ever have. Thank you. I can't stay long, but for now, well, I'll give them a little time. The boys obviously want that."

"But you don't?" That made her heart twist a little. She loved this ranch and didn't see why anyone wouldn't. But she understood. Honestly, she knew she'd been biding her time for too long since her broken engagement. She couldn't just remain here at the Two Harts for the rest of her life. Yes, she helped in the house and in the dormitory, but she needed her own place in the world, not just to forever remain the adult child who lived at home.

With a solemn frown, Brody said, "I can't, Ellie. I owe a man money, and I gave him my word I'd come back. He's elderly, a doctor who needs help to care for his patient. He taught me a lot and paid me well as I learned by his side. And he loaned me money to go fetch my brothers, based on my promise I'd return to Boston."

For a moment, Ellie stood in the soft lantern light, her eyes meeting his, and then her mind went in a very strange direction. Her feeling anything for Brody MacKenzie struck her in a way that was a little too warm.

"I'd better get on. We'll talk more tomorrow." And she ran—well, she walked really fast before any more strange feelings cropped up.

———— ✧ ————

Pretty little Beth Ellen Hart. He was close enough that he could have grabbed her.

Loyal Kelton let her go, but he had a smile on his face imagining getting her under his control. He could still feel the bruises. Oh, they had long since healed, but he remembered because of the beating her brother Zane had given him. Loyal wanted some payback for that, and taking Beth Ellen away with him was a good way to pay them back.

He watched her stride across the ranch yard and then disappear into the house. She slept in the school building most of the time. It looked like tonight she'd sleep at home.

Easing back into the shadows where he hid behind the row of shops on the Hart ranch, including a doctor's office, he reveled in how close he'd gotten this time.

Loyal had left the city behind in the last couple of years. He'd learned the woods, the trails, how to track. He knew how to slip around unseen. He knew how to handle a gun.

Of all the trails he'd traveled since his father had kicked him out of the bank, nothing was more pleasant than the nights he crept onto the Two Harts and watched for Beth Ellen and fantasized about grabbing her. And the day was coming. Ellie, he'd heard them call her. Beth Ellen was the name she'd grown up with, and she used to complain to him—when he was courting her, and later engaged to her—that her family had insisted on her staying with the childish name.

Both names were childish in his opinion. When they married, he'd've insisted she call herself by the more respectable name Elizabeth. But they hadn't gotten to the altar. His mistress had come to Ellie's attention, and his finicky little fiancée had objected and broken it off.

And Loyal's father had cut his money off.

Now Loyal stood enjoying the cool night breeze and the sounds of the sleeping ranch.

Josh didn't post a night sentry.

Loyal was tempted to walk straight off the ranch to the overlook where he'd left his horse, whistling, walking right out in the open. The Harts were too stupid to take notice.

Instead, just because he so thoroughly enjoyed it, he slipped along buildings, hid in shadows, like a ghost haunting the ranch. When he got to his horse, he was reaching to untie the reins when a gun cocked and pressed into his spine.

A voice hissed, "My name is Sonny. Sonny Dykes. I seen you sneakin' around here. I think we both want something from this ranch. I wonder if you'd like to work together?"

FIVE

"They need you here, Brody." Lock was rushing around, following orders.

Thayne was across the small examination table from Brody, helping calm a little girl with a cut on her leg, deep enough she needed stitches.

Her ma was standing at the foot of the exam table, holding a crying baby, with a toddler clinging to her ankles.

Lock brought a basin of warm water to the table beside Brody, who angled his body away from the anxious mother and whispered, "See if Ellie is busy."

Lock arched his brows, a look of relief sweeping across his face. He quickly but quietly left the doctor's office. He didn't even slam the door. Brody appreciated that because he was afraid the distraught mother might've jumped high enough to crack her head on the ceiling.

"Now, don't you cry, Belinda," Brody said in his crooning voice. The girl didn't stop crying, but she did look at Brody.

He smiled his best, gentle smile at her. She was his fourth patient of the day. He'd been awakened just after dawn by a cowhand with a sprained wrist. Not broken, thank heavens.

Next, a very pregnant woman had come in to say hello

and tell him she was worried because she felt like she was having labor pains, and it wasn't time yet.

Brody calmed her down with talk of false labor and got to know the woman a bit. It was her first baby, so she was delighted that she'd have a doctor's care.

Then a blacksmith came running in and clutching his throat. He'd burned himself pretty severely from a burst of flying sparks.

Now a hysterical mother, and it wasn't even time for the noon meal yet. It wasn't breakfast time either, since Brody hadn't had time to eat anything before having to treat patients. What did these folks do two days ago when there was no doctor? He decided to ask her that very question.

"We always went to the big house with our injuries and illnesses." The nervous mother was squeezing the baby too tight. Probably not strangling the tyke, but the kid wasn't going to calm down as long as his ma was halfway to crushing him.

"Mrs. . . ." Brody went blank on her name, if he'd ever known it. He turned to make eye contact with her. Her gaze was riveted on her daughter. "Excuse me, ma'am? Momma?" He was practically shouting before she finally looked at him. "Can you please come and hold Belinda's hand? Give the baby to my little brother, Thayne."

Thayne was reading Brody's mind by this point. They were doing everything they could not to say anything to make the situation worse and still do what needed to be done.

Thayne moved slowly but relentlessly toward the fretful mother, then had the littlest possible tug-of-war with her over the baby.

"Go on and hold Belinda's hand," said Thayne. "I'll watch your two little ones." He wrestled the baby loose, substituted his own leg for the one the toddler was clinging to, and the mother, startled into action, rushed to little Belinda's side.

"Just hold her hand and talk quietly to her." Brody saw Thayne pluck the toddler up into his spare arm. He was a decent hand with the little ones. Maybe they'd taught him that at the school.

Momma held Belinda's hand and talked quietly to her, as if her good sense finally had a chance to assert itself without the two fussing babies to tend.

Thayne walked and bounced and crooned. Momma bent low over her daughter and got her full attention. Belinda's wailing eased to sobs as she threw her arms around her ma's neck.

"Why don't you sing to her. Does she have any favorite songs?"

Brody took a deep breath, dreading the stitches he had to set on this little girl. To keep the family in a calm state, he sang along with "Rock-a-Bye Baby," the lullaby the mother had chosen.

Brody pressed a cool cloth against the leg and held it as tightly as he could to stop the bleeding and numb the pain. He needed Thayne or someone with a free pair of hands. This little girl was going to have to stay still. He didn't think asking the mother to hold her down would be wise. The woman looked as though she was barely holding on to her calm for Belinda's sake.

And Thayne sure enough had his hands full.

Once Brody had threaded the needle, he drew a deep breath, dreading what came next. He held the two sides of the wound together. It was a nasty cut three inches long. There'd been a broken glass of some kind involved. Brody had looked carefully and double-checked that no shards remained in the girl's leg.

He braced himself, wishing he'd kept Lock here or that his brother would get back. If he couldn't find Ellie, then Brody needed his brother.

Everyone was calm for now, but he knew it wouldn't last, and the wound was bleeding stubbornly. She'd lost too much blood. He had to close the wound.

Brody met Thayne's eyes. Thayne arched his brows. He wasn't going to be much help. The young ones were still fussing, and honestly Brody thought the toddler was slipping. Dropping the little boy wasn't going to help things.

Brody reached for Belinda's leg with the needle, then heard running footsteps. He said a quiet, desperate prayer it wasn't someone else in need of doctoring.

The door swung open, and Lock came in. A pace behind him, Ellie arrived.

"Good," said Brody, "you're back. Lock, show Ellie where to wash her hands. Then help Thayne—he's got his hands full."

"Debra, Belinda cut herself?" Ellie, who knew the names of all these folks, brought an immediate sense of peace and order to the room. She stood beside Debra, nearer Belinda's legs.

Brody said to Ellie, "You hold her still while I stitch up the wound."

He saw Ellie look at the cut, and all the color leached out of her face. But she squared her shoulders and took a firm hold of Belinda's knee.

The next half hour was anything but calm. Momma, baby, toddler, and Belinda were all crying again before Brody was done setting the ten stitches needed to close the wound.

Then came a bandage and a few instructions to the mother and a promise to bring Belinda back at the first sign of trouble. If all went well, she'd return in a week to get the stitches out.

"Thayne, can you carry Belinda home if Debra leads the way?"

He glanced at Belinda, who nodded and swiped tears from her face.

Thayne handed the baby to her, then picked up Belinda.

Brody said, "Lock, take your little guy along."

Ellie went to Lock and spoke so quietly, no one else could hear her. Debra led the way out. Thayne and Lock followed.

Ellie fumbled her way to a chair and sank into it.

"Thank you for not fainting.

"It was a nasty-looking cut." Ellie breathed in and out slowly. Her face had regained a bit of color simply from the fight to hold Belinda still.

Brody needed to clean the place up, but for a few moments he decided he'd go ahead and take a seat beside Ellie and rest a minute. "What did you say to Lock?" he asked.

"I told him to come straight to the house for a meal. I heard you had an early patient. When you didn't come for breakfast, I knew that was why."

"This was my fourth patient today. Is it always like this?"

"I wouldn't have thought it was. Randy spraining his arm, Josh was there for that. His horse did some crow-hopping, as many of our green broke horses do when a rider first mounts up in the morning. Josh sent him over. If you hadn't been here, he'd've just checked to see if the bone was broken. If it wasn't, he'd've wrapped Randy's arm and told him to take it easy for a few days."

Brody nodded. "Which is exactly what I did."

"I'll bet you did a much better job of it than Josh would have." Ellie stood and began gathering bloody rags.

Brody felt like he could do no less than help her tidy up the doctor's office.

Ellie went on, "Josh might've ended up sending him to town if he wasn't sure there was no break. Having you here helped us and got Randy care much more quickly."

"Then a woman called Harriet came in to talk about her baby that's soon to be born. It's her first, and she's thirty-five. She's a level-headed lady with a few premature contractions, which made her nervous. Early contractions like that are normal, nothing serious. We had a nice talk about what to expect. She was glad to find out there was a new doctor, and she wanted to meet me. The blacksmith burning his throat, it was plenty painful, but he'll be fine. Is there anyone on your ranch who can set stitches?"

The two of them talked as they straightened the room.

"Come on over to the house," said Ellie. "It's well past the noon meal, but there's plenty of stew left over. Did the boys eat lunch?"

"They had breakfast at the school but nothing since. I've been working them hard." Brody smiled at just how hard. "I haven't even had a chance to talk to them yet. I hoped today would be about spending time together and enjoying being with family again. I've been gone most of the last three years, attending medical school. The train connects Boston to New York, but money is always tight. Instead of buying a train ticket, I always sent the money home."

He didn't say it because there was no point, but he was regretting agreeing to this job. If he and his brothers could have just ridden off together . . .

"Let's head out before anyone else finds a reason to visit the doctor." Ellie went to the door, poked her head out to look left and right, then said, "Hurry, the coast is clear."

Brody laughed. He *had* taken the job, and one morning wasn't giving it a fair test. He moved quickly. Ellie had been at least partly teasing, but Brody didn't want to have any more wounded patients catch up to him. Not with his stomach growling like it was.

They reached the house just as Thayne and Lock came into view, jogging as if they were starving to death. Which, being growing boys, they probably were.

SIX

A plague of locusts had hit her kitchen.

Ellie watched the MacKenzie men take their third helpings of stew and their fifth biscuit each! She didn't protest because they were obviously ravenous. But she had planned the stew for both lunch *and* supper—supper for seven. Yet all of it was being eaten by the MacKenzies, and she'd invited them to supper, which meant she would have to start cooking as soon as they were done.

Sorting through her supplies, Ellie said, "I've got to run an errand. Go ahead and have a good visit. You've got the house to yourselves."

She went out to the root cellar and brought up a ham, a sack of potatoes, and another of apples—withered ones left over from last fall, but they'd taste fine in a cobbler. She had bread enough for supper, but none for breakfast tomorrow. She'd have time to make biscuits in the morning.

All these thoughts flooded her mind as she gathered food for another swarm.

Josh came down the cellar stairs. "Brody did a good job with Randy this morning," he said, then took the ham from her and the sacks of potatoes and apples. That left her free to collect a basket of eggs and some flour. "I got called in when Debra's girl cut her leg. Debra had two crying babies, plus Belinda was wailing. Brody looked a little overwhelmed. His first day and that was his fourth medical patient. Not all emergencies, but I think he's wondering what he got himself into."

They emerged from the cellar.

"We could really use him here," said Josh. "We kind of blackmailed him into staying by not letting him ride off with his brothers."

"Ride off on what?" Ellie shook her head. "We're supposed to hand over the children we have guardianship of and let him steal two horses?"

Josh laughed. "We could have just ridden into town with him and brought the horses back. I suspect Dorada Rio could use another doctor. The one there's getting older. He'd probably welcome the help."

"Brody said he has to get back to Boston. We just have to find a way to make him stay. And we're keeping him here— we're not sharing our doctor, Josh. Just forget it."

Josh rolled his eyes, grinning. "So how much do we pay him? Or do his patients pay him? Or do we pay him a little and let his patients pay a little more? Or is providing the office for free enough? Or—"

"Stop, I get it." Ellie swatted him on the arm. "We need to make some decisions." She looked over her shoulder at the house. "I wish Michelle were here. Whether she's right or not, she's always so *sure* she's right."

"Should we send a wire? Ask them what they think?" Josh and Ellie headed for the house. "Maybe they'd come home for a few days. With the train in Dorada Rio, they could get home, stay a day, and then go right back to the mountaintop. They'd hardly be missed." Then Josh added with a smile, "Jilly might even be glad for the break from her overly helpful sister."

It was no secret that the two older of the Stiles sisters squabbled. They loved each other and were profoundly loyal to each other, but both of them thought they should be in charge.

"Let's send a wire." Ellie looked at the food they carried. "Let me get the ham boiling, then I'll send the telegram." The telegraph machine was in the ranch house. No one else on the ranch fully understood Morse code, though Michelle was teaching it at school and had taught most of the Hart family the basics. "Then I'll go with you and give the MacKenzies a stretch to visit in private. Annie's at the school with Caroline today, and Gretel always stays home on Saturdays and Sundays."

"Sounds good." Josh hefted the ham. It was a big one, and they'd probably need every bit of it, considering the appetites of the MacKenzies. "I'll help you get things set up before you send the wire. Michelle or Zane can give us some idea of how much money to offer the new doctor."

As soon as the door swung shut and they were alone, Brody said, "I want you both to give up on this—" he looked around, listened, saw that the house was empty but whispered anyway—"this treasure nonsense. You should have lit that stove when Pa threw his journal in it. But I can't blame you for leaving the old man to stew alone, considering the things he said to me when I got there."

Pa had yelled and threatened and even swung a fist more than once. But he was so sick, Brody had ignored the noise, ducked the fists, and tried to make Pa's last days on earth as comfortable as possible. "Even so, I wished you'd waited for me."

"We couldn't stand it anymore," Lock whined, a bit too much like a youngster. "We had to—"

"You didn't wait, so we won't argue about it. That's in the past." Brody shook his head hard and swept both hands to erase what had already happened. It was over, no sense dwelling on it. "You want to stay here because of that journal. Ellie may not realize it, but I sure do."

"We do want that, Brody, but it's also a good place to stay. We've never eaten so well." Thayne seemed sincere, and Brody had to admit his brother was right about the food.

"The kids who've been here longer say the winter doesn't get all that cold." Lock picked up the story. "One of them lived in Dakota Territory for a while, so he knows what he's talking about. The beds are comfortable, our clothes are always clean, and school is interesting. Miss Hart told you I like geography."

"That's because you're obsessed with the scrawled map in that stupid journal."

"That's what got me interested to begin with, but I love the maps. I love all I'm learning about the world and how big it is."

"The reasons you're giving me are good ones to stay, but I told you: I gave my word I'd come back to Boston. I owe a man money there, borrowed against my promise I'd partner with him in his doctor's office. We'll find a good house once we're there. I'll make a decent living."

"You can earn money here and pay him back that way."

"It's not just about the money, Lock. It's about honor, too." Lock's mouth hardened into a mulish frown. "You can make promises for yourself, but not for us. We don't owe a man money in Boston."

"I sent that money to Ma and to you. You *do* owe him. Boston is a beautiful city. You'll love it there. Why keep chasing after a treasure that was probably born out of Grandpa's fevered imagination? I can make honest money being a doctor. You can finish school, and I'll help you go to college, get an education that will give you a good life. Thayne, you were a great help today. Maybe you'd like to consider medical school. Lock, there are schools where you can study cartography—that's maps. Let's build a life together back in Boston. I want us to be a family again. But I want you to hand over that journal and give up on Grandpa's strange notes and Pa's obsession. He ruined our family. He made life hard for Ma and for all of us. Stop the treasure hunt and search instead for something real."

"But Brodeeeee . . ." Lock, the worst of the two for certain, as good as wailed. He gave little Belinda a run for her money. "We don't—"

The door opened, and Ellie came in carrying a basket of eggs and a flour sack. Josh followed her in bearing a bounty of food.

Ellie made no secret that she'd heard what Lock had said, and she obviously wanted to know what was behind it. But beyond that hard, curious look, she got busy at the stove, Josh working beside her.

Since they couldn't talk anymore, and he seemed to be eternally hungry and there was a scoop of stew left, Brody served himself more food. Thayne and Lock both grabbed for another biscuit, but Brody snagged the last one.

Ellie said, "Josh and I are going to send a telegram to our brother, Zane. He and his wife have a better idea, we

59

hope, on how to handle paying you a salary, Brody. And we haven't moved beds into the doctor's office yet. Um, I'm not sure how we'll handle that. Maybe just mattresses on the floor for now."

"We don't mind sleeping at the school, Miss Hart," Lock said with a sweet smile, which usually meant Lock was up to something, though Brody silently admitted his experience with his brothers was long out of date.

"Don't add more work to your day, not yet."

Thayne added, "We can help if you want to build new beds and fill mattress ticks. Maybe others would like to help. We have a class on carpentry one day a week during the last period. For now, we're comfortable at the school." Thayne sounded as if he didn't want to create more work on such a busy day.

Brody added, "Don't do any extra work on the doctor's office because we aren't staying." He did need money to get back east, though, so working for a while would be necessary.

Ellie gave him a narrowed-eyed look, unhappy with his continued insistence on leaving.

"I've got a ham on for supper. It needs to boil for two hours. Then I'll bake it awhile. Annie's on duty at the school until suppertime. Gretel has the day off. After I get the wire sent, you'll have the house to yourselves for two hours. I'm sorry we interrupted you, but I wanted to get the ham started."

"Ham?" Brody's mouth watered just thinking of it. Decent food had been scarce for him for a long time.

Ellie nodded. "Please join us for supper. I hope to have a reply to my telegram by the time I get back. My sister and her husband are involved in the lumber industry, and there's a telegraph wire that runs right to their house in the mountains. I usually get a fast response."

Ellie and Josh left the room. Brody guessed it was for the telegraph. They were soon back. Ellie got a platter of cookies out of a cupboard, pulled the coffee forward on the stove, and set the cookies on the table. "Have all the milk you want—it's in the icebox. Or coffee if you'd rather." Her eyes shifted to Brody. "If someone needs a doctor, we'll come running for you."

Her eyes held Brody's for just a moment too long before she nodded, glanced at Josh, who tugged at the front of his hat, then left a pace behind his sister.

"Two hours?" Brody looked at Lock and Thayne.

"Two hours to get to know each other again." Thayne said it with deep satisfaction, which helped Brody let go of some of the hurt he felt when his brothers wanted to stay here rather than leave with him.

He took three cookies off the platter and munched on them while he poured himself coffee and got milk for his brothers. They all sat down to the delicious treat and chewed for a while.

Finally, Brody brought up the only thing his brothers probably didn't want to talk about. "Where's Grandpa's journal?"

Lock reached behind his back and shifted around until he'd pulled the journal out of his pants. The boy dropped the book onto the table, his eyes roving between it and Brody. "We think we know where to go. Come with us, Brody."

"Absolutely not. I'm not here to help you wreck your life. I'm here to make you see sense and give up on the nonsense Grandpa wrote down."

Lock's eyes flashed with the wild high spirits Brody knew might lead him to ruin. He'd seen them in his father's eyes. Furrows appeared on Thayne's forehead. A much more thoughtful young man, Thayne had felt the hardship their father's obsession had wrought on the family much more keenly.

"You have to hear us out before you go telling us what to do. We think we understand right where to go now. Pa didn't read that journal right."

"But you have?" Brody felt that whisper in his heart for fortune. He really did. He knew how they felt. But he fought it down. He had to—they all had to.

"Yes. And we're not going to let up until you listen to what we've discovered."

The almost fanatical light in Lock's eyes told Brody there was no dissuading Lock until he'd had his say. Brody braced himself to listen, really listen, then poured everything he had into showing his brothers the error of their ways.

SEVEN

"He really said all that, Harriet?" Ellie held her friend's hands.

"Oh, yes. He was wonderful." Harriet Sears was starting to be really round with her first baby. She was a bit older for a first pregnancy, at least mid-thirties. Right now she glowed with a different light than she had before. Her sister Nora had given birth to two little ones already, after three years of marriage. And Nora was younger than Harriet.

Harriet had begun to believe it would never happen for her and her husband, Bo. She'd been delighted to have a child on the way, but nervous. Women were much more likely to be done bearing children by her age than just starting.

Now Harriet's time to be a mother was finally coming.

"He helped me talk through a few things that had worried me. I don't expect trouble, but just knowing you've got a good doctor here now takes a weight off my shoulders. And Sally Jo had only good things to say about him."

"I was there to help bring Sally Jo's baby." Ellie smiled and felt the joy of that experience.

Harriet seemed to glow, and Ellie suspected she had the exact same expression on her own face.

Harriet hugged Ellie tightly. "I was with Nora for both

of her babies. And Michelle helped deliver them and did a fine job. And now she's gone to her lumber dynasty far away when it's my turn. Having Dr. MacKenzie working here takes such a load off my mind."

"With Sally Jo, he was calm and wise. He's had quite a bit of experience, though he's just out of college. But I guess part of college is treating plenty of patients."

Ellie glanced around, not wanting the whole ranch to know what she was worrying about. "I'm waiting for a telegraph from Michelle or Zane. I have no idea what to pay a doctor and whether my family should pay him or his patients or some combination of both. The more I wonder about details, the more I realize how much Michelle and Zane make the decisions around here."

"Your family is providing him with a doctor's office. It might be best to leave the details up to him. How much to charge his patients. I admit it never occurred to me to ask what I owed him, and I took at least an hour of his time. He never suggested I owed him a thing." Harriet smiled and patted Ellie's hand. "He's just as new at this as you are. You've given him a home and office. Maybe you should pay him for any treatment he gives to our students since they're not making any money. And let the folks who work for you pay. For now, make sure he doesn't starve and let the rest work itself out."

Ellie waved her hands in surrender. "Good advice."

Harriet took her turn looking around. "Tell me this: Is he as much of a scalawag as those two brothers of his?"

Harriet's eyes flashed with good-humored affection for Thayne and Lock. It was just the pure truth that the two were charmers. There was no malice in them, only high-spirited mischief—but there was an abundance of that.

64

Ellie snickered, then laughed. Harriet joined in. In the year since they'd built the school, as part of finding a way to share their wealth, they'd had several students who needed a lot of time, but none held a candle to the MacKenzie brothers. Those two had given the teachers all they could handle. At the same time, the boys were bright. In the midst of disrupting class with their pranks and their funny comments, they caught on to everything fast.

"So far, I think Dr. MacKenzie is very level-headed." Ellie had told Harriet a bit about how the boys had come to be so far from home, though she didn't exactly understand it herself. What child set out to run away from home and went from New York City all the way to San Francisco? "Maybe the boys will settle down now that he's here."

"Do you think he'd be willing to teach science classes and see if he can spark a child's interest in doctoring?"

"I haven't mentioned teaching to him yet, but oh, I hope so." Ellie didn't mention that Brody was bound and determined to go back east. Surely he'd be here long enough to deliver Harriet's baby at least. "The school would be so well-rounded then, although our history teaching for the older children isn't strong. Except . . ." Ellie hesitated and looked sheepishly at Harriet, who patted her on the arm.

"You're going to be all right, Ellie. You're handling the youngsters just fine."

Ellie grimaced. "We both know that's not true. You especially know that with your gift for bringing order to a classroom and finding a way to teach important lessons, even to unwilling students."

Harriet had stepped back from teaching as the day neared for her baby to come. And Ellie had taken over.

With disastrous results. Harriet had taught the older

students, boys and girls, in the morning. She ran an orderly class, the students behaved well, and they sped through their books. Harriet had a gift for finding what a child lacked and filling in the gaps.

Orphaned children were often slim on education. Despite their ages, the orphans might be well into their school years without knowing how to read yet. Harriet focused on those gaps and brought the children along swiftly. In the year since they'd opened the school, she'd done a fantastic job of finding the key to open a child's mind to learning.

Annie was good at it, too. And Harriet's sister, Nora, had a gift for working one on one with troubled children and showing them how education could open doors for them.

And then there was Ellie. She'd tried to take a class right at the beginning. The older boys ran roughshod over her. The older girls giggled and whispered. Finally, she'd been assigned to the younger children, who took merciless advantage of her mushy heart.

Ellie was a strong woman, or so she'd always believed, but her gift simply wasn't in teaching. She'd backed away from teaching when she could, but with Nora busy with her little ones, and with Harriet soon to be busy, Ellie had needed to step into the job.

She was a failure. It was why she'd decided she had to go elsewhere and find a place where she was valuable. Their school focused on finding the gifts each child had and developing them. Ellie had yet to find her gift, but she'd certainly found what it was *not*. She was no teacher.

These thoughts rushed through her head as she plotted her time to leave the ranch. To stop being the useless maiden sister. The decoration that people moved aside to make their own progress.

She had to go sometime, but when and to where?

Her thoughts went to Loyal, her betraying fiancé, and she knew she didn't want to marry, as most women her age did. She thought of Annie, her widowed sister, who still missed her husband every day. Ellie had decided she needed to take care of herself, and there was no way to do that here on the Two Harts.

Then she thought of how much she'd enjoyed delivering Sally Jo's baby. She could help Brody for now, but he wasn't staying.

Turning her thoughts from the inner turmoil, she told Harriet, "If Dr. MacKenzie stays, our people here at Two Harts would get excellent care. We've done so much changing and growing in the last few years. We're always working on some project or another. I like to think with what we are doing here, we're making the world a better place for everyone."

For everyone but her.

———— ✦ ————

"Oh, please, Mrs. Worthington, no. You can't fire me." Tilda Muirhead clutched her hands to her chest, half praying, half begging. All of it a waste of time.

Mrs. Worthington was her boss. She could fire her. And it's not like this was her first time making a mistake.

"We can't go around misplacing children, Tilda."

Misplacing was a kind way of saying it, and honestly, Mrs. Worthington was a kind person. Tilda had just messed things up one too many times. It's not like she hadn't been warned.

"Mrs. Worthington, you know about my life. You know the calling I have from God to help orphans. Yes, those boys running away was a terrible thing, but there was no sign they've come to any harm."

"By 'no sign,' do you mean their broken bodies discovered after they'd been run over by a train?"

Tilda flinched. As a rule, Mrs. Worthington wasn't given to sarcasm, but she appeared to be making an exception in this case.

"I mean there was no bank robbery, no gunfire. We saw no stampeding cattle or buffalo. Wherever those boys went, they went by choice. Fully healthy and with plans of their own. I believe they hid somewhere in town, then jumped on the train when it headed west again, but in hiding. It was the last stop on the orphan train route, and we were going back. I'm still confused about why the boys weren't adopted. There's always an interest in strong, healthy boys for farm work and the like. But at stop after stop, they were passed over. And then they vanished. I'm telling you, those boys were up to something."

Mrs. Worthington smiled, but it was a sad kind of smile.

Tilda went on, "Yes, the MacKenzie boys were definitely up to something. I suppose we knew that from the minute we included them in the orphan train. They were charming boys and a bit too eager to go west."

Shaking her head, Mrs. Worthington said, "I should never have let you take this group. I knew what kind of scalawags those boys were. They'd have gotten the best of many a caretaker. And this trip, your very first solo trip, it was like everything aligned in their favor."

Mrs. Worthington stared hard at Tilda, as if she could see right through her skull and read her mind. But why bother? She had always been an honest person, no secrets to ferret out.

At least none lately.

"The boys have been gone for a while, Mrs. Worthington." It had been over two months. "What brought this on today?"

"We're in a bit of a bad place right now, Tilda."

"B-because of the boys?"

"Losing them certainly makes it worse, but not strictly because of them. There is some pressure to end the orphan trains."

"End them?" Tilda rose from her chair. She'd been sitting like a docile sheep being scolded. Now she stood, angered at this nonsense. "But it's been going on for years. It's been incredibly successful at finding homes for abandoned children."

"Yes, I agree, but not everyone does. There have been instances of children coming to harm, I'm afraid, or finding themselves in miserable circumstances. A few have caused trouble and ended up in jail. A few had parents living who expected the orphanage to care for them until times got better. They've come to fetch their children home and found them missing. There are organizations trying to put a stop to our mercy mission, and, well, what really brought this on is . . . our biggest donor, just a few days ago, was threatened with a lawsuit. There is no good time to lose track of the children we are out-placing, but now it's particularly dire. We have to take steps to prove we are good caretakers of these children." Mrs. Worthington frowned in silent thought for a moment. "I'll tell you what we'll do."

Tilda gasped, and her hands clutched tighter. Mrs. Worthington was giving her another chance.

"I'm going to buy you a train ticket that stretches all the way to the end of the line."

"California?"

"Yes, and I'll give you a bit of money—we don't have a lot—for food along the way. You'll retrace those boys' steps. I suspect they went straight to California. They were always talking about their grandpa being part of the California gold rush. I think they had ambitions to find gold."

"Isn't the gold rush over?" Tilda knew her history well. She'd always had a special interest in frontier history, particularly California. She'd wondered at times why she found it so fascinating. It was as if something hovered just beyond her memory that had to do with old-time California. She'd read everything she could find on the topic.

"Yes, for about twenty years. But those boys, well, they were whip-smart, but sadly lacking in common sense. At any rate, you can't just go straight to California. You're going to have to get off in most every town along the way, beginning after that last stop you made on the trip where you lost them, and search for anyone who's seen the boys, including asking around town to see if anyone had food stolen right around the time a train came through. Then just follow them on down the line."

"Doesn't the train go all the way to San Francisco? That's a big city. How will I find them there?"

"You grew up in New York City. You're used to such a bustling place."

"But I've never done all that well here."

"I've noticed. Nevertheless, we have to find those boys. If word gets out that orphans can wander off, and we just let them and make no attempt to find them, our reputation will be in tatters. It might be the last straw that brings on a lawsuit. And that might end the orphan trains. We have generous donors, although not *that* generous, who could stop supporting us."

Tilda doubted that. Not if no one ever mentioned children had been "misplaced." But it didn't matter. Terrifying as it was to set out across the country alone, she was glad for this chance to go find the boys. And not just to save her job, but to save them. What might have become of them?

Yes, they were scalawags. Yes, they were sneaky and liars. But they were sweet, so sweet. She could only thank God for this chance to find them and she'd do it. She'd never give up.

Tilda lifted her chin and looked Mrs. Worthington in the eye. "I will go. I'll leave on the next train out of town."

"Thank you, Tilda." Mrs. Worthington shook her head fretfully. "I wonder where in the world they could have gone?"

EIGHT

"What do you mean they're gone?" Brody whipped his hat off his head and slapped it against his leg.

Ellie looked desperate with worry. "I stayed in the dormitory last night. On the girls' side. Josh was on the boys' side. When he woke up and started the youngsters stirring to get ready for breakfast, then church, he found your brothers' room empty. He sent me running over here while he searched more thoroughly in the schoolhouse. I was so sure they'd be here!" Ellie grabbed at her hair as if she might tear it out.

"You lost my brothers?" Brody looked around.

Ellie's panic flipped to anger, and she shoved Brody. "I didn't lose them. They've done nonsense like this before."

"Have you searched the barn and the chicken coop? Maybe they're in one of these buildings."

So many outbuildings and houses and woodlands near the house. Steep mountains rising, especially to the east. A person could easily get lost by accident, and if it was as Brody suspected, they could also get lost on purpose.

Ellie nodded. "Yes, we need to look everywhere. Josh sent one of the older boys running for the bunkhouse. We'll have a small army searching in a few minutes."

Brody froze in his rabbiting thoughts as he realized what she'd said. "What do you mean they've done nonsense like this before?"

"Um . . . well, we've lost your brothers a couple of times before today. They seem to have a love for running off. They've never been gone long, but this is how it was before—gone in the morning. We searched then, too. But when we've had one child run off before, he went toward town, headed for the train. We found him and brought him back, then tried harder to help him get settled in. So I'll have Josh send riders to Dorada Rio right away." Ellie paused and gave him a hard look. "But why would your brothers run from you? What happened?" She jabbed him in the chest with one finger. "You're not as worried as you should be. What do you know about this?"

Brody didn't want to tell Ellie anything. It was just too stupid, too shameful. But she looked near frantic, and she would probably search for as long as she could. Or at least she'd search until his two foolish brothers came sauntering back in. He'd handled them wrong. If only he'd told them—

"Brody!" She grabbed his wrist and shook it. Her voice was sharp. "Why aren't you worried?"

"Oh, believe me, I am."

"What's going on?" She plunked her fists on her hips.

Which set Brody free to let his face fall into his hands. Then he scrubbed his face, wishing he could avoid telling the truth to this woman who still hadn't told him what kind of money he could make here at the ranch, what people there were to treat, and when exactly his brothers could leave with him. A woman who was soon going to believe the entire MacKenzie family was made up of fools. And she might be right. But the truth was, they were wasting time by searching in the wrong places.

He swallowed hard, his throat bone-dry. "My little broth-ers . . . um, well, I think they engineered this whole business of being orphans—of coming to your ranch, even of running all the way across the country, because they . . ." He might as well get it over with and say it. "My brothers are searching for buried treasure."

Ellie's hands fell from her hips, and her forehead furrowed. Maybe she was worried there was something wrong with her hearing. "Did you say 'buried treasure'?"

Nodding, Brody went on, "The whole thing is a mad scheme. Pirate's treasure maybe. Ghosts. Gold doubloons. Lost mines or Spanish conquistadors." Brody shrugged. "My grandpa's journal is a little hard to decipher."

"So they aren't really orphans, hungry and cold, aban-doned by their family to live on the streets?"

He shrugged. "I suppose they were hungry, and Ma died, and Pa was awful. But he usually calmed down after some time."

"And they came here because . . ."

Brody wished she'd just finish it, so he didn't have to. "Because they have a journal, written by my grandfather and sent to my father when I was about five years old. Pa ran off, and we didn't see him for seven years. He came home for a while, but about the time my two brothers were done being born, he ran off again. He did that through the years, telling stories about how close he'd come to finding the treasure. The boys got caught up in the story. They got ahold of the journal, and with Lock's map-reading skill, they figured the Two Harts Ranch was closer to the treasure than where Pa had been searching. So they took you up on your generous offer to care for them, give them shelter and food and an education. But their aim all along was to use the ranch as a base to hunt for my grandfather's mythical treasure."

"So where is it?"

Brody studied Ellie more closely. He was struck by her question. Was she going to throw in on the treasure hunt? Was she going to become obsessed with lost gold or whatever it was Grandpa had supposedly found?

He sure hoped she was a better person than that. "It probably doesn't exist, but my pa believed in it to the extent he ruined our family. And now my brothers believe in it with all their hearts, especially Lock."

"Whether it exists or not isn't the question." She sounded impatient. Like she really, really wanted to know where it was rumored to be hiding. He watched her for signs of a fever—gold fever. "Where do the boys think it is?"

Sighing, Brody turned to the east and stared toward the mountain peaks. Miles and miles of mountains, millions of acres of rocks and forests, canyons and rivers. All of it was wasteland compared to this beautiful grassy valley in which he stood, this vast ranch. He waved a hand to encompass it all and answered, "They think it's out there somewhere."

———— ◇ ————

Ellie tore her eyes from the Sierra Nevada Mountains. She knew them. Knew how far and wide they were. As vast and unexplored as any stretch of land in the world. She looked at Brody and blinked. "How far will they go?"

"You said they came back before, but . . ."

She frowned at his strange tone. "But what?"

His shoulders slumped. He walked forward two paces across the front porch of the doctor's office and sank down on the top step. "But this time I'm here, and I told them their treasure-hunting days were over. This time they've got their helpful, encouraging, sensible big brother at hand to tell them to give up, hand over the stupid journal, and stop being treasure mad."

Ellie came down to the ground so she could look at him sitting there, demoralized beyond belief. "They may not come back because you as good as forbade them to search anymore?"

"I took the journal away and told them I was going to burn it to cinders. Just like my pa wanted to do when he tossed it into the stove. Before he could light it, though, my brothers snatched the journal out of the stove and ran away from home. Not that I blame them for that. Pa was terrible to them."

"Did you make them watch you burn it?" Ellie asked.

"I didn't burn it. They made me promise not to before they handed it over."

"Do you think they snuck into the house last night and snatched it away like they did from your pa?"

Brody shook his head. "No, I'm sure they didn't."

"How can you be so sure?"

Brody reached inside his shirt and pulled the journal out. "Because I told them I was going to sleep with it and carry it with me at all times. I told them they'd never get it away from me, not ever. I told them Pa was crazy and that I wasn't going to stand idly by and watch them act like Pa did. I wasn't going to let them ruin their lives."

"You're saying you had a bad fight with your brothers?"

"Hoo-boy, was it a fight." Brody, who'd been studying the tips of his worn-out city-slicker boots, looked up at her. "I don't think they were as happy to see me as they had been at first."

His lips tightened, and his eyes dropped again. The very image of a man who was purely downcast. "And they weren't that happy to begin with."

Ellie sat beside him on the steps and rested her hand on top of his.

He glanced sideways at her. She ached for the sadness she saw in his eyes.

"They were happy to see you," she said. "I watched them whoop and holler, hug you, disrupt class."

"But I wanted them to come with me, head back east where I've got a job waiting for me, and they didn't want to go. Yes, they were happy to see me, but they still picked treasure hunting over me. They knew I was finishing college last May. They knew I was coming home. They could have waited for me. They didn't just run from New York City to search for gold. They ran because they knew I was coming home. They ran away from me."

Ellie felt sorry for the lunkhead. Unable to resist comforting him, she slid her arm across his back. "Brody, how long were you away at college?"

"Three years. I had class all the time besides needing to work. I had to send money home to Ma. I should never have gone. I abandoned her with the boys. She wanted me to go, though. She was so sure it was the right thing to get us all out of being poor for good."

"And she was right," Ellie said, edging closer to him on the step.

"If you think dying gets a person out of poverty, I guess you'd be right." With a humorless huff of a laugh, Brody turned to look at her. His face was so close to hers, she was a little surprised. Yet she didn't pull back. There was too much pain in his eyes.

"What did she die of?"

Brody blinked a bit too rapidly and then straightened away from her. "I don't know. Ma died last fall, and the boys never told me what took her. I just now realized I don't know how or why she died. They never wrote to me the whole time I was gone, and Ma didn't write often. I sent money every month and always included a letter, but I didn't get much back. When she didn't write at Christmastime, I got worried. But getting her hands on paper wasn't easy, and Ma was no great hand at reading or writing. I didn't get home for Christmas, either. The train was expensive.

"The boys managed to hang on to the apartment after she died. Then Pa came home and made things so miserable for them that they took to living on the street. When I did get home, after college was over, all flushed with triumph and ready to take care of my family properly at last, I found Pa alone and practically bedridden. I had to work hard to find out what had happened to the boys, but I did it. And I followed them out here. And now, two days after I get here, they've run away." He turned to look past her at the rising mountains.

Ellie shuddered at the determination in his eyes. "Does that journal give you any idea where they'd go?"

Brody looked down at it. "The writing is garbled. Nonsensical at times. I think Grandpa must've had a fever or something. Lock thinks it's some kind of code or just deliberately opaque so no one could find and steal his treasure. Trying to make sense of this stupid book had been the work of a lifetime for my pa. I've read it, but I never really studied it. But my brothers know the book inside and out."

He punched himself in the forehead with the side of his fist. "What kind of fool idea did I have, thinking that taking the journal away from them would put a stop to their stupid treasure hunt? Besides, they probably got most of it memorized by now. I need to read it again. Try and decipher it, try to—"

"Stop!"

Brody looked up. Silently waiting. He wasn't punching himself anymore.

"You don't have to crack the code on a . . . what is it, a ten-year-old journal? Twenty?"

"Grandpa came out here a year after the forty-niners arrived."

Ellie's eyes went wide. "It's 1874 . . . 1849 was twenty-five years ago. And no one's figured out what your grandpa was writing about in all this time?"

Brody gave a sigh. "Well, my brothers think they know what it says."

"We're not going to solve such an old mystery right now."

"We have to find them, Ellie. They've gone off before and always came back, but we can't count on that. They could be in danger." He turned to stare at the mountains again, his eyes showing fear.

"You're in the West now, Brody, and you're on a cattle ranch. When things get lost around here, we track them. And we've got some fine trackers on this ranch. Honestly, none of them is better than Josh. Let's have him track down your runaway brothers before they come to grief."

The fear seemed to be replaced by hope. There was plenty of doubt too, but at least a little hope mixed in. "Let's go find Josh," said Brody.

———— ⋄ ————

A note was stuck on Cordell Westbrook's door when he arrived at his apartment after church.

Cord read it and groaned aloud. Grandpa had the bit in his teeth again.

Cord stepped inside and stared wistfully at the small piano he kept in his apartment. He'd had a vision of himself playing the afternoon away. Playing alone. Instead . . . he glanced at the note again and sighed.

He could have lived with Grandpa in his mansion and had access to Grandpa's beautiful Steinway grand piano. In fact, Grandpa had bought it and had it shipped by train all the way from New York City just to try to lure Cord to live with him.

Cord had felt honored by that. He loved that old man— even more than he loved that Steinway. But he'd learned he could only get along well with Grandpa if they had some distance between them—different floors of a mansion wasn't enough. Living in the same house would have put them at loggerheads.

So Cord had his own cramped apartment and had saved until he could buy the beloved, battered old piano. And he fulfilled his duty as Grandpa's only grandchild by visiting often. Or stopping by when requested. Like today.

Turning his back on the piano and stepping outside again, he hailed a taxi. Being it was Sunday, Cord had attended church like always and looked forward to his weekly day of rest as God commanded. Grandpa, of course, thought he knew better than God.

Sure, there was nothing wrong with visiting an elderly relative on the Sabbath. But calling Grandpa an elderly relative was like calling one of the powerful California earthquakes a little tremble. It was like calling the Rocky Mountains a bump in the road. And the terse, commanding tone of the note told Cord that Grandpa was up to something—something to do with a lost treasure. A hoard that was supposedly half his, although that portion had shifted over the years.

It used to be that Graham MacKenzie had borrowed money from Grandpa and never paid him back. A simple loan taken out from Grandpa's bank. Now Grandpa said the loan was personal, between himself and MacKenzie. As the years passed, the treasure—which Grandpa had allowed to grow in his mind into a huge gold mine—had become more and more Grandpa's. And his anger at the long-dead Graham MacKenzie and his fool of a son, Frasier MacKenzie, had turned into a grudge that bordered on obsession.

Mayhew Westbrook, for his part, never forgot a slight, never forgot a cent he was owed, and never forgot a broken contract. And he never, ever accepted defeat.

Cord had received many summonses like today, and almost always they meant that Grandpa had found some hint or heard a rumor that the MacKenzie family was on a gold hunt again. Graham must be dead by now, but his son, Frasier, had been a thorn in Grandpa's side for a quarter of a century. And there was a younger generation now, too. Like Cord himself who was twenty-eight. He'd heard his share of stories of hidden treasure and wealth.

He'd also been on a lot of wild goose chases, and it sounded like he was going on another one. The trouble was, Cord had his own plans now. He'd been putting in long hours at the bank to get ahead on his work, hoping he'd be out of the office for a while. He was tired of the city. Tired of Sacramento. City life had never suited him. His grandfather's house didn't suit him, either.

His mother's parents, Grandma and Grandpa Rivers, had farmed south of Sacramento, and Cord had grown up there after his father died. He'd loved the four years he'd lived there. But there wasn't land near them to homestead, and Grandpa Westbrook had summoned him to Sacramento, offering him tutors and a chance to work at his bank. Cord had suggested college, hoping to study music, but such an artistic pursuit was frowned upon.

For years, Cord had bent to Grandpa's will, living in the mansion Grandpa called Hill House until it all became too much. Despite how badly he wanted to save up to buy land, Cord had moved to his apartment before reaching a breaking point with Grandpa. But he'd since worked hard and saved with an eye to moving back to the country. His two loves were music and the country. Cord wanted both, and he wanted no part of the dull business of banking.

Of course, Grandpa didn't approve of the apartment, but Cord was adamant, and so Grandpa had allowed it, albeit with ill-grace.

Now he was nearly ready to buy his own land. Soon the time would come to make his break. He'd planned to spend the next two weeks searching for a likely place to set up his future. Grandpa wasn't going to like it.

Cord had intended to send a note to Grandpa's house on his way out of town to avoid a fight, but now he might as well face his grandpa with the news he was going to visit his mother, and that too annoyed Grandpa. Cord wasn't about to mention buying land as well.

He approached the main entrance of Hill House, hoping there would be time for him to play a few songs on Grandpa's Steinway. Fletcher, Grandpa's longtime butler, opened the door before he could knock. Cord had obviously been expected.

"Good afternoon, Fletcher."

"Welcome, sir." Stoic, tall, unbelievably self-contained,

and seventy if he was a day, Fletcher led the way inside. "Mr. Westbrook is waiting for you in his study."

As if Grandpa wasn't always in his study at this time of day. And as if Cord needed to be led to where that room was located in the mansion. But Fletcher observed the established proprieties of the house and never wavered from his duty.

Cord had never seen Fletcher smile or frown. The man was down to only wisps of hair on his head, but those he had left were always neatly in place. Fletcher, who seemed even impervious to a breeze, gave two perfectly correct knocks on the oak door of Grandpa's study, then waited.

"Come in, Cordell." Grandpa knew Cord would come.

The time to be less predictable was fast approaching.

One last time. Cord promised himself he'd start as soon as he obeyed whatever order Grandpa planned to give him this time.

Fletcher opened the door with a flourish, then stepped back. Cord entered the study, and the door clicked shut behind him.

Grandpa sat behind the expansive oak desk he'd owned since before Cordell could remember.

"About time you got here."

Used to Grandpa's gruff manner, Cord reached across the desk, and Grandpa gave a sheepish smile and shook his hand.

"It's good to see you, Cordell."

No one called him Cordell except Grandpa. "Your note was waiting when I arrived home from church." Grandpa knew he attended faithfully, so he knew exactly when Cord would get the note and exactly when he'd show up over here. Cord didn't bother to point any of that out as he faced Grandpa across his desk. "So then, what's happened?"

Grandpa had a sheaf of papers on the silken smooth

desktop. Beside the papers was a little book with an oddly marked leather cover. Cord thought the marking was an X inside a square, but it was so worn, he wondered if he was seeing it right. He'd never seen the odd book before and couldn't begin to guess where it came from.

Grandpa twisted the papers around for Cord to see but didn't give him time to read anything. "I've had a man searching old records, and he's come across rumors of a mining claim, or maybe it's a purchase of land. The rumors aren't clear, but it was owned by Graham MacKenzie. My investigator got word that Frasier MacKenzie has died. Frasier's youngest sons have vanished, but his oldest has recently arrived in the West and has taken up the treasure hunt. The MacKenzies are at it again. Trying to sneak into the area, find their grandfather's gold, and leave with it. They're planning to steal it right out from under my nose. The whole family is a nest of low-down vipers."

Cord was confused. "Whole family? You know that Graham, the old man who borrowed money from you, is dead. He has to be. You've searched and never found him. It's always been Frasier who's been the thorn in your side. What other family is there?"

Grandpa tapped the papers impatiently. "It's all in there. Frasier MacKenzie sent his son out here. Word has reached me that he arrived in San Francisco only days ago, and he headed straight for ranch called the Two Harts. Rumors suggest that's where my mine is. He's no doubt using the Two Harts as a base of operations while he looks for my gold to steal. Get down there, Cordell. Find Brody MacKenzie and squeeze him until he hands over the gold money."

"Where is it?" Cord asked, though he knew the general location. He'd heard of the Two Harts. A huge ranch, one that made Grandpa Rivers's farm look like a backyard garden. Cord's interest was piqued because he'd like an excuse to go see it. And he had cleared his calendar by working night and day. But he'd not yet told anyone he'd be gone. He'd planned to stop by the bank tomorrow to inform them he'd be away for a time. If he gave notice of his being away too much ahead of the date, suddenly the bank would be so busy, they couldn't do without him. It'd happened before when he wanted time for himself to go visit his ma and his other grandparents.

"Grandpa, how much money did Graham MacKenzie actually borrow from you?"

Grandpa's face screwed up in a way that told Cord exactly how he'd gotten all those wrinkles. They fell into deep lines to match his scowl. "He borrowed one hundred dollars back in 1850. At a rate of ten percent interest."

"Doesn't the interest payment end when a man dies? The last you've heard of him was almost twenty-five years ago. If you assume Graham died about that time, he owes you one hundred and ten dollars."

"The loan doesn't die when a man dies!" Grandpa slammed his fist on the desk. "And that interest has been building for going on thirty years."

"Ten percent is ten dollars per year times thirty. His descendants owe you four hundred dollars by your reckoning."

"No, it's been compounding. The first year, yes, he owed ten, but the next year it was ten percent of one hundred and ten dollars, and so on. It's far more than four hundred, and besides, he promised me a portion of the mine if he failed to pay it back."

"Grandpa, you know Frasier was a penniless old man. If there is a mine, it should go to his heirs. But there's no evidence Frasier MacKenzie could find it. You know that. Frasier was a penniless drunk who abandoned his family to live in poverty back east. He's never produced a penny out of that supposed mine or whatever he meant by treasure. If you foreclose on him, you'll get a full portion of nothing, or maybe a lost treasure—which will probably never be found. So once again, a full portion of nothing."

That set Grandpa off.

Cord backed away and sat down in one of the wing-back chairs Grandpa had centered in front of his desk. The chair didn't usually go there. It belonged to Grandpa's right, by the fireplace. But Fletcher always directed two footmen to move it into place, so that Cord could be comfortable while Grandpa demanded and dictated.

"Just so you know, I'm going to stop and see Ma on my way."

Irritation flashed in Grandpa's eyes. "I want this taken care of, Cordell."

Cord couldn't hold back a smile. "I work hard for you at the bank, and I don't see Grandma and Grandpa Rivers very often, nor Ma. If I'm going to be traveling, I'll stop and spend a few days with them."

With an impatient jerk of his head, Grandpa said, "Just don't forget what you're supposed to get done."

"I won't, sir. I suspect I've got plenty of time since that family has been searching for nearly thirty years. A couple of weeks at Grandpa's won't matter much. I hope we can finally settle this MacKenzie business to your satisfaction." Cord doubted it would ever happen, but one of these times, maybe he'd find enough to give Grandpa some peace.

"Now, remember I want . . ." Grandpa began.

Since Cord wasn't setting out on this journey until he'd

gone into work tomorrow and made sure the bank knew he was going away, he was in no hurry. And Grandpa seemed to enjoy issuing orders at the top of his lungs.

Cord settled in, hoping this wasn't the time Grandpa's temper tantrum gave him heart seizures. The man was in his mid-seventies, after all. He really ought to calm down.

When Grandpa finally settled down, Cord said, "I'll leave first thing in the morning. Would you like to listen to some music before I go?"

A bit of the red color faded from Grandpa's face. "Yes, I'd like that."

"I play the organ at church every Sunday. It's a majestic, finely made pipe organ. You should come with me. It's beautiful music, and it might soothe your soul, along with the preaching."

Grandpa managed to smile. "I will one of these days. It will be suppertime soon enough. Stay for the evening meal with me."

Grandpa really did love his only grandson. Cord knew that, and he returned that love.

He noticed Grandpa struggling to get to his feet. Cord knew better than to offer assistance, but he walked alongside his grandpa and prayed for the stubborn old man while they proceeded to the music room.

NINE

"They went this way." Josh led them up a trail Brody would have overlooked if someone else wasn't in charge. He paid extra close attention and saw boot prints. Two sets. His brothers' prints.

"How far could they hope to go on foot?" Brody brought up the rear. Ellie was ahead of him, with Josh in front of their single-file search team.

Josh looked over his shoulder with a purely scornful expression. "So you're upset they didn't steal horses when they ran off? That's a hanging offense, you know."

Brody flinched. "Is it a hanging offense if they ride off on them and then come back?"

"Yes." Ellie and Josh both glared at him and spoke at the same time.

"You're thinking of hanging my brothers?" Brody grabbed the saddle horn to keep from dropping to the ground.

Ellie added, "For land sakes, we wouldn't call the sheriff, Brody, but if you don't know stealing a horse is a serious business, then you need to learn."

"I'm not going to steal a horse!" Brody was no great rider. His family had certainly never owned a horse, nor had they been able to afford to rent one. But when in college, he'd gone home with friends a few times and learned how to ride. After a fashion. When he'd rented the horse in Dorada Rio, he'd been nervous about it, and he was down to his last few coins. He'd eyed the horse nervously. The swayback had stood with its head down. It looked suspiciously like it was sneaking in a nap. Even being saddled did little to rouse the horse.

Then Brody had asked for directions to the Two Harts. A fifteen-mile walk—which was what the hostler had told him—could be done, but he was driven by an almost frantic need to find out if his brothers were all right. At the mention of the Two Harts, the drover had given him a different horse and said to keep it for as long as he wanted. And if he stayed at the ranch for good, the Harts would provide him with a horse, and Brody should send the horse back to town with any of the cowhands who rode in.

The Harts were good customers.

Now, Brody rode on his gentle, well-trained horse and wondered if that hostler hadn't tried to rent one of his less biddable horses to a tenderfoot—until he heard the words *Two Harts*.

"Look there." Josh pointed. "They're running. I reckon the sun must've finally come up. They were moving slowly in the dark. Wherever they're headed, they're going fast."

Josh had been studying the ground, but now he picked up the pace.

"You said they ran off before but came back on their own." Brody swallowed hard and forced himself to ask, "Do you think they ran off this time to get away from me? Do you think this time they don't plan to come back?"

Josh didn't answer. He turned off onto a slightly less wooded stretch of trail and pushed his horse at a fast walk. Ellie dropped back to ride alongside Brody.

The way she was studying his face, Brody wondered what he looked like. He felt the weight of these mountains on his shoulders. "I was a bad brother to them. I should have quit school and come home to help. I wanted to be a doctor badly, though, and so did Ma. But it was too much for her."

"You said you sent money." Ellie reached across her horse and patted him on the arm. "Your ma managed for several years with your money and the boys' help. Why do you blame yourself for her death? She didn't die those earlier years."

"Going without finally caught up with her."

"She wanted you to be a doctor, Brody."

"Yes, but not to the point she'd give her life for it."

"You don't know that. She might have been happy to give all she had so you could achieve a dream you both shared." Ellie was silent for a moment, then said, "My ma died before I left home. In fact, her and Pa dying was part of the reason I moved away. A year after they died, I went to college near San Francisco. They had full bellies and plenty of money, but they died anyway. We can't know the time or the place where God will call us home."

Brody fell silent for long moments as their horses' hooves clipped along on a trail more rock than dirt. The trees had fallen back, and the blue sky came into view with a warm sun. Birds chirped in the trees, and a hawk soared overhead.

All of it was so beautiful it almost hurt—the mountain wilderness surrounding them, the gentle breeze, the country sounds, which were so different from what New York City and Boston had sounded like. No crowds of people rushing around. No streets busy enough so as to risk your life to cross them. The air was scented with pine and so fresh his lungs enjoyed each breath.

It suited Brody just fine.

"If we find them—"

"*When* we find them," Ellie interjected.

Brody forced his slumped shoulders to square and lifted his chin. Because of course they would find them. Probably. "*When* we find them, what should I do? Isn't this proof, right here, that I can't force them to see sense, to give up on Pa's obsession? Do I just help them with the hunt, even if it takes the rest of our lives? I can't do that. I made a commitment back east."

"I don't think you can force them to quit. Short of locking them in a room all night and posting a guard over them all day."

They rode on for a few minutes, Brody lost in thought, and he tried to figure out what in the world to do with his brothers.

"Can you present them with a reasonable way to search? Can you promise to . . . I don't know, take a week off twice a year and tromp around searching for the treasure? Or maybe promise to spend all day Saturday hunting? Maybe they'd see it as you supporting them without letting it disrupt your life and theirs."

Brody shrugged. "I don't think there's a treasure, Ellie." He sighed. "I guess I could see it as exploring the mountains. But I hate the idea of spending every Saturday the whole time I'm in California hunting for something that isn't there. That'd be a waste of time."

"Maybe you could start out with one Saturday a month. Maybe the boys would come to see how useless it is after a year or two."

Brody made a terribly rude sound. Year or two? No, he had to get back. "My pa searched for most of my life. He never gave up."

"The boys stayed here for a while." Josh interrupted their talk. "When they moved again, they took this trail, narrower and steeper. It's gonna get cold up higher. I wonder if they've got any idea what they're looking for?" Josh turned his horse onto an upward trail that pointed north rather than west.

Ellie went next. The trail was too narrow for them to ride two abreast.

Brody brought up the rear. He made out footprints, so the boys weren't trying to hide a trail. At least they hadn't figured out that level of sneakiness—not yet anyway.

Loyal watched Beth Ellen ride by with her brother and a stranger. The stranger Loyal had seen at the ranch when he'd been spying. A doctor, it seemed. He itched to grab the woman who'd brought him to ruin, but Josh Hart was a salty cowboy, well-armed and nobody's fool.

Loyal let them go, but his chance would come.

Sonny Dykes had decided not to shoot him when they'd both been skulking around the Two Harts. Instead, they'd teamed up.

Loyal didn't particularly believe in a treasure, but he could use one. Sonny believed with his whole heart.

As soon as the riders were out of earshot, Sonny talked about his favorite subject: "I got wind of someone with knowledge of MacKenzie's Treasure. I haven't tracked it down solid yet, but I heard rumors that the old man owned a mining claim. If we could find that claim, we'd find his treasure."

Loyal Kelton straightened and looked at his new saddle partner. "These mountains are full of myths and legends about lost treasure. Just because Frasier MacKenzie spent his life searching for it doesn't make it real."

"No, it doesn't, but we've never known the exact location of any of those myths and legends. If we found the old man's claim, we'd know right where to look. We need to search old records. And hope it hasn't been lost and has the location of the MacKenzie land."

"It's been dormant for years. They can't still own it."

"Way outside of town, there's no taxes, nothing to make it fall back to the state. If we can find it, it doesn't matter if they own it or not—we'll still have the location."

"And did you find it through that old fool Frasier MacKenzie?"

With a smile so sharp he could've cut someone's throat with it, Sonny said, "Nope. I stumbled on it through Mayhew Westbrook. He's had a secretary combing through old documents for most of the last year. His secretary hasn't found it either, but I got word he was huntin'."

The two of them lived in near squalor in a falling-down shack on the edge of the Sutter land. Most of the land had been claimed by John Sutter, whose mill had sparked the California gold rush. But Sutter's vast holdings had been overrun by the gold rush, and Sutter had lost most everything and moved back east.

Mining claims had resulted in shacks. Those had given way to farms. But plenty of old shacks tucked into rugged forest, not suited for farming, were abandoned. Loyal thought bitterly of his father cutting him off over his broken engagement to Beth Ellen Hart. He'd fallen a long way from his life working in his father's bank. Now he and Sonny lived in one of those hovels. He thought of Beth Ellen with hate in his heart and plotted ways to make his father pay, Beth Ellen pay—*everyone* pay who'd turned their backs on him when they'd found out his father had disowned him.

Revenge was the juice that kept his blood flowing.

He hated how far he'd fallen, but he also loved it. Getting kicked out of his rich life and finding Sonny had opened his eyes to a life he relished. A life severed from all the rules of polite society.

Yes, his father had a mistress for years. His mother knew and turned a blind eye. Both of them seemed content with their lives.

Loyal had found a mistress just like his father had. Of course he had. All men did that. But Beth Ellen, his then-fiancée, had found out and left him. Father had called him a fool for not being more discreet.

That, along with Loyal's hefty gambling debts, funds missing from the bank, and Loyal's open contempt for his father's hypocrisy had gotten him kicked out of the bank job. The tidy mansion his father had bought for Loyal in anticipation of his marriage to Beth Ellen and the money father had deposited in his account, along with his bank salary, had all been taken back.

All of that for simply admitting with no remorse that he led the same life as his father . . . well, except for the gambling.

Loyal had admitted it, even bragged about it. When his father, enraged, had slapped him across the face, Loyal, with pent-up anger after years of such slaps, had hit back.

Father, his nose bleeding, his eye swelling shut, there on the floor of his library in the mansion on Nob Hill in San Francisco, had looked afraid. Furious, but afraid. It was an expression that swelled Loyal's heart. Filled him with fierce satisfaction and made him want to punish everyone who'd turned their backs on him.

Most especially his father, his mother, who'd slipped him some money on the sly, but wouldn't stand up to his father.

And that little fool Beth Ellen. So superior, so much better than everyone else.

Yes, he hated this life, but he loved what had been turned loose in him after years of trying to put on the front of a proper, wealthy son of a banker.

"Tell me what you know about MacKenzie's Treasure."

Sonny, with a mean expression, drew his knees up and rested his forearms on them. "First, you need to know we're going to have to get the money to polish you up a bit. The folks we need to talk to will only do business with a man in a good suit, a man with flashing good manners. You've got them. I can't even pretend to fake them."

And Sonny was a decent liar, so he must want Loyal to really shine for someone. His smile sharper than ever, Loyal said, "To find that hoard that's supposed to go along with MacKenzie's Treasure, I'll put on a suit. I can find the money. Just tell me who I have to kill."

Sonny laughed, and it stirred Loyal's cruelty to say something pure evil and have a friend who'd enjoy it.

"I wondered about your pa."

"I'd kill him and not miss a minute's sleep, but the sheriff would come looking."

"We don't need to kill him."

Loyal felt a wave of regret, and yet he knew it was best.

"We just need to steal from him."

And that made Loyal laugh again.

Ten

"We have to go back." Thayne rolled onto his back and stared at the sky.

"Brody ruined everything, so if we do, we'll never get another chance to find MacKenzie's Treasure." Lock enjoyed calling it that, as if the treasure were a known and sought-after king's ransom.

"We had to make him feel real bad running off two days after he showed up." Thayne ran both of his hands deep into his dark hair. Thayne looked like Brody and Ma with his blue eyes and height. Lock took after Pa—shorter and with blond hair. Lock had Pa's love of treasure hunting, too. He pitied Brody, who seemed to want a boring, quiet life.

"You know he was worried about us," Thayne went on. "He wants us to live together. It'd be nice. And I liked that he searched for us and found us. He loves us, Lock."

Lock shoved aside the twinge of guilt. Yes, Brody loved them, just like Ma had loved them. But Lock could almost taste that treasure. He knew Pa had done them wrong by abandoning them, but Lock knew that longing for adventure. And he knew Pa had loved them . . . he just knew it. It had to be true. A father loved his children. But Pa knew how to dream. He wanted more for them than a small apartment and living hand-to-mouth. Pa had gone treasure hunting for his family, not just for himself. "He's never going to give us that journal back. And if he drags us back to Boston, we'll lose our last chance. Even in the doctor's office at the ranch, it's going to be next thing to impossible to sneak out. It was hard enough before, but we managed it."

"Twice." Lock smiled to think of it. It wasn't easy slipping out of the school. They'd tried a dozen times and managed it only twice.

Add in a big brother who was probably a light sleeper, just because that was how their luck ran, and it would be impossible.

"I'm hungry, and we didn't bring enough food. I can snare a rabbit, but it takes a long time. You know Brody is hunting us by now."

"I've been practicing spearing fish. We won't starve out here, Thayne." Lock got his pocketknife out, unfolded it where he sat cross-legged on the ground beside his stretched-out brother, and stabbed the knife into the dirt. "I reckon we did hurt Brody's feelings, though. Why can't he help us instead of making things harder?"

"I don't know. We've got directions to a hoard of gold or maybe a mine." Thayne sat up, his eyes shining with excitement. "You're right. We can't go back, not yet. We've got to keep hunting for the treasure."

"What do you think the treasure is exactly?" Lock looked at his brother, and the two of them smiled. It was their favorite topic, guessing at what the treasure was Grandpa had found.

"A pirate's treasure. Pirates hiked inland and buried it out of reach of other pirates. Then they got killed in battle, and there it lay until Grandpa found it." Lock stabbed the ground again with the knife, sharpened by his own hand. He'd earned the knife by helping around the ranch. None of the students were required to work, but they were required to explore what interested them.

Lock liked horses and cattle well enough, and he had gained some cowboy skills, yet they didn't grab his attention the way geography and cartography did. Cartography was the creation of maps. Josh Hart was the teacher for that subject because he'd been at sea and traveled all over the world.

How could he stand to travel all over and then give it up just to settle in the wilderness of California? Lock was fascinated by Josh's stories.

Mrs. Hart, Michelle, was the one who urged them all to explore different jobs and study different things to find out what was the most interesting to them. She was an inventor herself, and Lock was interested in that, too.

"I think it's a diamond mine." Thayne was partial to that theory. "The weird way he talks about it in almost a puzzle that we're meant to put together. Diamonds would be something he'd never dare write down. If the journal had fallen into the wrong hands, it would need to be sneaky."

Lock liked the theory. He wasn't sure it was right, but it gave him a thrill that sent shivers up his spine. "But if it was a mine, why didn't Grandpa just chisel the diamonds out and bring them home? He took a lot of time writing his journal. In that time, he could have gathered enough money to bring us all to California."

"I wonder what happened to Grandpa?" Thayne sat up, his eyes flashing with impatience. They liked talking about the treasure, but both of them hated talking about Grandpa. His disappearance seemed to rob their whole family of a fortune. And in the end, with the journal, it robbed them of their pa, too.

Brody and Ma had been disgusted with Pa and his treasure hunts. Lock and Thayne had been hurt. As very young boys, all they'd known for years was that Pa was gone and not for the first time.

"Let's go. You took notes from the journal, right?" Thayne clambered to his feet, and Lock knew their rest was over. And they were both still hungry.

"Yep, but I didn't have time to write out everything. I never expected Brody to find us. But once he arrived, I knew he'd want the journal, so I wrote everything I could. I think the last time we went too far north. This time we go west."

"There's a mountain in the way." Thayne turned to look at the peak looming ahead. It had snow on top.

"Do you think that snow stays up there all summer? Or is it just too early in the spring?"

Lock had no idea if the snow would melt or not. Did it last all summer? "It's already June, full summer to my way of thinking. If it doesn't melt soon, it isn't going to. But one of the reasons we went north last time was because we let that mountain turn us aside. This time we tackle it. Let's go."

Thayne fell in beside him, peering ahead. "How far is it to the mountain? And it's huge. What do we look for when we get there?"

Lock swept one arm at the monster ahead. "When we get there, then we'll decide where to look. And it's right there. It can't be far."

— ✧ —

Josh shoved his Stetson to the back of his head and turned to Ellie with a strange expression on his face. "No, they'd never go that far."

"What is it?"

Josh pointed at the ground. Ellie was no champion tracker, but even she could see two sets of footprints heading . . . "Oh no. They're going straight for the mountain. What can they be thinking?"

She whipped her head around to Brody. "That's a cold mountain. If they press hard all day, they'll manage to get into high ground about nightfall."

"It's June." But as he said it, she saw Brody's brow furrow with worry as he stared at the white peak ahead. Brody brought up the rear and was leading two horses. "And the mountain is right in front of us."

"Distance is deceiving when it's as big as Big Windy Mountain." Ellie hoped they'd catch those boys. When they did, the two of them would need a ride back to the ranch, which was why they'd brought along spare horses.

Josh sounded ominous. "It's summer down here, but up there it can be full winter all year long and bring cold right down on your head any time it takes a mind to. If you get up on that mountain in the daylight, you'd better be heading down before nightfall. It's nowhere you want to spend the night."

It was still early in the day. And the days were long in June. But then a cool breeze washed over her. "You could survive up there overnight if you knew what you were doing. If you could find shelter and start a fire and you wore the right clothes and brought blankets. Your brothers don't know a lick about wilderness living."

Ellie was no hand at it, though she reckoned she was

better suited for it than Brody, and for sure his two half-wit brothers. And good or not, none of them had packed for cold weather.

Josh added, "That pleasant little wind you're feeling right now? It gets ice-cold on the mountaintop. It draws the heat right from your bones. This trail is straight up that mountain. Plenty of side trails, so we can't just go galloping after them at top speed, and for a fact I hope they turn aside. Those two scamps are heading for Big Windy Mountain. It's a long day's ride and exhausting because of the slow climb. You don't really realize where you are until you find yourself climbing out into a treeless, white wasteland with night coming down fast. It can snow up there year-round, and it's no place for a tenderfoot. Which describes your brothers right down to the ground."

"It's no place for anyone. Let's go, Josh. No time to fret about it. We've got to catch those boys before we all find ourselves lost up there."

Josh kicked his horse into a fast walk. "I know where the trail divides. I'll push hard and slow when I need to and hunt for sign."

With a worried look at Brody, Ellie fell in behind Josh. Brody brought up the rear. She focused on keeping up with Josh's increasingly fast pace and prayed God would protect two foolish children—who were a little too old to be involved in such nonsense.

———— ✧ ————

"They're still heading straight for Big Windy."

A gust of icy wind carried Josh's terse words back to Brody, almost as if it were laughing at them.

Brody only now realized that welcome cool breeze at the

lower levels held the chill because it was coming off a snow-cap. Dreading how miserable his brothers must be by now, he was glad when Josh picked up the pace. They'd trotted as much as they could, but the trails didn't always allow it. Mostly they'd held to a fast walk.

The boys were on foot, though. Josh had to be closing in on them. They'd ridden steadily, eaten beef jerky and drank from their canteens, all while staying put in the saddle. Taken only absolutely necessary breaks.

Now the sun was setting behind their backs, and the wind had picked up and whistled between the rocks and trees, finding them even when Brody would have thought they were in a sheltered spot.

They'd left the ranch in eighty-degree weather. Brody hadn't even considered a coat. Ellie had changed into a riding skirt, and her blouse had long sleeves. But it was all lightweight.

And now it was near freezing.

He imagined his brothers in this weather and shuddered from fear more than cold.

Josh cut through a narrow gap in a jumble of boulders, with trees growing out of every crevice. The path was shady. The sun would have been welcome. It was a beautiful place if Brody could put aside his worry long enough to enjoy the view.

One of the spare horses tugged at the rope tied to the back of Brody's saddle, hard enough it drew Brody's attention. He looked across the backs of the two horses and was stunned by the sun setting over the hills and valleys they'd crossed. The woodland and crags of rock, all painted orange by the approaching dusk. He drew in a slow breath at the beauty and at the sheer size of it all. The sunset seemed to stretch on forever, with the ranch hidden somewhere far below them.

He had no idea they'd come so far. How had the boys kept ahead of them? What time had they set out? Right at bedtime? They have to be this far on the trail by now.

Josh said over his shoulder, "We'll hunt for as long as the light lasts. If we don't find them, we'll find a place to build a fire and shelter through the night. We can't survive out here riding."

"What about them?" asked Brody. "Why should we be comfortable when my brothers might be freezing to death?"

Josh and Ellie both looked over their shoulder at him, their expressions grim.

Ellie said, "We won't give up easily, Brody. But it does them no good if we die out here searching. We won't be able to save them if we don't take care of ourselves."

Brody fought down the angry retort that sprang to his mind. This wasn't the Hart family's problem, and both of them were probably tougher than he was. They could go on for a long time in the cold. He'd be the one to fold first.

The shadows lengthened as the sun sank lower. The orange had settled to gray when the first flutter of snow came down on a rush of wind.

Brody couldn't believe it. He lived in a cold state. New York had harsh winters. But never once in all his years living there had it ever snowed in June. Mountains apparently made all the difference.

"They'll be easier to track in the snow," Josh said. "But once we lose the light . . ." He shook his head. "Not much chance of seeing a footprint in the dark."

"There, look." Josh jabbed a finger at a rock.

Brody didn't see anything.

"You boys get out here right now." Josh's voice thundered and echoed.

Brody's heart sped up to think Josh had found his brothers.

Ellie's voice cracked like a bullwhip. "We've got to get off this mountain now, before we lose the light. People have been known to freeze to death when they get caught out in the cold overnight."

Lock stuck his head out of a scrub pine, shivering, his lips blue. "Miss Hart?"

"Get out here now and mount up! Let's get out of here before the snow falls any faster."

"Brody?" Thayne stood, stumbled forward, caught himself, and hurried toward the closest horse. "We're freezing. We never thought it would get so c-cold."

Brody should have dismounted and boosted his brothers up. They both looked close to done in. Cold, hungry, exhausted, disheveled. They were both shaking in the swirling snow.

Thayne paused as he walked past Brody's horse. He looked up, his cheeks so cold there were white patches on them. He rubbed his hands together and looked as sheepish as possible considering his face wasn't exactly mobile. "I'm sorry we ran off, Brody."

"We'll talk later." Brody heard the harsh tone, much of it caused by his throat being chilled, but there was anger and hurt there, too.

Thayne flinched and looked down at his hands.

"Mount up. Both of you. Let's get back home." Except they didn't have a home. Not really. Everything they had was thanks to the Hart family, and his little brothers had returned all that generosity by sending the Hart family into the cold for a long, hard day.

Lock passed Brody with his head down and didn't even bother to apologize.

Brody chose to look on that lowered head as shame when it was probably something else. Lock was probably planning their next getaway, next time with warm coats and a better supply of food.

They reached their horses and struggled to drag themselves into the saddle. In the time that took, Josh turned his horse around on the narrow trail. He rode past Ellie, then Brody, and without being overly helpful, managed to boost Thayne into the saddle of the horse he was trying to mount. Then he reached Lock, who'd managed to climb up, and steadied the nervous horse. With a few swift moves, he untied Lock's horse and got the critter turned around. Then they all set out for the ranch.

Ellie passed Brody next and got Thayne's horse. Brody was bringing up the rear again.

He was glad of it. The boys were now surrounded. There was no chance they could run off again. Not that they looked apt to do that. Not today at least.

Instead, they looked purely relieved. A slightly wider spot in the trail came along. Brody rode up beside Thayne and handed over his canteen, then shoved a few strips of beef jerky into his brother's hand.

When their hands brushed, the icy chill of Thayne's fingers worried him. Brody had riding gloves on, and Thayne had none. Thayne drank deeply, then handed the canteen back.

Brody handed his gloves over. "You can wear them for a while. Then we'll give Lock a turn."

Ellie heard Brody talk and looked back. She shouted, "Josh!" Her brother looked at her. "Give Lock your gloves—their hands are dangerously cold."

Josh stripped off his gloves and handed them back to Lock.

Then, seeing what Brody was doing, he gave his canteen and some jerky to the boy as well.

They were back heading down the trail in seconds. Brody's hands were freezing, and he could only imagine how bad his brothers' hurt.

It crossed Brody's mind that the boys were too big for a whupping. Ma had handed out such years ago, but she'd given it up when she'd thought they were old enough to be reasoned with.

Except the youngsters had never really reached that age, and Brody was sorely afraid they never would.

Eleven

"You'll stay at Brody's tonight." Ellie dismounted.

Josh caught the reins of all the horses. "I'll put them up. You two, get inside."

None of them were cold anymore. They'd been riding in warm weather for hours, so the boys weren't in desperate straits.

Annie emerged from the back door of the main house, carrying a kettle Ellie recognized as a stewpot. Annie would have been keeping it warm all this time and watching for them.

The boys fell off their horses more than dismounted. Brody watched them with a furrowed brow and sad eyes. "Give yourselves a few days to regain your strength before you run off again," Ellie said with ample sarcasm.

Lock responded to that by collapsing. Brody was on his knees beside his brother instantly. Ellie decided to stay by Thayne.

"He's probably just out on his feet. But it's not a natural sleep." Brody stood, then hoisted his little brother, who wasn't that little, into his arms. Ellie ran ahead and got the door open. Brody took Lock into his examining room, and they followed him in. Annie set the pot on the stove and busied herself setting out plates and utensils on the small table in the same room as Lock. Ellie looked around and saw that Annie had kept busy today. The house was more fully furnished.

"We've set up two beds in the smaller bedroom and moved the boys' things over." Annie looked at Thayne. "Come and eat or you'll be the next one to collapse. Ellie, you stay and make sure they're fed. I'll go get Josh a meal. Caroline is asleep. I shouldn't have left her alone in the house."

Annie scooped up food on one tin plate only and tapped her ladle hard against it. Too hard.

Ellie flinched. Her sister was annoyed, and Ellie couldn't blame her. These two imps had made this day much harder than it should have been.

She left and closed the door with a slam.

Thayne gave his brother a worried look. As if he couldn't resist, he went to the table and sat. He wolfed down the food. Ellie would have told him to stop, but instead she took a seat across from him and ate with almost as much enthusiasm.

As soon as her plate was clean, she went to Brody. Lock's eyes were open now.

"Is he able to sit up, Brody? Good food and some rest will probably fix him up."

Brody nodded, and together they eased Lock to sit up. With Brody's arm slung around his brother's back, they walked him back to the table.

Ellie quickly filled two plates, then gave Thayne seconds, herself too. The four of them sat there eating in silence. At last, as her plate emptied again and her belly quit complaining, she said quietly, "I think we need to work out a plan where you MacKenzies can hunt for the gold—"

"Treasure," Lock interrupted.

Ellie resisted slapping him on the back of the head. "Treasure, then. You're obviously very determined, and we don't want any more incidents like today. Boys, please don't run off again. And, Brody, you need to find a safe and orderly way to search for the treasure with your brothers."

The boys, exhausted and nearly asleep on their feet, perked up enough to look at Brody, who nodded and said, "Fine, we'll search for it. I'll get the journal out tomorrow evening after you're back from classes, and we'll start planning." He eyed his brothers. "Is that good enough for you? Will you please agree not to run away again?"

"We're sorry, Brody," Thayne said, his head lowered. "We just sort of ran wild when you took the journal away. It felt like our last chance at MacKenzie's Treasure, so we went after it. I promise not to run off again."

They all looked at Lock, who didn't speak, but he was on his third helping of supper, so maybe he wasn't plotting another escape.

A dull thud sounded from under the table.

"Ouch!" Lock glared at Thayne. Ellie suspected Thayne had just kicked his brother in the ankle.

"I promise too." Then Lock turned to Brody. "I mean it, I won't run off again. That mountain is a lot farther away and a lot colder than we expected. We'll come up with a plan, and we'll do it with your approval and help."

Brody nodded at Lock. "Now let's get you both up to bed. It's late."

———— ◆ ————

Tilda was exhausted and had been for days. She'd lost the MacKenzie boys somewhere in Cheyenne, Wyoming. When the boys vanished, she figured they'd hopped off the train, waited until she wasn't looking, and had gotten right back on. With all their whispering about gold, she doubted very much they hopped back off until they'd reached Sacramento, California.

Sutter's Mill. The destination of the forty-niners during the gold rush was close to Sacramento, which was a large city. How could she ever find those boys there? And had they stopped there or traveled on? They'd been missing for going on two months now. The thought of finding them was overwhelming.

Tilda rode on day and night, through storms and long stretches of silence. Finally, what seemed like endless prairie gave way to majestic mountains that took her breath away.

Every time the train stopped, she wandered whatever small town it happened to be and asked about the boys. In a big city like New York, two mostly grown boys might slip into an alley and live without anyone noticing. But in these small western towns, if someone saw two boys alone, no doubt skulking around searching for a meal, they'd be remembered for sure.

In Fort Bridger, Wyoming, someone remembered a rash of thievery right about the time the boys would have been passing through. Only food was stolen, and it was put down to stray dogs or hungry children. But that explanation didn't satisfy everyone, so it was discussed and remembered.

In Reno, Nevada, she heard a report on the boys that made her feel like she was indeed on the right path.

"Why, yes, those boys were here," a woman said, stepping out of the kitchen, wiping her hands on an apron. "At the time you're asking about, two boys showed up at the back door of my diner. They seemed like good boys, but very hungry. I could see they were in a bad way. I saw no sign of parents, and usually when folks get off the train, they eat at my diner, so I'd have noticed a family with two boys. I feared that something had gone wrong for the boys; I tried to get them to tell me what trouble they were facing. They denied any such trouble, only offering to work to pay for a meal."

Tilda nodded. "Two boys. One taller and with dark hair? They're brothers, and the younger one has blond hair."

"That has to be them," the woman replied. "Said their names were Joe and John Smith. I suspected they were lying, but I didn't fuss about it. They offered to sweep up or wash dishes. I let them do both. Told them to eat first, though. No hungry boy is going to come to my door and walk away without a full belly. I was a little afraid they'd eat and then run off, although I wasn't about to scold them if they tried that. In the end, they were a lot of help to me and more than earned their meals. I invited them to stay around for a while longer, but when that train whistle blew, they were off and running."

"Thank you, ma'am," said Tilda, "for helping them out. Those boys' real names are Thayne and Lochlan MacKenzie. They were riding on an orphan train, and I was in charge of them. I wasn't watching them closely enough, and they jumped on the train that was pulling out and rode away. I didn't even know they were gone for quite a while."

The lady kindly nodded. "There are other small towns ahead and water tanks where there are no towns. The train had to stop every fifteen miles or so to fill up, but I'd say the boys were headed for California. I heard them talking, something about a treasure. It made me think of the gold fields. I don't know for certain, of course, but the way they ran for the train told me they had a destination clearly in mind." She paused, then added, "I watched to see that they made the train, and if not, to fetch them back here. I never saw them climb on as any regular passenger would have. I suspect they stowed away. Railroad detectives and conductors can be harsh on unpaid riders. 'Course, if they were riding since Cheyenne, I suppose they found a good hiding place. I surely hope so."

"Thank you again for your help. It eases my worries knowing they got a good meal here." Tilda gave a sigh. "But only a bit. I've no idea what they are after."

Tilda reached Sacramento at last, although she had no idea how to find two resourceful . . . or to be more exact, two *sneaky* young men in such a big town. As she sat there thinking, she felt a bit overwhelmed and demoralized. Did Sacramento have street urchins like New York did? After praying for inspiration, it occurred to her that a parson might know where to find children around here who had no home.

When she got an idea while praying, she took it very seriously. Gathering her strength, she stood, took a firm hold of her satchel, and headed down the cobblestone street. She set out to see what the business section of the town looked like. Along the way she kept her eyes open for ragamuffin children, churches, and a sheriff's office. Information might be gained from any of those three sources.

Tilda had been walking for a while when she came to a crowd of people exiting a small white church. It was the first time she wondered what day of the week it was. She had to guess Sunday.

An older man with a Roman collar shook hands as folks left the building. Several friendly people greeted her. With a smile pasted on her face, she nodded at each of them.

A nicely dressed woman, standing beside a man—no doubt

he was her husband—noticed Tilda and came down the steps. "Hello, I'm Mrs. Moore. Parson Moore is my husband. Are you new in town?"

"I'm Tilda Muirhead. Yes, I've just stepped off the train."

"I heard it pull in. It creates a real commotion, and this morning it arrived right during my husband's sermon. He had to speak up."

"I'm in town searching for a pair of young boys who are runaways. I have no idea if they stopped in Sacramento, but I have reason to believe they came at least this far. I was with them in Cheyenne, Wyoming, and I've been after them ever since. It occurred to me that a parson may know if two boys with no parents have been seen in town."

Mrs. Moore's brow furrowed as she listened. She rested a hand gently on Tilda's arm. "You poor thing, you must be worried sick."

Tilda nodded and felt the burn of tears. Mrs. Moore's kindness almost did her in. She fought back the urge to start crying and dump all her problems on this kind lady.

"Have you eaten? I have a chicken roasting at home, and it's more than my husband and I can eat. It's just the two of us these days. We'd love company. I can't think of two boys wandering around in town lately, but my husband might have noticed something. And if he hasn't, he'll know who to ask next." Mrs. Moore's arm slid across Tilda's back. "Please, come with me." She waved at her husband, then pointed to the house next door.

He nodded his understanding. Mrs. Moore then guided Tilda to the first comfortable place she'd seen in a long time. The warmth of it almost made her burst into tears.

Loyal had been forced to hand over the key to his parents' front door. They didn't know he'd made a copy of the key that unlocked the French doors that led from the garden into the ballroom. He'd known better than to steal the actual key, as Father paid too much attention to detail for it to go missing. But Loyal had thought to make a copy before their last ugly fight. He'd picked this less-used door deliberately, hoping Father wouldn't change the locks on every door in the house. Turning the key, feeling the well-oiled lock give way with a quiet click, gave Loyal deep pleasure.

Father never should have turned him out. The whole world was told the story that Father was displeased with his son for treating his fiancée poorly. But that was just part of what had happened. Loyal had helped himself to money from Father's bank. And from Father's safe. And to pieces of Mother's jewelry. Loyal had turned up drunk a few too many times. He had a liking for a good poker game, and the ticking of a roulette wheel made his mouth water.

Yes, Loyal had kept his mistress in fine style, but that was something he'd learned from his father.

Mother had to know about the string of women Father kept. Yet nothing was ever said about it. It was only later that Loyal learned he wasn't supposed to let Beth Ellen Hart know about his mistress, at least not until the ink was dry on the marriage license.

Beth Ellen had found out and had broken off their engagement. Father had been disgusted with Loyal's carelessness, but it was the gambling and stealing that had been Father's last straw.

How was Loyal to know Father had a last straw? He was rich beyond belief, and he'd always turned a blind eye to Loyal's expensive hobbies. That is, until he hadn't.

Slipping through the ballroom, Loyal made his way to Father's office. The house was dark. Loyal had watched as the lights went out one by one before he'd come in. Once in Father's office, Loyal moved to the picture hanging on the wall behind his father's desk, tipped it sideways, and with his fingers trembling with excitement, he opened the safe.

The old fool hadn't changed the combination lock.

Swinging the safe door open, he saw the stacks of bills Father liked to have on hand at all times.

Loyal might be able to help himself again if he could avoid detection, so he reached behind the cash that was up front and pulled out a few nice-sized stacks of hundred-dollar bills. Loyal had worked in Father's bank for years, and he judged the stacks to amount to two thousand dollars. On impulse, he reached in again and took a few more stacks and itched to take it all.

He resisted with a grim scowl. It should all be his.

Tucking the cash in his pockets—he'd been sure to wear clothes that had generous pockets—he crept up the back stairs. Had Father thrown Loyal's clothes out? Had he stripped the room clean?

Mother had always been staunchly protective of her only son. He hoped her sentiment had kept the room as a shrine. Or maybe she'd kept it hoping Loyal would be restored to her loving arms one day.

Sonny had said Loyal needed to steal enough money to dress himself up. But if he could just steal one good set of clothes, he'd be able to keep the money. All this because Sonny had heard stories about buried treasure.

Well, it'd be fun to search for it, and so Loyal played along. He vividly remembered which floorboards squeaked from years of sneaking in late at night. And not many squeaked. Such things annoyed Father. He went into his old room.

It was a shrine for a fact. Good old Mother had kept Loyal's room just the way it was when he left it. He went straight to his dressing room and then to the large closet. It held all his clothes. Probably out of style now. Loyal hadn't asked if that was important to Sonny's plan. Just who were they trying to impress anyway?

Loyal found a satchel on the floor and quickly filled it with a suit and shirt, boots, a neckcloth. Everything a well-turned-out gentleman needed.

He stepped out of the closet just as a lantern lit up. Whirling toward the light, he saw Father.

A grim-looking old man. He'd had gray hair the last time they'd met, but now it'd gone all white. His shoulders were bowed, and there were deep creases in his face.

"I see you've stooped to housebreaking now." Father sounded disgusted. And tired.

Loyal hadn't seen him in years. They didn't run in the same circles these days.

"You look like you could use a change of clothes." Father's eyes slid over the jacket Loyal wore. His eyes paused on Loyal's bulging pockets. "How much did you steal?" Father huffed out a laugh with no humor in it. "I never thought to change all the locks and change the combination on the safe. Foolish error."

"You've gotten old." Loyal felt a strange desire to hurt this man. "You should have kept your son close. I could have taken some of the workload off your shoulders."

"The bank would have folded at the rate you were stealing money from it. That *added* to the load. I made the right choice to get rid of you. Now take what you've stolen and don't come back. You won't be able to get in a second time."

Loyal walked toward Father and stopped when they were face-to-face. Their eyes met and clashed. They'd always been the same height, though now Loyal was taller. Father had shrunk with the passing of time.

"You're not even going to try and stop me?"

"I'm putting a stop to this, but no. I don't trust you not to turn violent. You look worn down, drunk as usual. But I'm sure you could still do harm. You're bloated up. Those clothes may not fit you anymore."

Then Father's eyes changed. Loyal saw something in them he hadn't seen since he was a child. Not love. Father didn't go for such soft emotions. But maybe there was a wish in Father's gaze.

"If you made promises to me, Loyal, we could try again. I wouldn't trust you, at least not at first. Money would be locked away, and you'd have no access to funds at the bank or to your mother's jewels. But if you want to get off of this dark trail you've set your feet upon, we could try. You could come home. Your mother would like that."

It wasn't begging, and Loyal would have liked to see the old man beg. But it was close, and it gave him some satisfaction.

"Here's my answer." Loyal slammed a fist into his father's stomach. With a dull grunt, Father clutched his belly, curled forward, and slumped to the floor. Loyal snatched the lantern out of Father's hand to keep it from breaking on the floor, maybe burning the mansion down. The idea had merit, but not today.

Standing over him, Loyal set the lantern aside and said, "I chose to punch you in the stomach so you'd have no bruises on your face that needed explaining. You're welcome."

He picked up his satchel, smiling as he patted the cash in his pockets. Then he left the room, and left his father in a heap on the floor. He went down the back stairs and out through the ballroom. He didn't bother locking the door behind him.

TWELVE

"This isn't that big a ranch." Brody sat a platter of fried chicken on the table along with mashed potatoes and a plate of biscuits. He'd learned to cook for himself in college, and now he could do it for his family.

"How can so many people need a doctor?" He slid into a chair, his heart aching to look at his brothers. He was thrilled and hurt and desperate.

Passing the bowl of potatoes, he watched his brothers dig in to the food before he said, "I know how determined you are to search for the treasure. Can we agree to search for a while, but before we get started, pick a date when we will call off the search? Because I've still got to get back to Boston."

Lock quit chewing and sat up straight, as if someone had poked him in the back. His eyes flashed with an excitement Brody recognized from his father.

"Really, Brody?" Thayne sounded less thrilled, as if just maybe he was taking Brody's feelings into consideration.

That would be a switch.

"Yes, but if we really search for it and we find nothing, will you agree the treasure is a fable and come back with me?" Brody took a bite of a chicken thigh and chewed while he waited to see if Lock would insist being reasonable would only slow him down.

Thayne and Lock exchanged looks.

Thayne said, "I want to stay with you Brody, but I think we're on the trail Grandpa left. Why do you have to go back? You can be a doctor here."

Brody looked hard at his brothers, each in turn. "I told you—I gave my word. The doctor I worked for is trying to care for people, but he's getting older. He had no one to share his burden. I got to know him, and he was a good man. He paid me well too. A few times, when we weren't that busy at his office, he went ahead and paid me, then loaned me money to go to New York and fetch you. He did that on the promise I'd come back and work for him. It's a decent job, and he needs me. It wouldn't be honorable to change my mind."

"But if we find the treasure," Lock said, "you can send him the money you owe him."

Brody's stomach twisted to hear his brother dismiss honor. "What about being trustworthy?"

Both boys lapsed into silence. Lock looked more sullen than Thayne.

Thayne buttered a biscuit while he chewed on his bite of dark meat.

Brody went on. "I want us all to go through that journal more carefully before we set out."

Both boys nodded as they chewed.

"Then I want to see if we can get any notion of a true direction. If we've got to climb that mountain, then we need to pack lots of food. We need to buy or rent horses from the Harts. We need to either wait until the height of summer and hope it's warmer or wear good coats."

"That sounds pretty smart." Lock looked calmer. No gold fever flashed in his eyes. Or not much gold fever anyway.

"And we need to decipher that journal enough to narrow our search. We can get everything ready, then ride out for weekend trips. Maybe sometimes we can go longer. Once we know how far away the mountain is, we may want to set aside a week or two for our searching."

Lock's face spread into a wide grin. "I like that idea, Brody. When Pa went out, he had to take the train across the country, so he couldn't come home. But if we're close, then we don't have to make an endless journey out of it."

"I've given this a lot of thought since you two ran off yesterday."

"Brody, I'm sorry. I hope you—"

Brody brought his hand up to cut off Thayne's fifteenth apology. He sat across the small table from Thayne. Lock was on Brody's right, their backs to the cookstove and dry sink.

"I've never really believed there was a treasure."

"Brody, we can't—"

"Let me finish, Lock."

Lock fell silent, but it was obvious he was fighting back words of protest.

"I've never believed in it, mostly because Pa running off the way he did hurt Ma so badly. Not just because we had no money. Ma worked hard taking in washing and working as a cook in a diner. I was delivering groceries. We both watched Theresa die, and Ma and I felt like she may have made it if we had been able to keep our apartment warm and give her good food. If we could have afforded to go to the doctor. I blamed Pa for all that, and it set me against believing in that stupid treasure."

Brody saw the mutinous expression in Lock's eyes, but

his little brother didn't start in pushing for a treasure hunt. Brody saw too much of Pa in Lock. Would Lock abandon a family someday in a futile search for treasure? Certainly Pa wasn't the only man who'd ever done so.

"But it occurred to me today, maybe for the first time, that Grandpa believed in it."

Lock's jaw relaxed. His shoulders relaxed, and a smile crept onto his face again.

"Grandpa found *something*. I doubt very much it's a gold mine or pirate booty, but it's something. And we are going to figure out the clues he left in his journal and find that treasure. I've already written to Dr. Tibbles and told him I'd be delayed. Now I'll write again and tell him I'll be a bit longer."

"He did, Brody. Grandpa found something he was excited about. We don't know what, but you're right. It's something."

Brody nodded his head firmly. "Don't forget your promise. I'll help you hunt for the treasure, but only on the condition you don't run off again."

Both boys nodded.

"It'll be fun." Lock ate a biscuit in a couple of bites. "And with your help, we have a lot better chance of success. You've never really studied the journal, have you? You're smarter than us. Maybe you can understand things about it that we never could."

"That's settled then. Yes, it's time I studied the journal."

"There are words in it we think are maybe a foreign language. We've never been able to read it, and there are strange numbers here and there that don't make a lick of sense."

"Now I'd like to talk about something else," said Brody. "Can you boys tell me what happened to Ma? Did she take sick or—"

A soft rap on their door brought all their heads around.

Brody quit talking. They were upstairs eating, the boys done with school for the day, Brody done doctoring. He hadn't locked the doctor's office door on purpose. That way, folks could get in to call for help if need be.

He fought back a groan to think he might have a patient. He liked helping people and found that doctoring suited him, but he'd've liked some time with his brothers.

Brody hurried downstairs to the door and swung it open. He found Ellie on his doorstep. She didn't look one bit unhealthy.

She held up a plate, covered with a red-and-white-checkered cloth. "Gretel made gingerbread today. I brought some for you."

Brody smiled and stepped back. "That sounds delicious. Come in."

"You would be very welcome to eat at the main house with us anytime you want." Ellie had a lemon-yellow dress on with white lace at the neck and wrists. It was like letting summertime into the room.

"Give us a little notice," she went on, "and we'll make sure there's plenty. I was told you had a steady stream of patients today. And the boys had school. It's a wonder you had time to cook."

"I have coffee, and there's milk. Will you join us for dessert?"

Ellie smiled and nodded, then Brody led the way upstairs. He looked at his brothers. There was so much more to talk about. He wanted it to be just the three of them, but gingerbread wasn't to be ignored.

"It sounds like you've been really busy," Ellie said.

"Is your ranch usually so full of people needing a doctor's care? How have you survived all this time without it?"

Ellie shook her head. "It does seem like you're overrun. There were a couple of accidents, like the cowhand with the broken arm. We'd've had to take him into Dorada Rio. A long, painful ride. I suppose most folks would have just gotten well on their own. But it put their minds at ease to talk to a doctor. And you've helped most of them heal faster, I hope."

Brody hoped so too. "Do no harm."

Ellie smiled. "That sounds like a good idea."

Brody looked at Ellie, then at his brothers. "No, that's an oath I had to take when I became a doctor. It's more complicated than that, but the basic idea is to help all you can and make sure you don't make things worse. It comes down to 'Do No Harm.'"

"The Hippocratic oath." Lock nodded. "Michelle mentions it sometimes."

"You've mentioned Michelle a whole lot of times. More than Zane."

Lock said, "She's the smartest woman who ever lived."

Thayne shook his head. "Nope, she's got two sisters. The three of them are the smartest women who ever lived."

Brody thought that was a little rude. "Not smarter than Ellie and Annie, your teachers."

Ellie waved off his defense of her. "I'm bright enough, though teaching isn't really my gift."

"It's really not." Lock shook his head.

Shocked, Brody said, "You apologize to Ellie."

With a wave of her hand, Ellie said, "It's the simple truth. I have a strange effect on children. I seem to stir them up instead of settling them down. I've often wondered if the children don't actually get stupider when I'm working with them."

"Now, Ellie."

"It's not my gift, nor my calling, Brody. I need to find a higher purpose for my life that also suits my skills—except I don't yet know what those are. Michelle assures me I have them, but even she can't quite discover them. Watching Michelle arrange the school to discover the children's talents and develop them has made me accept that each child has a gift. Not having a teacher's skill doesn't make me unintelligent, so Lock isn't insulting me. But Michelle and her sister Jilly, they are a wonder. Jilly has a strange quirk to her memory—she can remember everything she's ever learned. It's amazing.

"She's an engineer who helped build a railroad up a mountainside that they use to haul lumber. She helps us when we've got a construction project. She built this doctor's office and the school. They've got another sister, Laura. She's never lived here on the ranch since I came home from going to school in San Francisco, but they say she's studied chemicals and has a particular talent working with dynamite. They came here with a mission group, who lived with a poor community on the far end of the ranch until the community broke apart. Afterward the mission group settled here on the ranch. Harriet is one of them."

"The lady I talked with about her coming baby?"

"Yes, and Sally Jo, whose baby you delivered that first night. Gretel's the one who made the gingerbread. Wait until you taste her apple strudel! And she makes a Bavarian cream pie to make the angels weep."

"Well, this gingerbread is excellent."

His brothers had wolfed theirs down, which was testimony to its fine taste.

"Tell Gretel thank you for us. And thank *you* for bringing it over here. I'm sure you've had a long day, too. I look forward to meeting Michelle and her sisters."

"Now, what can I—?"

"Doc, come quick. Harriet's gone into labor!" The man's voice reached them before he'd made it to the door.

Brody sprang into action. It was instinct at this point. He grabbed his doctor's bag and said, "Boys, the journal is under my pillow if you want to stay and study it."

"We can come along if you want. You may need our help." Thayne was out of his chair, Lock only a pace behind.

"I'm coming too, Brody. Harriet might appreciate a woman being close by, and I loved helping with Sally Jo."

They were all thundering down the steps before the frantic husband could come up.

Bo Sears looked scared to death, just like most every father Brody had ever seen, especially first-time fathers.

They all raced after him.

THIRTEEN

"I'll walk you home, Ellie," offered Brody.

She looked at him, a little dreamy-eyed. "Watching a new life come into the world is something I will cherish for the rest of my life. And especially Harriet. She has been so much help with the school. She's a wise woman of faith who wanted to be a mother with all her heart. Seeing her look down at that baby boy, the pure love in her eyes . . ." Ellie stopped talking, as she couldn't get the words past the lump in her throat. "Please, come for me whenever there's a new one on the way."

He kept walking, so she caught his wrist in a tight grasp. Stopping in the pale moonlight to face him, Ellie added, "Please say I can help you, Brody."

Patting her hand, smiling bright enough to shame the moon and the stars above, he said, "Of course you can help. I'd appreciate it very much. You were a great help, by the way. And a doctor needs a nurse. In fact, you can learn enough to take over midwife duties when I leave."

Ellie, still hanging on to him, patted herself on the chest, just to touch her warm heart. "Really? You'll teach me what I need to know?"

"I'd be glad to teach you. It's a good idea to have the

knowledge spread beyond just one person. Harriet would have been fine. Once Nora showed up, she'd've brought the child without help."

Ellie felt a cool night breeze and wondered if the stars were stirring around. "When Nora arrived with her two little ones, I was glad the boys were there."

Brody chuckled softly. "Jesse had his hands full with those babies. The older one especially kept things lively."

"Nora had to bring the baby along, who's still nursing. And Jesse spends most of his time riding the range. He was overwhelmed caring for them alone. Your brothers were wonderful helpers. They really are good and generous boys."

They resumed strolling toward the main house, Ellie holding his wrist.

The coo of a pigeon broke the silence of the cool night. Ellie shivered from the wind. "It has to be nearly morning."

"Bo had a pocket watch. We checked to know the time of birth. The baby was born at two. And we were another hour getting them all settled." Brody shook his head. "The sun will be rising almost before either of us get to sleep. That's the way of doctoring, though—you go when you're needed. Help all you can."

"And *do no harm*," Ellie said. "A strange thing to have to swear to. Why would a doctor ever do harm?"

"Sometimes there are treatments a doctor might think are helpful, experimental things. It can make things worse. It's not always clear whether you're helping. If possible, I like to let a patient heal on their own."

A wave of exhaustion swept over her, and she found herself leaning on Brody. He slid an arm across her back. "You're almost asleep on your feet."

She murmured her agreement, then yawned until her jaw cracked.

The house waited just ahead, and she leaned more completely on Brody. "You're exhausted too, and probably more than I am. Yet here I am leaning on you."

When they reached the back door, Ellie straightened away from him. "Thank you for letting me help tonight. That's two babies now I've helped bring into the world."

A distant rumble drew her attention to the sky. "We'll have rain by morning. The grass and fruit trees need a good drink."

"Fruit trees?"

"That's right. Michelle read about orange and lemon trees, limes, and some others as well. They're supposed to grow well in the type of soil we have here."

Brody laughed. "I've barely even seen an orange. Not many of them growing in New York." Then he looked down, and Ellie met his gaze, warm and kind and so full of the miracle they'd just witnessed.

"Ellie," he whispered, "you're so beautiful in the moonlight. Your hair shines almost as brightly as your eyes. Can I . . . can I kiss you?"

She'd never been asked before. Her fiancé was the only man she'd ever kissed, and he had never asked but just assumed and taken his kiss. She'd allowed it at first, but then put a stop to it before long. And with that single thought, she shoved all memories of the unfaithful Loyal Kelton from her mind.

"Yes," she said. "I'd like that very much."

He lowered his head slowly, blocking her view of oncoming clouds and the moon. And then his lips touched hers, and her eyes closed, and the whole world beyond this one man and this one moment faded until there was only Brody, and only this kiss they shared.

He raised his head. His eyes opened, and she saw that he would have liked another kiss, a deeper one. She also saw his restraint and respect.

"That was a mistake. I shouldn't kiss you when I have to leave."

That stung like a whiplash. The sweetest moment of her life and he was sorry it had happened.

She wanted to beg him to reconsider, to stay here at the Two Harts. But that wasn't the way she wanted it to be between her and any man. She covered her hurt with anger. "No, you most certainly shouldn't have, Dr. MacKenzie."

He stepped back as if she'd attacked him. "I'm not sure how hard you're working in the house and in the school. I suspect you work hard all day long. But if you need a *third* job, I could use your help at the doctor's office."

His easy rejection of her after the kiss, now inviting her to work with him as if he felt nothing, wrenched at her heart.

And who would teach at the school? One of the older girls had expressed an interest in teaching. Ellie would be easily replaced, and that was another hurt. Better to hurt than to be a fool and fall in love with a man who was determined to head for the far end of the country the first chance he got. So she'd work with him and learn from him and let the hurt make her wise. Maybe she'd know enough to fill in here when he left, or maybe she'd go somewhere to study further. Did they let women become doctors? She wasn't sure. "I'll talk with Annie at the school, and Gretel in my kitchen, and see if they can get by without me. I find I love doctoring."

She nearly squirmed at the word *love*. But it was true.

True or not, it might be best not to speak of love of any kind around Brody.

"I'll see you tomorrow, I hope. You should try and get a few hours of sleep to get you through the day. Tomorrow I'll stop by Harriet's house and probably Sally Jo's, too. I won't start office hours early. Get some rest."

Brody opened the door and held it for her while she stepped inside. The warm glow of helping bring a baby into the world was wiped out by Brody's thoughtless rejection. She was determined not to let it hurt her too badly. Instead, she'd consider a new path: learning to be a doctor.

After Brody shut the door behind her, she made her way to bed, upset and confused. But she was determined not to let any of it show.

———— ✧ ————

"Grandpa Westbrook is sending me off to search for those low-down MacKenzies again." Cord shook his head at his grandpa's obsession with the MacKenzies and their supposed treasure.

Ma sighed so hard, Cord watched to see if she'd deflate. "I'm sorry, Cord. When will the day come that you stop doing his bidding?"

"You know why I do it, Ma. He's a lonely old man—"

"By his own choice," Grandma Rivers interrupted.

The three of them sat at Grandma's kitchen table. Grandpa was out milking the cow. Cord had offered to go find him and help with the chores, but Grandma insisted he'd be in any minute.

Cord had ridden up to the tidy cabin just ten minutes ago. He'd had time to shed his hat and coat, just barely needed in the cool spring air, and wash his hands. Grandma had poured him coffee and given him a slice of custard pie, along with the chiding that it would ruin his supper. Which Cord had assured her it wouldn't.

He smelled the roasting chicken and the bread baking. Not much kept him from eating Grandma's good cooking.

"Yes, but he's not a bad man . . . in his own way. I love him, and I hate cutting him off. I'm about the last connection to anyone outside that mausoleum he lives in."

The so-called mausoleum was one of the biggest mansions in Sacramento, but Grandpa had as good as buried himself in it, and so the word suited.

"He doesn't even go into the bank anymore. He owns it, but he's finally let go of the reins. His gout keeps him close to home. He reads his books and stews over the MacKenzies." Cord smiled. "He said he might go with me to church one of these days."

Ma arched her brows.

Grandma clucked over Mayhew Westbrook's heathen absence from church. They all prayed for his soul nonetheless.

If Mayhew Westbrook had plans to repent at the last minute, he was running out of time. He was far older than Cord's grandparents. Cord's pa, Wayne Westbrook, Mayhew's only child, had come along very late in life. Whereas Cord's ma had been born when Grandma and Grandpa Rivers had been young.

It was the pure truth that Grandpa Westbrook needed someone, and Cord was all he had.

Grandpa shoved open the back door, and his eyes landed smack-dab on Cord. A smile widened his friendly face. Cord got up and took the milk bucket from him and the egg basket, which Grandma whisked away.

Cord gave him a hug. "Why didn't you put up your horse?"

"I will, but I had to come in and see Ma first, and Grandma trapped me in here with her custard pie."

"Sneaky woman, your grandma." He looked past Cord and smiled at his wife, then clapped Cord on the back.

"I'd like to stay a couple of days if it's all right, and then I'm off on a treasure hunt."

Grandpa snorted. He knew exactly what Cord was after. "I'll take the visit for as long as it lasts. I've got a corral I need to repair, and I'd welcome some help. One of these days, boy, you're gonna give up on city life and settle here with us for good."

It was Cord's fondest dream. But there wasn't room on this small farm for another man. And though in his fifties, Grandpa was a reasonably strong man still—he didn't need much help.

Cord's dream was to save enough money to have his own place. He hoped it'd be near enough to his family that he'd see them often. But for now, Grandpa Westbrook, cranky man that he was, also loved his only grandson, and Cord couldn't betray that by leaving Sacramento behind.

"Where are you heading?" Grandpa asked.

Cord's eyes lit up. "Have you heard of the Two Harts Ranch?"

FOURTEEN

Al norte de la Bahia de Los Piños con Capitan Cabrillo en una espesa niebla.

Brody shoved the book at Lock. "What does this mean?"

Lock had studied this book more than any of them. "I've looked up most of these words in the library back in New York. *Capitan* is Captain, I think, in Spanish, so it must all be written in Spanish. I think he's the captain of a ship—maybe a pirate ship?"

"He? Who are you talking about?"

"Capitan Cabrillo. I couldn't find a pirate named Cabrillo, but then I didn't find much about any pirates. Captain Cabrillo, the pirate, makes sense."

"Los Pinos sounds . . . well, there's Los Angeles. So is Los Pinos another California town?" Brody tapped on the journal. "Los Angeles, that's a town named by the Mexicans who owned this part of the country before America took over. Los Pinos is a place maybe."

Thayne, always more sensible than Lock, said, "We need to find someone who speaks Spanish. I think a few of Zane's cowhands speak that language. I've definitely heard a language

I don't understand. Maybe it's Spanish. Mrs. Lane might know who we could ask."

Brody had to think for a minute. He remembered that Mrs. Lane was Annie, Ellie's sister. Which brought Ellie to mind, and he felt the tips of his ears heat up like they sometimes did when he was blushing. Mostly it was confined to his ears, so he hoped his brothers couldn't see him turning red, wonder why, and end up tricking him into admitting he'd kissed Ellie.

He shouldn't have done that.

"But why would Grandpa MacKenzie, who didn't speak Spanish, write down Spanish words?" Brody pointed at the unreadable lines. "See how they're written, not in Grandpa's usual script. I wonder if he copied the words from somewhere. Or maybe someone said the words to him, and he tried his best to write down what he'd heard, then study it later."

"Or so *we'd* study it later." Thayne sat around the corner of the square kitchen table to Brody's right. Lock was on his left. Thayne turned the journal so he could read the words directly instead of looking from the side.

"We should ask around, see if any of the Hart cowhands can read this." Brody studied the wall in front of him as he considered what to do next.

Lock was shaking his head before Brody could finish the sentence. "What if the words mean 'here's the exact location of the pirate's treasure'? We can't show this to anyone outside the three of us."

Brody was drawn out of his pondering to look at Lock. "Then what do we do?"

"I was here when Michelle was, before she left for the lumber company on a mountain her family owns. I think she speaks several languages." Lock turned to Thayne. "Do you remember if one of them is Spanish?"

Thayne shrugged. "I think I heard Russian once, and maybe French. Those aren't near as common around here as Spanish. Seems to me if she was going to learn languages other than American—"

"English," Brody interjected.

"Right, anyhow, you'd think she'd learn the language first that's all around her. I'll bet she can speak it."

"So do we abandon the treasure hunt until she comes home and hope she doesn't steal the treasure?"

"The Harts are mighty rich, and they're good people. I doubt they'd steal our treasure." Rebellion sparked in Lock's eyes. "But she won't be back for weeks. If we wait too long, that mountain we need to climb will be colder than ever. It might set us back another whole year."

"We can't wait that long." Strange that Brody felt the urgency to go treasure hunting just like his brothers, but for a different reason. This was a waste of time, and he wanted to be done with it. "I wonder if Ellie speaks Spanish." He was ashamed of how badly he wanted an excuse to go see her. He quickly shoved that aside. "Let's ask her and get on with translating this journal."

After last Saturday night's fiasco when he'd forbade them to search for the treasure ever again, and they'd run off, he was determined not to treat them with a heavy hand. Thayne was sixteen now, and many sixteen-year-olds were on their own, working and providing for themselves. An adult man couldn't really run away from home. Brody knew a few who were already married men with children. And Lock was nearing full height and certainly thought of himself as a man. Brody wasn't going to lay down the law with them ever again. Instead, he'd talk to his brothers man-to-man, and the three of them would make decisions together in a reasonable manner.

Lock leapt to his feet with a shriek. "You think if we can get that line translated, that'll lead us to millions of dollars in pirate treasure?"

Body didn't remind Lock that there were quite a few lines Brody couldn't read. Fine, he would make reasonable decisions with Thayne.

Thayne punched the air. "I think it's a diamond mine, not pirate's gold." He pushed back his chair so hard it went crashing to the floor.

Lock rounded the table, hooting with laughter. "Pirate booty, a dead man's chest full of gold doubloons. Yo-ho-ho!"

"Diamonds!" Thayne righted the chair, stepped onto the seat, and leapt off, shouting, "Diamonds, diamonds, diamonds!"

The two of them started dancing a jig.

With a sigh that came all the way from his toes, Brody decided being reasonable was going to be his job and his alone. "Boys, we've spent enough time on the journal today. I'll talk with Ellie tomorrow once work slows down. Now, I want to know more about what went on at home while I was away. I sent money enough to pay your rent. And Ma was working. Did you two work? What was it like at home?"

The boys, their chests heaving from the exertion, finished their dance. Their spirits high, they went back to the table and sat down again. Thayne and Lock plopped down in their chairs, and finally Brody was given a chance to talk about something other than hunting treasure.

FIFTEEN

"I read a little Spanish," Ellie said in reply to his blunt question. She was a bit surprised to see Brody so early in the morning. She'd intended to avoid him except for when she was working with him. She never should have kissed him.

Well, honestly, he'd kissed her. She hadn't kissed him. But she hadn't exactly run away screaming, now, had she?

Brody held up the ragged old book he'd waved at her the other day. The one that he'd refused to give to his brothers. The one he'd threatened to burn. "It's written in a way that's almost, well, not a puzzle exactly, but I get the feeling Grandpa was afraid it might fall into the wrong hands. He wanted to write his thoughts down. He sent it to Pa. But I think Grandpa only did that as a last resort when he was afraid of someone. He was writing this and taking notes for his own use. How confusing it is makes it less of a fascination and more of a nuisance. My pa abandoned us, *three times*, to chase after treasure."

"Three times?"

"Yes, and each time he was gone for years."

"Come in." Ellie waved him inside. "I've got coffee on."

"I'd better not. There might be patients soon. If I could just tell you what I want and leave the journal with you . . ."

Ellie found her fingers almost itching to snatch the journal out of his hands. It worried her a little just how badly she wanted it. It was a strange urge she hadn't felt before, which might be pure greed. Or was it just curiosity, a fascination with the idea of a treasure hidden away somewhere? Undecided, she gave up and said, "I'll walk over to the doctor's office with you." She turned to the kitchen and called, "Gretel, I'm leaving to go help Brody with his patients."

Gretel poked her head through the doorway that led from the back entry to the kitchen. She had a baby perched on her hip and a toddler clinging to her skirts. She probably needed help a lot more than Brody did. Even so, she smiled and looked not a bit worried. "All right. Lunch will be ready at noon. I'll plan on feeding Dr. MacKenzie, too."

Nodding, but without inviting Brody to lunch yet—she would later maybe—she followed him outside into the California sunshine. A perfect June day. "Can you believe how cold it was up in the higher elevations the day we were searching for the boys?"

Brody walked beside her. "It's almost impossible to believe. I sure felt it, though, and so must accept it. The weather can change suddenly in New York and in Boston, but . . ." Brody shook his head and turned to her. "Ellie, I don't want to talk about the weather." He gestured with the journal. "There are plenty of things in this journal that don't make sense. We decided the unreadable language in several sections are in Spanish, but none of us know it well enough to be sure. You say you can read a little Spanish?"

"Yes. I can try to figure out what it says."

"I thought about talking to one of the cowhands I met

who was speaking Spanish to his horse. But I don't know how many people I want to know about this journal."

They reached his doctor's office and went inside. There was a front entrance with several chairs and little else, and a door that led into the examining room in the back.

They walked to the back, where Brody set the book down on a table. He remained standing as he flipped it open. Ellie sat down. He then turned to the page he wanted and handed the journal to her, pointing to the mysterious line: *Al norte de la Bahia de Los Piños con Capitan Cabrillo en una espesa niebla.*

"Hmm. Well, the first part says 'North of Los Pinos.' I think *Bahia* is Bay. 'North of Los Pinos Bay with Captain Cabrillo.'" Ellie looked up at Brody. "But I've heard of no one by the name Captain Cabrillo, nor does Los Pinos Bay sound familiar."

Brody straightened away from her and sank into the chair across the tiny round table from her. "North of Los Pinos Bay. I suppose we can try to find it on a map. One of California probably."

"We've got good maps in the house. You're welcome to come in and look."

"Thank you. What about the way it's written? You see those tidy block letters? We think Grandpa copied them from something else."

She nodded and said, "I think you may be right."

"How about the rest of it?"

"*Niebla* means fog. I think *espesa* means something like . . . like it's especially foggy, but I'm not sure about that. Maybe lots of fog or heavy fog or thick fog? So we're north of Los Pinos Bay, and it's really foggy."

"I think my grandpa found something that had those Spanish words written on it, and he copied them down." Brody looked sharply at the open journal. "But Grandpa didn't speak Spanish, which means he copied it to translate later."

Ellie closed the cover, keeping her place with one finger. "Tell me more about this book."

"Grandpa sent it to us. He came out here to hunt gold along with the forty-niners, and he never came back. He later mailed us his journal, shipped all the way from California, and Pa came to believe he was holding the key to a treasure. In fact, Grandpa used the word *treasure*."

Ellie turned the journal over, running her hand over the back cover. "That's what the journal *says*, but what about the journal itself? It's no normal pad of paper like you'd buy in a general store." She lifted it to study in the light streaming in from the window. "This is very old leather."

"Well, Grandpa wrote in it near thirty years ago now."

Shaking her head, she passed it to Brody. "It's not thirty years old. It's much, much older. And look at the cover. It's badly worn, but there's something on it." She pointed to it. "What is that?"

Brody held the book up to the light, tilted it, then back. "Looks like a rectangle with . . . with raised lines cutting it into quarters. Four triangled quarters." He looked at Ellie with wide, startled eyes. "Like an X. Could it be like 'X marks the spot'?"

Ellie's thoughts were rabbiting around. "What I think is, it's *very* old—much older than your grandpa when he was alive. He *found* that journal somewhere." Their eyes locked. "Brody, your grandpa didn't buy it at a store."

"You think it's part of the treasure, don't you? You think Grandpa really did find some old treasure."

Ellie shrugged a shoulder. "If it's as old as I think it is, it's proof your grandpa found *something*. The writing isn't that old, though, and it's in English except for those strange Spanish words. That has to be your grandpa's writing, or at least it's the writing of someone much more recently than when the book was made."

"It's Grandpa's notes, I'm sure. He had terrible, scrawled handwriting. He makes mention of my folks a few times, hoping he can bring Pa and Ma out to California. And me and my little sister."

"You have a sister?"

"Yes, Theresa. She died while Pa was away following Grandpa's journal notes. Ma kept a roof over our heads, but we were always hungry. Always cold. It wore all of us down—most especially my sister, Theresa, who was still very young. Theresa woke up one day with a raging fever, and she wasn't strong enough to fight it off."

The bitterness in his voice went deep, and Ellie was sorry he carried such a weight around.

"When Pa finally came back, he had given up on finding the treasure. He settled back into our cold little rooms, went back to work, and stayed a few years. That's when Thayne and Lock were born. Things were good for a while. With him working, we lived better, had enough to eat. But then he started reading this infernal journal again." Brody shook the old book as if it were to blame for all his troubles growing up.

"Pa said he'd come up with a new idea about where to search. Not long after that, he was gone. Leaving Ma and me with the two little ones. I was about half grown so I could earn a little money. Ma wouldn't let me quit school, so I worked after school and on weekends. Pa came back one more time when the boys were ten and eight. The train was running by then, and it made coming home easier. Neither

Ma nor I trusted him this time. He was drinking more often; he worked some but couldn't make much. Finally, he ran off again, and I didn't see him again until I came home at the end of college. I got there in time to bury him. Then came looking for my brothers."

"I'm sorry about your pa, Brody. But this is from your grandpa. Was your grandma still alive?"

"No. Grandpa headed west soon after she died."

"Set aside the bitterness and hurt from your father if you can." She took the journal back into her hand and waggled it at him. "This is from your grandpa. He didn't abandon anyone; he just struck out on an adventure. And he wanted to get word to you about what he'd found." She pursed her lips and stared at the old book. "And it truly does look like he found something. This book is part of what he discovered. This alone is a treasure."

She saw the pain fade a bit from Brody's eyes. Not gone, but pushed away for now, replaced with a spark of excitement she hadn't noticed before now.

"I've honestly never spent much time reading the journal. It's high time I did some studying."

"I'd love to help if you'll allow it. I mean, to get involved with your treasure hunt." She smiled brightly at him. "I hope that doesn't mean I'm infected now."

"Not sure if gold fever is actually a sickness, but it sure is a bothersome condition."

They smiled at each other. She felt her smile growing wider to match his.

"Ellie, about that kiss the other night. I had no right to take such . . . such liberty with you when I know I can't stay here at the ranch. That's what I was trying to say. The starlight, the joy of delivering the baby, I let myself get carried away."

Her smile faded, as did his.

Someone burst through the door. It was Alice. "My son cut his hand, Doc!" she cried. "It's cut bad, too."

The noise was like a rifle shot starting a race. Ellie jumped to her feet, knocked her chair over backward, and said, "You take care of that. I've got to see if Gretel needs my help. Come for lunch."

"No, wait a minute. I might need help. You're my nurse, remember?"

That kept her from just rushing all the way back to the house. "Oh, that's right." She whirled to face Alice, the wife of one of their most dependable cowhands. She had her youngest son, Jimmy, about four, in one arm. He was wailing. Sure enough, his hand had a nasty cut on it. She held her baby, Ronnie, in the other arm, crying just as hard.

"Set the boy on the table," Brody said, snapping into his job as doctor.

Ellie resented it a little. Here she stood, still addlebrained by the memory of that kiss, and yet somehow he was all business.

Alice placed Jimmy on the examining table.

Brody turned to Ellie. "Miss Hart, get a basin of warm water, and fast. Then I need sutures—you know where I keep a needle and thread—and bandages." Once he stopped issuing orders, he leaned over the boy, talking in that soothing voice of his. Talking to both mother and child.

It calmed Ellie just enough to get her moving.

Sixteen

"Boys, we're going on a treasure hunt this weekend."

Lock leapt so high and shouted so loud, Brody hoped the neighbors didn't run over to see who was hurt.

Thayne laughed. It was pure glee.

Brody hated to say it, but they'd been patient. For them at least. Twitchy and pestering him nonstop, but they hadn't run away from home again, so that counted for something.

"The clinic is quiet." They were upstairs after a long day of work. The boys went to school, of course, but they'd come home and there'd been so much to do, yet they'd both helped so willingly and with increasing skill. Thayne might be halfway to becoming a doctor soon.

Lock didn't quite have the right attitude for it, but at least he was kind to the patients. He had a special knack for soothing any babies that tagged along with flustered mamas. And the boy fetched and carried for Brody without complaint.

They'd earned this weekend of chasing their dreams.

"I told Ellie that if anyone has to have a doctor's care this weekend, they'd just have to ride into town." Brody waved the boys over to the table. "Now, let's sit down and study the book one more time. Why did you decide to head for the mountain last time? You said you were going around it on your other searches. What clue did you see?"

The three of them pondered the journal. There were about twenty pages of notes in Grandpa's scrawled handwriting.

"Miss Ellie says she's found no evidence of a Los Pinos Bay." Lock tapped on the strange sentence. "A bay's got to be part of the ocean, right?"

Brody considered that. "Lakes can have bays too, but there are no large lakes around here. There's one over in the Sierra Nevada Mountains that straddles the state line between California and Nevada, but I don't think Grandpa went that far east. I think it must be talking about a bay on the Pacific Ocean. The California coast has one after another. None of them named Los Pinos, according to the maps I saw."

"But if this is really old . . ." Thayne ran his hand over the open page, thinking. Both boys were treating the journal much more gently now that they knew it was so old.

"This page here." Lock flipped the page to one with a sketch on it, a roughly drawn map. Ellie had a good map in the house, and she'd let Brody and the boys look it over. The two looked nothing alike. "Why did he sketch such a worthless map? It might make sense if we knew where he was when he drew it. But it doesn't set the map in a specific location. It could be anywhere."

"We know he came out here with the gold rush. That's Sutter's Mill, and that area became Sacramento. If Grandpa made it to Sacramento, why did he end up down here so far south?"

"He sounded like he thought Sacramento was a madhouse," Lock said, staring down at the sketch, "and he wanted no part of it."

"Could be," said Brody. "Not that many people got rich

hunting gold. The Harts did well once they started raising cattle and selling the beef to hungry miners. Michelle's father, Liam Stiles, became wealthy when he abandoned gold mining and went into the lumber business. Maybe Grandpa saw some opportunity like that. Maybe he washed his hands of gold mining and set off to start a ranch or cut timber. He doesn't say it, but he sounds discouraged."

Brody had taken his own notes while reading through the journal and had them in front of him. There were five sentences that Ellie said were Spanish. Brody had them all printed out before him. "Los Pinos means *The Pines*. Ellie says the pine trees are much thicker and much taller in Northern California, so based on that clue, she thinks Captain Cabrillo was sailing up the California coast and came ashore somewhere and named the bay himself. This journal is old enough that the name may have no meaning beyond whoever saw it and named it."

Lock's excitement drained out of him.

Thayne said, "I read that Lewis and Clark named all sorts of things on their expedition, but they didn't get the names sent to others right away. By the time they did, other people had already named a lot of the same things, and those names got recorded first."

Thayne looked up from the journal. "How old do you think this is?"

Shaking his head, Brody said, "Most of the bays on the map I studied aren't newly named. San Francisco Bay was named before Ellie's father came out here. And he came about the same time as Grandpa did. Here Grandpa writes, 'Looking for gold where others might not find it. It's beautiful here. Might build a home and own a piece of the old sod for my family.' And over here he says, 'Might find a place in the mountains to the east and settle down. Find the treasure a man needs.'"

"He mentions the Sierra Nevada Mountains in at least one place," Lock said.

Nodding, Brody wondered why his family couldn't have been more like the Harts—working, building something real, something lasting. Why had the journal so haunted their lives? After thinking it over, Brody decided that Ellie was right: The journal was something Grandpa had found. Or it was part of what he'd found.

"That's why we came here to the Two Harts." Lock closed the journal and sighed. "He seemed to be heading back east and probably keeping to the California Trail. The only trail Grandpa would have known about."

"That would be true when he was coming out. But he'd been here a while. Maybe he found something else."

"But he mentions that mountain we were headed for—or what sounds like that mountain."

"His description does sound like that one peak. It's the highest around these parts. And only a few pages further, while he talks of the land and his exploring, he first mentions treasure. His writing becomes more puzzling from then on."

A knock on the door had Brody rising.

"May I come in?" It was Ellie.

He hurried to the door and swung it open.

"I've come to help you plan our trip." Ellie smiled brightly.

Brody blinked. "*Our* trip?"

SEVENTEEN

These three didn't know just how big the West was.

Ellie trailed along beside Brody. Josh had thrown in with them because he refused to let Ellie ride out into the wilderness with three greenhorns and a strange map. Ellie thought that was wise. Josh was in the lead, Lock riding beside him, with Thayne just behind on the narrow trail.

They sure as certain didn't know how big a mountain was. And Ellie didn't know how to narrow their search.

The MacKenzies were never going to find whatever it was their grandfather had found unless they tripped and fell on top of it. And yet here they were riding east, chasing some clue Ellie found dubious about the mountain ahead. Ellie wished Michelle and Jillian were here. Those two had steel-trap minds; they'd be able to draw information out of the journal that none of the rest of them would recognize as important.

Usually, Michelle and Zane went to the lumber camp owned by Michelle's family and stayed there about a month. It used to be that the Stiles family would run the lumber camp for about six months of the year. The camp would then close for the cold weather, and the Stiles would move to their home in San Francisco.

But since train tracks had been laid all the way to their mountain, they could extend their time, which meant the Stiles lumber dynasty made more money now than ever before because they were working nine months of the year. Ellie knew Michelle always itched to stay up there. She and Zane had agreed to be gone for a month, yet it was a bit longer every year.

Zane seemed to like it on the mountaintop too, but eventually he dragged Michelle home. Now that they had a baby coming, Zane liked it down here better. He thought ranch life to be superior to lumbering. And Michelle was a great help on the ranch, just because she was full of innovations and ideas. She spent time every day in a shed Zane had built, where she worked on new inventions. The baby would curtail that somewhat for a while, but Michelle did love to invent.

Yet they were needed in San Francisco as well during the winter. The rest of the family lived there and conducted important business that Michelle helped with. That meant another month gone.

They got along here without Zane, but they missed him. He was a skilled rancher and ran the Two Harts wisely. They all did better when he was around, although she sometimes sensed a little resentment in Josh, who'd done a fine job with the ranch but had to let go of the reins when Zane returned.

This winter Michelle's sister, Jillian, and her husband, Nick, were coming to the Two Harts. They had a few construction projects to do here, such as improving the telegraph wire they'd had strung from Dorada Rio, and Jillian wanted to build a couple of bridges across creeks that tended to flood in the spring. She'd spoken of damming up one of the creeks to create a pond to be stocked with fish. Ellie couldn't quite imagine that. How did you move fish without them dying when they were out of the water? She wasn't sure what all they had in mind, but she liked fish and no one was better at creating things than Jillian, so Ellie decided she'd just stay out of the way and watch.

Ellie wondered what those two bright, curious women, and Zane too, would make of MacKenzie's Treasure and that mysterious journal. No one knew this land better than them.

"What were the landmarks your grandpa mentioned again?" Ellie enjoyed listening to the MacKenzies talk about the journal, and she thought talking it through might kick up a few new ideas. "There was more than just talk of a mountain, right?"

Lock twisted in the saddle, his eyes shining with excitement over the hunt.

She sincerely hoped when they found out there was no treasure, he wouldn't be too disappointed. Ellie liked to dream of treasure as much as anyone, but she was also a California rancher, which made her a realist. Finding hidden treasure didn't happen very often, probably because it didn't exist.

Then again, Graham MacKenzie had definitely found something.

"He mentions a spring that pours out of a crack in the mountain and cascades down into a small pond. He said it was summer, and the pond was as green as Loch Uaine."

Brody interjected, "They say Loch Uaine is a mystical place. I for certain have never seen it, and I doubt Grandpa had ever seen it either. He was from a little town in the southern Scottish Highlands, while Loch Uaine is in the north. But it's legendary for its beauty. The MacKenzies are pure Scottish, as I'm sure you've guessed."

"A green loch?" Ellie had heard of Scotland and its many lochs and rugged highlands.

"Loch Uaine means 'Lake Green.' They say the little people, elves and such, go there to wash their stockings, which has made the lake a turquoise color."

Ellie laughed at the whimsy of it. "It sounds beautiful."

"Our pa was born there, the youngest of eight children. His family came here to America when he was just a boy."

"Eight children? Where were they when your pa ran off? All those aunts and uncles . . ."

Brody shrugged one shoulder. "Pa was a straggler, and several of his older brothers and sisters died back in Scotland. That was part of what drove Grandma and Grandpa to travel to America. They brought five children with them. One didn't survive the crossing but died aboard the ship they sailed on. One was a daughter who was nearly an adult by the time Pa came along. She married and headed west on a wagon train with her husband, and one of my uncles went with them. The other one died fighting in the Civil War. I never knew him. They were all gone before I was born. And Pa was barely old enough to remember them leaving. I think that was part of what lured Grandpa west. He hoped to find some sign of his kids. I'm just imagining that, though. I never heard Grandpa speak of it."

"We never knew our grandparents," Thayne said. "Ma's folks died before she married Pa, and Pa's folks died before we came along."

"I heard Grandma and Grandpa tell stories of the old country." Brody shifted in his saddle. "They missed their home, but it was a hard life there and America beckoned them."

"So your grandpa said there was a spring that poured into a little pond as green as Loch Uaine." Ellie looked at Josh. "Does that sound familiar?"

"No," Josh replied. "Lock, what else is in there?"

"He said to take on the mountain but watch for a broken monster tree. Not sure what that means."

Josh nodded. "There are some huge trees out here. Sequoias mainly and redwoods, but usually they're closer to the ocean. I suppose those would seem like monster trees to a man from New York."

Ellie didn't bother to mention the range of redwood trees along the western slope of the Sierra Nevada Mountains. Anyway, it wasn't much of a clue, as trees broke off all the time in storms and such.

"Well, we're taking on the mountain. What are we to do when we see this broken monster tree?"

"He said there's a trail there, rugged and narrow, that turns left at that tree. I wonder if that tree blocked the trail, or maybe his horse ran away with him. Grandpa was no more of a rider than we are. There are other clues as well."

"Let's hold off on them for now and instead keep an eye out for a tree that could be described as a monster."

"The trouble with Grandpa's clues is we're mostly adding up little hints," Brody said. "But it's an arithmetic problem that doesn't give enough information. We may be coming up with nothing but wrong answers."

Thayne looked behind him at Ellie. "Thank you for letting us take your horses, Miss Ellie. We appreciate it. When we ran off before, the mountain seemed as though it was right in front of us. We had no idea how far away it really was."

"You're welcome, Thayne," Ellie said. "You know, you're getting to the age when you need to be thinking about what you want to do with your life. You've had a chance to work on the ranch. Do you like riding? Or we can focus on continuing your studies. You could become a doctor like Brody. We can get books on just about any subject, whatever interests you. Michelle and Jilly could work with you if you want to study arithmetic or science at a higher level. Laura is a chemist if you wanted to study that area of science."

"All right," said Thayne. "I'll think about it."

Ellie made them stop for the noon meal. The MacKenzies were going to be saddlesore after today, and a break from such a long ride was necessary, even if the men wanted to push onward.

Loyal strode into the Sacramento Straten, the finest restaurant in town, and shook hands firmly with the man Sonny had told him was the key, a man who'd expect his dinner companion to be well-dressed. For although he was a stranger, Loyal knew the type. "Mr. Westbrook, good to meet you."

"Mr. Kelton. I've heard of your father over in San Francisco but never had the pleasure of meeting him." Mayhew Westbrook had steely-gray hair with a bald dome. He stood up straight, unlike Father who was bent these days. He was dressed elegantly, so Loyal was glad he'd picked his best suit, even if it was uncomfortably tight.

Westbrook moved slowly as he led the way to the dinner table as two waiters, dressed in finery, held their chairs for them.

The clinking of silver utensils against china plates set the backdrop of the hushed room. Loyal quickly scanned the place, looking for anyone who might know Father.

Father likely hadn't spoken of being punched. He'd always done his best to keep the family name out of any scandal. But men who knew Father might mention Loyal's presence here with Westbrook, and Father might make it his business to reach out to Westbrook to spoil any business the man had with Loyal.

Loyal recognized no one, but he didn't dare study the room overtly. Because he wasn't sure how far gossip about his dismissal from the bank had traveled, he began with, "I'm on my own these days. Banking didn't suit me. But I saw my father not too long ago. He's doing well." Not counting a bruised stomach.

"My grandson is working with me at my bank. It's a fine profession. Maybe you'll return to it one day." Westbrook was old. Older than Father. And he had those same sharp eyes. The man was smart, but then no one could rise in the competitive banking world of California and not have a keen mind. Loyal didn't underestimate the man.

Yesterday Loyal had contacted Westbrook and said, "I heard you're on the trail of an old treasure, one I've also taken interest in. I love talking about the fables that fill the Rocky Mountains. Come and join me for lunch."

Mayhew Westbrook had done his best to sound casual, as if buried treasure and lost mines were a simple pleasure. Even so, Loyal had read the change in his voice and knew the old man cared.

That's why Loyal was here. Sonny had found just enough details to lead them to Westbrook.

As they settled in, a waiter served them coffee and took their orders. The two of them exchanged pleasantries, mostly about the weather. Loyal got the impression Westbrook didn't give much away.

After their meals were served and they'd both had a few bites of tender roast beef, Loyal said, "I've come across rumors of an old mine claim registered to Graham MacKenzie. Included was your name, saying you were a stakeholder."

Westbrook sat forward. "I did stake MacKenzie to a claim years ago, but then I never heard from the man again."

Loyal didn't believe the old man. He wasn't telling the full truth. He remembered punching his father and wondered what more information there was to glean from Westbrook if a little force was applied.

"Can you tell me where this claim is?" Westbrook licked his lips in a way that indicated thirst to Loyal . . . or was it hunger? "I've also heard a rumor or two, namely that Mac-Kenzie had found something, but it's not clear what exactly. Then only silence for years. I figured he headed back east or died. But he has family—they'd own that claim now. And that family owes me money."

"I don't have much information, Mr. Westbrook, just enough to believe such a claim exists." The rumors had come to Sonny through Westbrook's investigator. "Honestly, I'm a little surprised the whole thing has even a shred of truth. But I was in Sacramento, so I thought I'd look you up."

"I wonder if the old prospector actually found some-thing." Westbrook seemed to look back through the years, probably remembering promises that had been made.

"Can I call on you again?" Loyal asked. "I can't think of any way to get to the truth short of going from town to town and digging through old claim records. This is from thirty years ago. I suspect some of those towns with land offices no longer exist. It's been interesting to go explor-ing, although I'm sure it's pure folly. But if I find anything, I'll remember your claim to it and bring what I find back to you."

Westbrook's eyes flickered with indecision for a moment. Then he answered, "My grandson, Cordell, is out following a clue I recently received about the MacKenzie family. I wish we could get this information to him; it might change the course he's following."

"Where is he? I've got some traveling ahead. If we happen to be in the same area, perhaps . . ." Loyal let his voice fade, hoping to have said enough but not too much.

"He's south of here. Close to Lodi, I believe."

"Lodi?" Loyal remembered the last time he'd been in Lodi. He'd run across his worthless fiancée . . . former fiancée by then. Loyal had tried to win her back, hoping to restore himself in his father's eyes.

Instead, he'd ended up running afoul of Beth Ellen's brother Zane Hart—and her brother Josh too, though it was Zane who'd punched him. Loyal had found himself writhing on the ground below the train station platform. Ever since then, he'd longed to exact revenge on the whole family, especially Beth Ellen.

Westbrook nodded. "I got word that one of the Mac-Kenzies, a grandson of the first MacKenzie, had been seen at the Two Harts Ranch."

A wave of fury swept over Loyal.

Westbrook had been leaning forward in his urgency, but as his eyes sharpened on Loyal, the old man straightened in his seat.

Loyal felt the need to come up with some excuse and quick. He skirted close to the truth for simplicity's sake. "I-I used to know Beth Ellen Hart. She lives on the Two Harts, or I should say she lived there a few years ago. I've lost track of her. I used to . . . to have hopes for the two of us. I'm sorry to say she broke my heart. Ah, to be so young again." Loyal laughed to dismiss it as if just a childhood romance. Unimportant now. That his interest in revenge and Sonny's interest in treasure would intersect gave him a savage satisfaction.

Westbrook seemed to relax some. "Well, I won't expect you then to go down there. I'm sure you don't want to see her. If you find the location of that mining claim, I'd appreciate it if you'd wire me the information. I certainly don't expect you to make another trip to see me. A telegram would be welcome, though."

"I'll most certainly do that," Loyal promised.

"Now," said Westbrook, grinning, "we can't eat at the Sacramento Straten without trying their apple dumplings. They're famous for them. They even make their own ice cream."

Eighteen

The afternoon was half gone, and as the altitude rose, the temperature dropped.

"Look. That looks like a monster tree, and it's broken off." Pointing, Lock's voice rose with excitement.

Brody snapped his head up and realized he'd been dozing in the saddle or the next thing to it. His heart sped up. "Is . . . is that a sequoia?" He was awestruck by the massive size of its trunk. "It *is* a monster tree. I can see why Grandpa described it that way."

The tree was so wide at its base, all five of them, arms reaching out, couldn't stretch around the trunk. And yes, it was broken off, but so high up that Brody couldn't estimate its full height. Was it thirty feet, forty, fifty?

Still standing, the trunk showed rot on one side that had formed an opening like a cave, deep enough for a man to step into without ducking. Looking at the dark crevasse in the giant tree made Brody feel as though he were staring into its heart—its broken heart.

Before breaking and falling, the treetop must have dominated the rest of the forest. The underbrush hid the extent of the once-majestic sequoia from view.

"There are huge old oaks back in New York." Brody spoke in a hushed voice as he might have when in church. He was struck hard by the beauty of God's creation. "I've taken the train from New York City to Boston. Along the way, I've seen some mighty big trees." He paused as he took in their surroundings. "Nothing compares to this."

"If we head north," said Josh, "there are some of these same trees closer to the ranch. Every summer, Pa and Ma used to pack a picnic lunch and take us out to see them and spend an afternoon in the shade of the sequoias. My brothers and Annie and I would pretend they were giants, and we'd play hide-and-seek around their trunks. I'll never get over the splendor of these trees."

Brody felt like this was the chance of a lifetime to see something so magnificent.

"And that," said Josh, pointing to the left, "is a trail fit only for a jackrabbit."

Despite Josh's unflattering assessment, Brody never would have recognized it as a trail. Josh turned left. The trail went straight down, cut right into the side of the mountain.

Brody had to tear himself away from the tree when he wanted to stay and just absorb the grandeur. He rode forward while vowing he'd come back and spend more time in this stand of trees.

The broken colossus blocked the trail in front of them, so it was just as well they needed to turn off. It was a rocky stretch, yet there were sprouts of life shooting up from the roots of the broken sequoia, as if the tree were fighting for life.

Patches of green grass wrapped around the base of the tree, and with the mountain rising up to the west and against the blue California sky, the beautiful view was fit to be a masterpiece painting.

Thayne looked over his shoulder at Brody and asked, "Do you know, is the green pond the next landmark?"

Brody shook his head. "No. Next we search for a hole, *then* the green pond."

"The trouble with using landmarks," Ellie said as if wanting to warn them against getting their hopes too high, "is that rocks cave off or break. Trees can get swept away in a landslide. With the earthquakes California is so famous for, we've had creeks jump their banks and carve new routes. We even had one dry up completely. There was a crack in the creek bed, and the stream plunged underground."

Ellie looked at Brody. "Can creeks do that? It's not like there's a tunnel for it to follow under there."

"I don't know much about earthquakes—or vanishing streams, for that matter."

"You'll get a chance to learn more. We get little quakes quite often. It gets so I don't pay them much mind. Anyway, with your grandpa's journal, a lot can happen in thirty years."

"Your grandpa," Josh called back as he rode down the treacherous slope, "should have given you better directions, but I reckon saying that now is a waste of time."

Brody agreed with Josh on both counts.

"Do you suppose Pa ever got this close to Grandpa's trail, Brody?" Lock was almost bouncing in the saddle. "Do you suppose he rode this exact path?"

It was a steep trail and barely wide enough to ride side by side. Brody thought, at the rate it was narrowing, it'd be single file soon.

Brody looked at Ellie. "You never met a man out here, mad with gold fever? Pa only came home this last winter, so if he was treasure hunting, he might've even come by the ranch to fetch a meal or something. He looks more like Lock than Thayne and me. We took after Ma."

"I can't remember such a man, but it's a big mountain. Your pa might've wandered far from the trail we picked. Do you reckon he ever came this way?"

Brody shook his head. "What Pa did was a mystery. We're on the trail left behind by Grandpa."

"We need to be hunting for that hole Grandpa spoke of," Lock said. "Problem is, his clues are cryptic and buried in lengthy descriptions of scenery. Some of his sentences don't seem to go with the rest of his writing. I've tried to pay special mind to that. I think Grandpa was hoping to hide directions to his treasure by salting them with flowery words."

Brody had little doubt that his brother had the journal as good as memorized.

They rode on downward. Strange to have such a steep descent on a mountain where the trails went mainly upward. Soon the trail twisted, rising occasionally, though mainly they were going down. Finally, they reached a wooded stretch where the trees blocked out the sky. In the deep shadows, Brody felt as if he were sliding down into the belly of a huge beast. A chill rushed up his spine at that thought, and he shoved all such thoughts from his mind to watch where he was riding.

"That might be what Grandpa was talking about." Thayne pointed to a rockslide.

"Why? That's not anything I'd describe as a hole." Brody glanced at Ellie, wishing she knew enough about this mountain to help with Grandpa's mysterious clues.

"Look just above those scattered rocks. There's something there. I think if it wasn't for the rockslide, we'd see it better. Let's look closer."

Josh reached the slide, which covered the trail. "That's called a scree. Like we said, the trouble with landmarks is they can change. That could be the right spot, but the rocks are hiding it." He reined in his horse. "It does look like there's something there." Josh turned to Thayne and nodded.

Brody rode up behind Lock and halted, watching as Lock let his horse walk out onto the scree.

"Should he be walking across that?" Brody asked.

Ellie gasped. "Lock, no. Come ba—"

Lock's horse slid on the loose pebbles, then caught itself and took lurching leaps back onto the trail. Lock fell backward off the horse with a shout of terror. He landed hard on the crumbling rock, then slid out of sight over the edge of a cliff.

Brody jumped down off his horse and ran to the spot where his brother had disappeared. He felt the rocks give and went flying after his brother into midair.

Brody hit the ground hard, then slid downward, twisting to claw at the jumble of small rocks. He heard his name being screamed from above. It was Ellie.

He caught hold of something, which jerked him to a stop. Then he broke loose and started tumbling again. He kicked up dirt, choking as he fought to stop his fall. A tree growing out the middle of the talus slide slammed into his belly and stopped him for a second. He glimpsed Lock below him, still skidding down the nearly sheer slope.

The tree wrenched out of the rocks, and he fell again, faster this time. A solid blow to the head left him addled. Suddenly he stopped, his head still swimming. He forced his eyes open and saw he was on a ledge half as wide as his body. There, gasping for breath, he looked down and saw Lock, who was still falling.

163

Brody's ledge gave way, and he started tumbling again. He hit a boulder, hard enough it knocked the wind out of his chest. He realized rocks were sliding with him as he'd created an avalanche.

If he survived this mad fall, he might well be buried with the rocks he'd shaken loose. Gasping for breath that wouldn't come, he saw another pine tree ahead, bigger this time. He surged forward with his battered legs and flung his arms around the tree.

The rough bark of the scraggly tree scraped his face. Branches slapped him. But it held.

Still not breathing well, he looked down. The world whirled and faded. He dragged a leg over the tree so it held his weight in case he blacked out. Panting, aching in every bone and joint, he looked down again. He spotted Lock below him at the bottom of the slide, lying flat on his belly. He wasn't moving. Little rocks cascaded down, bouncing off his brother's back and legs and head. Lock was bleeding.

Brody's mind cleared enough that he could see he'd fallen most of the way down, and what was left wasn't as steep.

Sickened and with no idea what else to do, Brody eased himself off the tree branch. With some modicum of control now, he slid the rest of the way down the slope. He felt his pants snag on a sharp point. Tearing fabric followed.

When he reached the bottom, he crawled across the rocks, with more of them peppering his back, and threw himself over Lock. And there he lay until the rocks quit pouring down. Feeling dizzy and halfway to having his wits knocked out of him, Brody pulled away from his brother.

He pressed two fingers against Lock's neck. With a near sob of relief, he realized Lock was still alive. Brody slid his hands expertly over Lock's arms and legs. No obvious sign of broken bones. Lock's face was bleeding, scraped nearly raw on the right side. But Brody knew just how many injuries there could be that didn't show and were nearly impossible to treat. Broken spine, broken or cracked ribs, skull fractures, ruptured spleen. A body could be busted up inside in a hundred different ways.

Brody heard a shout and looked up to see Ellie. She was coming down. They'd found a path off to the side where they could climb down safely. He saw Josh ahead of her, with Thayne, white-faced and terrified, right behind him. All three of them were heading down to lend their help.

Brody's vision narrowed. It was like looking through a tunnel, and with each passing second the light lessened, until the only thing he could see was Ellie. She glanced over her shoulder in her recklessly fast descent. Their eyes met.

He wanted to shout to her that he was all right, but he was too dazed to manage it. And too tired and hurt.

He was still trying to muster the strength to reassure Ellie he was fine when the tunnel closed. He was only dimly aware of his slumping flat onto the ground in utter darkness.

NINETEEN

"Brody!" Ellie scrambled faster, her heart thudding. Rocks and scrub brush that she grabbed to slow her descent tore at her hands.

Josh glanced up at her, but she only distantly noticed as she rushed down. She'd've tried to slow down, move with more care, but she didn't have that much control of her descent. She slid suddenly and doubled her time, skidding right past Josh.

He reached out and snagged her by the back of her coat. "Ellie, be careful."

She nodded, and with just a bit more control they continued on their way down.

Rocks pelted her head, and though she didn't look up, she knew Thayne was coming. She'd probably get a face full of dirt if she looked up. She'd heard the cry of terror break from his throat when his whole family had vanished over a cliff. She'd screamed right along with him.

How could either of them be alive? But she'd seen Brody moving. Just a little, but that meant no broken spine, didn't it? No broken arms and legs?

He'd knelt over Lock. Then he looked up at her. Never

had she seen so much in another's eyes as that moment when her gaze latched onto his. She was mindless to anything but speed and prayer.

At last, they reached the bottom of the treacherous slope. Distantly she heard water flowing and wondered where in the world they were.

Ellie was ahead of Josh. She saw him pause to make sure Thayne got down all right.

She ran for Brody and dropped to her knees beside him. He was facedown. Gently she rolled him onto his back and pressed a hand flat on his chest. His heart was beating solidly.

Josh reached Lock. "He's alive."

Brody moaned, and his eyes fluttered open. "Ellie, Lock, I-I checked. There's a pulse. No broken bones. But he's bleeding . . ." His eyes closed.

"Brody, no. Stay with me."

"Lock seems to be knocked insensible, but he's in one piece." Josh was checking over Lock just as she checked Brody.

Ellie looked up to see Josh sit back on his haunches.

Thayne, beside his little brother, slumped to sit on his backside. "You think they're going to be all right?" Thayne sounded like he might burst into tears.

Josh nodded. "There could be things wrong we can't see, but let's hope they've both just taken a pounding and will come around." He shifted his gaze to Ellie. "It may be a while, though. I'm going back up to the horses. I'll scout around and see if I can get them down here." He pointed to the left. "There may be a more passable slope over that way. It looks promising. And there's grazing here, with water aplenty sounds like."

Ellie looked away from Brody, and it took all her strength. Water was definitely flowing somewhere nearby.

167

"If I can't get the horses down here, I'll tie them up and haul down bedrolls and such. We'd planned to camp out tonight. It looks like we're going to make that camp right here in this spot."

Brody moaned again but didn't open his eyes or speak.

Ellie felt hope and fear in equal parts.

"Thayne, you'd better go up with me. If I can't get the horses down, there'll be a lot to haul. It'll take us both to carry it all."

Thayne's eyes slid from one brother to the other. Ellie sensed him wanting to refuse to go. He wanted to stay with his family instead. Yet he would be more help by going with Josh.

He nodded and rose to his feet. "Be careful, little sister." Josh's words were simple, although they seemed to be something more than their most obvious meaning.

Josh's eyes flitted between her and Brody. Then he and Thayne started heading back up the slope, leaving Ellie alone with two battered, unconscious men.

———— ✧ ————

"Lock!" Brody's eyes flew open with a start. "Lock! No!"

Ellie's face filled his vision. "Brody, you're awake."

"Lock . . ." Brody rolled to the side and was hit with agony in every joint. "I have to—"

"He's right here. He's still unconscious." Ellie helped Brody to sit up.

Brody blinked at the sight of his brother, who was tucked snugly under a blanket. A fire crackled on past Lock. Brody smelled savory meat and saw a steaming coffeepot. He looked overhead to the night sky, exploding with stars. "How long have I been asleep?"

"You fell in the middle of the afternoon. And the days are long."

"You set up camp?"

"Yes." Ellie came to his side as he looked down at Lock. As he struggled to focus on his brother, his head began to throb. There were two of Lock, then one, then two again.

A concussion. Any blow to the head bad enough to knock him out for hours was very likely to qualify as a concussion.

"Josh got a couple of rabbits," said Ellie. "He's had them cooking a long time now. The meat should be tender enough to chew, even with a terrible headache. First, you'd better check Lock over. I'll fetch the canteen. Then if you're up to it, you should eat something."

Josh reached for the coffeepot sitting on the red-hot coals at the heart of the fire. "I'll pour you a cup of coffee, fix up a plate of rabbit and biscuits."

Brody nodded slowly, then slid his hands up and down Lock's arms and legs. In the flickering firelight, he noticed a nasty gash on Lock's forehead. Running his hands over Lock's skull, he felt two bumps the size of chicken eggs.

"Has he been awake, even for a minute?" Brody looked over Lock's abdomen, checking for swelling or bruises, watching for his brother to react in pain.

It wasn't that he wanted Lock to feel pain; Brody just wanted Lock to react to the world around him.

Ellie was back at his side so quickly, Brody had barely noticed she'd left. "Josh and I have been watching over him," she said. "Thayne too—that is, until he fell asleep about an hour ago."

Thayne slept near the campfire, covered with a wool blanket against the chill of the mountain night.

Brody drank deeply from the ice-cold water in the canteen.

It was fresh water, not the tepid water they'd been hauling on their journey. Again Brody heard the rush of water nearby. He saw their horse beyond the fire and heard the quiet cropping as they ate grass.

Thayne sat up, shoving aside the blanket. "Brody, how are you?" His brow furrowed as he crawled the few feet between them to rest a hand on Brody's arm.

"Looks like I'm going to be all right. Tell me, has Lock been conscious at all? Even for a little while?"

Thayne shook his head sadly.

Brody frowned as they both stared at their brother Lock's still form.

Ellie said, "I've been watching him closely. Josh and Thayne and I sat him up just a bit, and he swallowed a little water. I think his sleep is more normal, a true sleep rather than being unconscious. We haven't tried to wake him up, hoping sleep was the best thing for him right now. But he's breathing at a steady pace. He even snored for a while and shifted a bit, as someone who's asleep is apt to do." Ellie knelt between Brody and Lock, who lay to Brody's left, with Thayne kneeling on Brody's right. "Do you think we should try to wake him?" She rested a gentle hand on Lock's shoulder.

Lock's smooth breathing became uneven for a few seconds, then went deep and steady again. Brody got to his knees beside Ellie, closer to Lock's head. Thayne came around until he was directly across from Brody.

Josh, who'd been handling everything involved in a night under the stars with two injured companions, stood by to watch. He hadn't poured coffee or gotten Brody his food yet, leaving Brody to tend to his brother first.

"He must have a concussion," said Brody. "I suppose I do, too."

"I've never heard that word before," Thayne said. "How serious is it?"

"It just means the brain is bruised. Like a blow to your arm will leave a bruise, a blow to the head leaves a bruise as well. Usually it heals right up, but a person needs to be careful. You can get dizzy. Your vision can blur, or you see double. Headaches can be a real problem. There are other symptoms, too. Some concussions have a few of them, others none. But with time they almost always heal up just fine."

Brody checked Lock's head again and winced at the two large bumps. One on the back of his skull, one on the right side. His face was scraped up badly. Just moving told Brody he was almost as battered as his brother.

"I'm going to see if he'll wake up. It's a good idea to interrupt even normal sleep after someone's taken a blow to the head."

Brody reached for the canteen, then pulled a kerchief out of his pocket and soaked it with cool water. Lock's face had been washed. His cuts and scrapes looked clean but were unbandaged. There were enough of them it was hard to know where to start.

Pressing the cool cloth to Lock's forehead, Brody said quietly, "Lock, can you hear me? Lock, wake up."

Brody used his best doctor voice while pressing the cold kerchief to his brother's face and neck.

With a quiet moan of pain, Lock's eyes fluttered open. He lay there staring up at Brody.

"You're awake. Good. You fell over a cliff. We've been worried about you."

"W-we?"

Brody nodded. "Thayne and me, Ellie and Josh. We set

up camp right here where you fell. You've been sleeping a long time. Would you like some food or a drink of water?"

"The water sounds good."

"Thayne, can you help lift him?"

"I'm glad you're awake, Lock. I've been powerful worried." Thayne slid his arm under Lock's shoulders on Lock's right while Brody did the same from the left. They eased him into a sitting position.

Ellie got the canteen. "I'm here too, Lock. And Josh." She held the canteen to his lips, and they all watched as he sipped from it, then drank long and deep.

"How about something to eat?" Ellie asked. "Josh cooked up a couple of rabbits, and there are biscuits. He also made coffee. A warm drink might suit you."

Lock shook his head, then stopped and moaned. "Thank you, Miss Ellie. Josh, thanks for making the food, but none for me. I hurt all over, Brody."

"It'll hurt like you've taken a Saturday night beating, but it's all bumps and bruises near as I can tell." Brody prayed he was right about that. "You'll heal up in time. Would you rather we left you alone so you can sleep some more?"

"More water first, please."

After Lock took another drink from the canteen, Brody and Thayne lowered him gently to the ground. Instantly his eyes closed, and his breathing fell back into that same steady rhythm.

TWENTY

Ellie sat up, crossed to the other side of the fire, and knelt beside Lock. She gently shook his shoulder. "Lock." She spoke softly, hoping to rouse him during this, her third check of the night, but without waking everyone else.

She heard movement behind her and saw Josh tossing kindling onto the campfire's still glowing embers. She hadn't managed to move quietly enough for him but smiled because she wasn't sure that was even possible.

In the first gray light of approaching dawn, she kept up the gentle shaking, hoping to ease Lock into wakefulness. She'd gotten him to stir the other times, so she was hopeful he'd come around this time, too.

Brody had been fully prepared to keep watch of his brother all night long. It had taken some urging, but the poor battered doctor had finally agreed to get some sleep. She'd left him alone, each time wondering if she should make him wake up as well. Yet he hadn't told her to, and he'd been alert and rational, so she'd decided to let the man sleep on.

"Lo-ock," Ellie crooned. It made her think of the soothing way Brody often spoke to his hurting patients. "Lochlan MacKenzie, wake up now." She saw the first shifting of his eyes behind closed lids. The rocking continued, but she quit talking for the sake of quiet.

His eyes fluttered open. They focused. She hadn't realized how worried she was, but each time he'd awakened throughout the night, tension uncoiled within her, and she relaxed a bit more.

Brody had spoken of concussions and how important these moments of wakefulness were. She wasn't sure why, but Brody was tired and so she didn't question him, just promised if she couldn't wake Lock, she'd wake Brody and let him help.

Lock smiled. He'd had a dazed look in the night, but now he looked alert. He shoved his blanket aside and sat up, then yelped.

The whole camp was awake now.

Brody moved to Lock's side, with Thayne coming to his brother as well.

"Every inch of me hurts." Lock reached for his head and winced. He kept moving his arm until his hand rested on the back of his head.

Supporting him, Brody got Lock to sit all the way up.

"I need . . . um, that is, excuse me, Miss Hart, but if Brody and Thayne would help me, I'd like to . . . step away from the camp for a minute." Lock's cheeks turned ruddy in the dim light.

Ellie said, "I'll help Josh get breakfast on." She moved away quickly to minimize Lock's embarrassment.

She busied herself getting out the skillet but heard the boy moan in pain as Brody and Thayne as good as lifted him to his feet.

Josh came up beside her with a saddlebag and pulled out a side of bacon. From the corner of her eye, she could see how painful each movement was for Lock. She noticed Brody seemed to be feeling every move, too.

"I'd offer to help, but they're managing. Mostly." If it was modesty keeping them from asking for help, maybe she should offer. "I think Brody could use a hand."

"We'll help if they ask," said Josh. "And I think Brody has the sense to ask, so we can keep cooking." He nodded at Ellie, and the two of them did their best to get a meal on and not worry about the MacKenzie brothers.

They soon rejoined the camp, and Thayne eased his brother onto a fallen log Josh had rolled near to the fire.

Brody asked questions of the young man, inspecting again the bumps on his head and the scrapes and bruises on his face. The three of them were a while getting settled, and by then Ellie had prepared biscuits and baked them in one skillet while Josh fried bacon in the other.

Ellie poured fresh coffee for Brody and Thayne, handing each of them a cup. "Would you like anything to eat or drink, Lock?"

He gave her a sheepish look, then rubbed a hand over his belly. "I can't tell if I'm starving or I just got punched in the stomach lots of times during my fall."

"I'll get you a little bit of coffee and a biscuit, and we'll see how that sets in your stomach. If you feel up to it, I'll get you more."

They were soon all fed and drinking a second cup of coffee. Lock had eaten a little. But he kept it down and claimed to only be seeing one of everything now.

Ellie hated to say it, but she thought it was wise. "We may as well head for home—I mean, if you think you can ride, Lock. Looks as though our treasure hunt is ruined for this weekend. We'll try again later."

Josh, quietly packing away the washed skillet, said, "Before we go, I need to show everyone something."

"What is it?" Lock asked.

Ellie could tell he didn't want to head back. But he couldn't go on either.

"Where I got the water for the horses and to refill the canteens." Josh paused, and Ellie thought he was maybe doing it just for the dramatic effect.

"Go on." She wanted to kick him but opted for decorum instead.

"Come and see. Lock, it's only a few paces beyond that clump of scrub pines."

Brody exchanged a look with Ellie, who shrugged.

Lock was helped to his feet, and they all followed Josh around the pines to see . . .

"Loch Uaine." Brody said it as if he were too awestruck to speak louder.

A spate of water poured down from a crack higher than their heads, coming out of solid rock. It splashed down into a bowl about six feet across that was green as the grass of spring.

Josh smiled. "This must be what Grandpa was talking about in his journal."

Brody looked at Ellie, then Josh. "I've never seen anything like it."

"I'm no chemist—not like my sister-in-law, Laura, who I reckon could tell us for sure what caused that bowl of rock to turn green." Josh scanned the area. "We're well off the Two Harts Ranch here, but Zane and I spent a lot of time running in these hills. I've never been down here, though, and I've never seen anything like this anywhere else either."

"You think Grandpa's treasure is right here?" Lock's voice shook with excitement.

176

"Not right here, but close. Real close." Thayne spoke with a reverence he probably should have reserved for church.

"Can we stay here, Lock?" Thayne rested a hand on his brother's shoulder. "Just for a little while to look around? If not, we'll come right back here soon as we can."

Ellie saw how Lock trembled. He was standing up through pure force of will. How was he going to ride the whole way back to the ranch? It wasn't just staying here; it was what they'd have to do next that was going to be the greater challenge.

"I have to sit down." Lock's knees buckled.

Brody and Thayne were so close that they caught him and eased him to the ground without his falling and maybe hurting himself further.

It was very clear Lock wouldn't be doing any searching.

"I want to help." Lock gave Brody such a beseeching look it hurt Ellie's heart. "I want to be with you when you find the treasure."

Brody knelt by his brother's side. Thayne dropped in front of Lock and bent his knees, spread wide, his ankles crossed behind him.

"What should we do?" Thayne rested a hand on Lock's shoulder. "We wouldn't be here if you hadn't pushed me into coming west, which brought Brody west. This is your treasure hunt as much as it is anyone's.'"

Lock clamped his mouth shut as if he hated letting the words out, but finally, stiffly, he said, "I'll rest here by this green pond, maybe study it while you all scout around. I can't stand the thought of being this close and not hunting at least some. Maybe if I rest awhile, I'll be able to help. If you find the treasure, it'll all be worth it whether I'm there or not. And if you don't find it, you'll have eliminated a few places to look for when we come back. But this is the best clue we've ever had. I believe we'll find it right around here somewhere." Lock's excitement came through even as his shoulders sagged.

"I'll fetch you a blanket." Brody sprang to his feet, then staggered. He wasn't in the best shape either.

"I'll go." Thayne was on his way to the campsite, which was only a few dozen paces away.

"Bring a canteen, Thayne." Ellie looked around, wondering what the green pond could possibly have to do with the treasure. It was certainly an odd feature. Chances were it was what Grandpa MacKenzie had referred to in his journal. "Lock, you get comfortable and gather your strength."

Lock nodded and tilted sideways toward Brody, who shifted to let Lock lower himself to his side. Thayne came with the blanket, and Brody took it and covered Lock.

Thayne set the canteen on the ground next to his little brother should he wake up and want a drink. "Lock, I—" Thayne fell silent. He and Brody looked down at Lock.

Ellie, standing behind Lock, said, "What is it?"

Brody looked up. "He's fast asleep." Shaking his head, he added, "Let's go hunt around. Give Lock some quiet."

Ellie asked, "Is there anything else in the journal where your grandpa wrote about this pool, something we could be missing?"

Brody looked at Thayne, who answered, "I think he mentioned it was near Loch Uaine . . . or in sight of it maybe. Or some such reference of closeness. We best just look around."

"Keeping in mind," Brody added, "that whatever Grandpa found, he found thirty years ago."

As the three of them turned toward the search, Josh said, "I'll go to the west of this green pool, each of you pick a direction. Keep your eyes peeled for anything unusual, such as an unnatural-looking mound. Whatever your grandpa saw might be buried under thirty years' worth of falling pine needles."

Ellie walked slowly, studying the ground in her direction, which mainly went straight back to the rockslide to the south. In all other directions, there was no end to the thick woods, the underbrush, the stony soil, weeds and fallen pine needles. They were surrounded by Sequoia trees mostly, though nothing compared to the massive ones she'd seen before, like that one broken tree.

As she headed toward the bottom of the cliff, she wondered if the scree slide was newer than thirty years. If it was, the treasure could be buried beneath tons of shattered stone.

How could they ever hope to find the treasure in such a vast wilderness?

Twenty-One

"I can't believe we're so close to finding Grandpa's treasure." Thayne grabbed Brody's arm and shook it.

All Brody could think was that every move, every breath, ached. And Lock had to feel worse than him. He sure acted like he did. How were they going to get him home?

"Ellie went south." Thayne pointed. "Josh is going east. I'll go north, and you west."

Brody looked up to see Ellie disappearing around a tree, headed for the cliff he'd fallen over yesterday. Not much searching to do there. In fact, Josh was moving east along the face of the cliff while Brody was to head west alongside it.

"Get to hunting." Brody could barely think of the treasure for worrying about Lock. "Keep an eye out for anything Grandpa would have left as a marker—a pile of rocks that looks like it was stacked by hand, a carving in a tree trunk, those kinds of things. Even after thirty years, they might still be visible."

"I'm going to ask Ellie if she'll let me search along the cliff face. I want to stay close to Lock."

Thayne nodded and headed off to have a quiet little look at hundreds of acres of forest.

Brody couldn't help but feel pessimistic about their chances of finding anything. Minutes later, he caught up with Ellie, who was standing, hands on her hips, glaring at millions of small rocks.

She heard him coming, gave a wild wave of her hand at the rocks, and said in disgust, "How am I to search all of that?"

"Let me do the searching for a nonexistent treasure in a mountain of broken granite. I think it's best I stay close to Lock."

Ellie nodded. "Where were you supposed to search?"

Brody gestured in a westerly direction, to his left along the cliff face. "That's my assigned area."

Ellie peered hopelessly toward the west. "We know your grandpa found that journal. And he wrote of treasure, so there must be *something* around here."

Brody tried to imagine where Grandpa had been. "Do you suppose he fell over that cliff, too? How in the world could he ever find the green pool otherwise?"

"It's impossible to know which direction he came from. He might've hiked in from an old trail that led to the pool. No falling over a cliff required. But he must have found it somehow. Which means, if he wrote of a treasure, there was more than just the journal."

"And he wrote in ink. Almost no chance he had ink with him. So he found something, went to a town for ink, and started writing about it. Now that I think of it, you can tell his writing begins early in his search, but that's just because once he had the journal to write in, he started taking notes about all he'd seen and done."

"Is there anything else in that journal to give us a clue?"

Brody could tell she was stalling, avoiding a Herculean task, but then so was he. "I don't have it memorized like my brothers do. I hardly read it before I got to the Two Harts." He stared through the bushes as if he could see Lock. "My brother is lying over there and battered half to death because of the journal. I've always hated that book. I blamed it for Pa wrecking our lives. Now I'm blaming it for Lock being so badly hurt."

He shook his head and turned back to Ellie, who'd done nothing to earn his grumpy discontent. "The little bit I read since we got here focused mainly on that line about Captain Cabrillo and the bay he mentioned. I thought that line and others similar to it held the best chance of clues. And I did it all while not really believing in the treasure until you said the journal was old. Lock could probably recite the stupid book line by line, while I don't remember anything after the Loch Uaine line. If we don't find anything before Lock regains his strength enough to ride home, I'll go over it more carefully before we come out here hunting again."

Ellie rested a hand on his arm, and he felt her strength and warmth. "There *is* something here, Brody. Your brothers know that now, so we can't pretend otherwise. They're going to want to search this land and search that journal and never stop. Maybe we can just think of it as a hobby. Like some men play cards. Like some women . . . oh, I don't know." She threw both arms wide. "Play the piano or read a book? What hobbies do women have? I myself don't have time for hobbies."

Brody grinned. "I don't spend much time playing cards either." He turned toward the rockslide. "Is it possible this slide happened after Grandpa was here? Could the treasure be buried under there?"

"I have no idea." She took a couple of steps to the west. Brody caught her arm, and she faced him.

"Ellie, we need to find time to talk about . . . well, about what might be going on between us. I've got to return to Boston. I've got to see to my brothers and learn to be a proper doctor, but there's something—"

"Beth Ellen?" Josh's voice had Brody dropping her arm and Ellie turning to her brother. Who was closer than Brody realized. The man had snuck up on them for a fact. Brody wondered what Josh had seen or heard. From the glint in the man's eyes, Brody figured he'd seen and heard enough to think he needed to interfere.

"Yes?"

"Can you come with me for a bit?"

Ellie gasped, and her pulse sped up. "Did you find something? Evidence of a treasure?"

"No, I just want your company while I hunt." Josh crossed his arms and glared at Brody.

Brody figured he knew what Josh was about.

Ellie glanced at Brody, her cheeks flushed.

"Beth Ellen?" Brody said quietly. He hadn't heard that name before today.

"Only my family calls me that," she explained. "I've been trying to break them of it." She looked at her brother. "And thought I had."

"Which means you're in trouble. My ma would use my full name only when a scolding was coming: 'Brodick Graham MacKenzie, you get yourself over here!'"

"Brodick?"

"Aye, lassie. 'Tis a fine Scots name." Brody added a thick burr he'd learned from his grandpa. "And my ma could wield it like a claymore."

Ellie narrowed her eyes and gave her brother a mean little smile. "Just guess who's not my mother or father?"

"At least he didn't call you Elizabeth Ellen. Nay, he's not your da or ma, just your big brother. He cares about you, even though he shows it by treating you as if he has no trust in your judgment or respect for you knowing your own mind."

"Yes, even though . . ." She headed toward Josh, a militant light in her eyes.

Brody didn't watch her go because he was afraid of what might gleam in his eyes right in front of Josh. Instead, he turned to the fall of rocks and walked along the cliff face, trying to think of what sign might survive thirty years. Surely Grandpa would have left something behind.

———— ✧ ————

Ellie went to Josh's side, then turned without saying anything and tromped through the underbrush.

She wanted a fight. Of course, she didn't want her big brother to scold her, so she wanted a fight where she did the fighting while he kept his mouth shut.

"I saw a dark shadow behind a tree," said Josh, "right at the base of the trail we rode down. I want to see what's behind that tree."

But she needed him to be grouchy and bossy and a generally annoying brother before she could start her shouting. And he wasn't helping her.

Josh led her to a gnarled, stunted oak tree growing out of a jumble of boulders. And he was right—there was something behind this tree.

"You like the doctor?" he asked. "He seems like a good man. If he heads back east with his brothers and his treasure, and you go along with him, I'll miss you."

Ellie stopped right where she was and closed her eyes. She

brought her hand up to cover her face, suddenly weary. "I haven't slept out on the hard ground for a long time."

"That's no answer."

It most certainly wasn't.

Both of them stood there studying the tree, the boulders around it, and that shadow.

"I'm not going to fuss at you, little sister. But I remember how things were after you broke things off with Loyal. I came home before you were over him."

"I was over him the day I found out he kept a mistress while we were engaged, and he told me directly he had no intention of sending her down the road after our wedding."

Josh turned from the tree and rested both hands on her shoulders. His hands were so callused they felt like leather. He'd been at sea. Through the years of hard work, setting sails, battling winds, and tying off rope aboard ship, his shoulders had broadened, his frame had been whittled down to pure, corded muscle, and his skin was weathered a bit too much for a man of his age.

When he'd come home for good, he'd thrown in to work the ranch and that had only honed his strength, though the regular meals kept him from looking gaunt.

He was a pair with her, or so everyone always said. They were the blond-haired, blue-eyed children to match Ma, while Zane and Annie, the two eldest, looked more like Pa.

Josh was one of her favorite people in the world.

"Your love might have died, and the breakup was absolutely final, but you hurt for a long time. It's been three years, Ellie, and I've never seen you so much as flutter your eyes at one of the cowhands."

"Flutter my eyes?" She swatted him on the upper arm.

He grinned. His white teeth shone amid his tanned face.

Long hours in the California sun had darkened his skin and bleached his hair. "Whatever it is that you women do to cast a lure."

Ellie closed her eyes in pain at her brother's oafish talk of lures and fluttering lashes.

"Whatever you do," he went on, his hands tightening and then loosening on her arms, sincerity shining bright in his eyes, "you haven't done it before. Why now? What is it about him that so draws your attention?"

Ellie wrapped her arms around her brother's waist and held him tight. "I don't know what it is about him. I haven't flirted with any cowhands because it never occurred to me to do so. None of those men has interested me, even mildly. I suppose that has its roots in distrust. Loyal taught me that hard lesson. He seemed like an upright and decent man— until I found out he wasn't. How could I trust my judgment after that? But Brody brings something out in me. Something good that is nothing like what I felt for Loyal."

Josh snorted. "What a terrible name for that low-down, *disloyal* coyote."

"Brody has a lot to do before he can turn his attentions to a woman. He's a near stranger to his brothers. He's got to stick with them while he tries to solve the mystery of this treasure. And he insists he's honor-bound to return to the east. He owes some doctor money, which his family used to survive. Loaned with the promise that Brody would return and be his partner in the doctor's practice. And I have no interest in moving to Boston, far from my family."

"*He* would be your family, Beth Ellen. That's how it works. The Bible says 'a man shall leave his father and his mother and shall cleave unto his wife.'"

"Stop. I've just had a moment or two with Brody that

were . . . intriguing. I'm in no way ready to talk about any cleaving, for heaven's sake!"

Josh laughed. "Well, if you do want to talk about it, pick Annie, not me. Now let's get on with the treasure hunt."

Ellie sighed, shaking her head. "That journal had to have come from somewhere. And to mention that pond?"

"That means it's most likely pointing to something around here, but that's a long way from certain. For now, let's keep looking around. We have a slow trip home ahead of us. We've got work tomorrow, as does the good doctor, and those boys have school. Thayne and Lock agreed to short trips. Finding the pond is a good first step. We can search until the sun is overhead. I hope by then Lock will be rested enough to ride. I can rig a travois if he's not."

"Agreed, whether the MacKenzies like it or not. We'll go home and study the journal for further clues, then come back here. Because without more clues, we're never going to find the treasure in this wilderness."

Loyal snatched up the weathered document. "I've found it."

Sonny tossed aside the stack of papers he'd been combing through. "Finally."

"The Two Harts Ranch was the clue we needed." Loyal read the description of the claim written on the water-damaged document. "We can find this. It must be where MacKenzie discovered the gold mine."

Loyal still had his fine suit on. He'd realized he missed dressing this way. He had just the smallest twinge of regret for punching his father. Oh, he'd enjoyed it. No doubt about that.

But there was no going back now. He should have at least

strung the old man along. Let him hope there was a chance Loyal would reform and come home.

It had been too tempting, and Loyal knew he was a miserable failure at resisting temptation. Now he in his fine, if overly tight, suit, and Sonny in his rough western clothes stood in a claims office near the Two Harts Ranch, sorting through old records.

"It's a treasure, Loyal. He staked a claim for mining, but don't get your head stuck in the rut of thinking it's a gold mine. We don't know what exactly he found. An old rumor called it 'MacKenzie's Treasure.' And there were no gold mines in this whole area. Why then would he stake a claim up there in the mountains? No. I think he found something else. A stash that he wanted to legally own. There are all sorts of stories in the West of lost gold, lost diamonds and other jewels. Whole lost cities of gold, for heaven's sake." Sonny licked his lips as he listed all the possible wealth to be had.

Loyal had to admit he liked thinking of it himself.

"Old Graham MacKenzie showed up out of the wilderness, headed straight for the claims office, and filed this exact claim. There was a story that he mailed off a package, then vanished back into the wild. Like a puff of smoke never to be seen or heard from again. Next thing you know, his son came out west and searched, and he was here for years."

"Those rumors you heard were stirred up by this?" This was the most Sonny had told him so far. He'd given out information in dribs and drabs, just enough to keep Loyal strung along. It was maddening, and yet at the same time Loyal had to admit that Sonny knew him well. Knew better than to trust him.

That old saw about honor among thieves was laughable.

"That's right, but the son, Frazier MacKenzie, was poking

around Sutter's Mill. He had whatever he'd learned from his pa lumped in with the California gold rush, only now we know his pa was farther southeast. Right around here, in fact. That's what this here claim tells us." Sonny slapped a hand flat against the paper Loyal had set on the table.

Loyal jumped at the loud slap, then looked around. The man behind the desk watched them, a small frown on his face. How loud had they been talking? Had the agent heard too much?

They were in a land office in Cornerstone, California. A tiny town that hadn't grown with the rest of the state, partly due to the rugged land around it. It was the third small town they'd searched that was near the Two Harts. Around here there was no ranch land, no fertile farmland, no river, and no gold mines, ever. It didn't even have a particularly beautiful view to attract tourists. The train had passed it by.

But it hadn't descended into a ghost town as some had. The land office, with its moldering records, remained still.

When Loyal and Sonny had asked if they could comb through the old mining claims, the land agent had shrugged and gone back to reading his book.

"Keep your voice down," Loyal hissed. "Now, how do we make our way to this claim?"

"There should be a map in this office somewhere."

Loyal's voice dropped to a whisper. "The agent is watching. We don't want to draw any more attention. No sense starting a brand-new gold rush."

Sonny nodded. Then, with a quick glance at the agent, he shoved the claim toward Loyal. "I was hoping to slip this into my pocket and take it with me. Instead, you'd better copy down the description of the land. He'll notice if we try to steal it."

189

Loyal knew Sonny could read and write, but they weren't his finest skills. "We don't want him chasing after us, maybe kicking up a fuss. In a town this small, the less attention we draw, the better. We don't want anyone coming looking for us."

Loyal knew it was probably too late. There probably weren't many who came into the land office asking for old records to search through. But that couldn't be helped now.

"Then we'll see if we can locate this mining claim on a map and head for our pot of gold." Loyal grinned as he wrote. He knew he was already counting his money, and that wasn't wise.

But like resisting temptation, no one had ever accused him of wisdom either.

TWENTY-TWO

It wasn't easy getting Lock to cooperate. It helped that he was still addled some from his fall. But even at that, the boy was grumbling the whole ride home.

As the sun lowered in the sky, Ellie said, "I'm going to ride on ahead. I can make sure there's hot food waiting and Lock's bed is ready for him. At the rate we're moving, it's going to be full dark when we make it home. We won't eat until the middle of the night."

Looking at Josh, Ellie offered, "I could send back a wagon."

"I don't think that'd save us much time. You go on."

"Thayne, will you ride along with me?"

"Sure, Miss Ellie. It's a peaceable place here in California, but I don't like you riding off alone. I should stay and help with Lock, let you and Josh go, but I'm not sure we Mac-Kenzies know the way home."

Brody regretted their slow pace. While the trail was plenty wide and well-traveled, there was no way they could ride faster than a walk, what with Lock and his precarious condition.

"Josh, if this trail goes all the way to your place, you can go on ahead, too." Brody's stomach twisted to think of being alone out here with the sun going down. Soon it'd disappear altogether. Well, he wasn't really alone—he had Lock. Then again, he was no help at all.

Ellie looked at Josh, who shook his head. "I'll stay with you. Sometimes there can be trouble on the trail."

Brody only had to look at his injured brother, and feel his own aches and pains, to know that was the absolute truth.

"I'll take a meal over to the doctor's office so you can get Lock straight to bed." Ellie and Thayne trotted off, and Brody heard with envy their horses' hooves change to a thundering gallop as they faded into the distance.

Brody didn't ride any faster, but Josh, who'd been ahead, slowed until they rode three abreast, Lock in the middle. His head nodded low, and Brody heard a soft snore.

When Lock slumped sideways, Josh's hand shot out and kept him in the saddle. Brody helped hold Lock in the saddle from the other side.

"Thanks," said Brody. "I've had a grip on him for most of the trip. I hope he's all right. I probably shouldn't have moved him, but I didn't know what else to do."

"I think we should have ourselves a talk," Josh said.

Brody looked across Lock to study Josh. Then, before a scolding could start, he said, "You know I came to your ranch thinking I'd be confronting child-stealing vermin who'd pressed my brothers into forced labor."

"Like we shanghai children, but instead of selling them to be shipped off somewhere, we make them learn to lasso and brand cattle?"

"Something like that."

"It only works to shanghai someone if you put them on a boat and set sail across the sea. It's hard to keep that type of slave labor corralled on a ranch. They can just walk away."

"You seem to know a lot about being shanghaied."

Josh chuckled. "Not personally, but I was a sailor for years."

"You were?" Brody asked. "I figured you'd been here all your life. Grandpa MacKenzie was a sailor before he married Grandma. I've often wondered if that was what made him long for adventure."

"I wasn't here all my life. I wanted to see the world, so I abandoned my family."

Brody heard self-disgust in Josh's words.

"I didn't come home for two years, and then I stopped by to visit and ran off again. The next time I reached the San Francisco Bay port and came home, I found my parents had both died. My big sister had married, Ellie had gone away to school in San Francisco, and my older brother was running the ranch alone. My whole family had been blasted apart. Zane was living alone in the big house. He was lonely and wanted me to stay. But I claimed the sea was my home now, my first and only love. As soon as we shoved off from port, I knew then I'd let grief push me away. I regretted it from the moment we set out. I was two years gone again."

"You've sailed on a lot of journeys," said Brody.

Josh nodded. "I've been to Europe, India, New York a few times. When I finally came home again, I planned to stay for good." He gave a quiet laugh. "The family had changed just as radically as before. Annie was a widow and a mother, and I'd barely met her husband. Ellie had come home from San Francisco with a broken heart."

"What?"

"And Zane was a married man. He and his wife, along with his sister-in-law and four missionaries, were all crowded into the house."

"Go back to Ellie."

Josh plowed on. He had a glint of amusement in his eyes.

He knew what he'd said would goad Brody. "There was barely room for me. Then Jilly started building all those houses we have on the ranch."

"Who's Jilly again?"

"The sister-in-law who'd helped build a railroad as well as the houses."

"Right. She's the sister-in-law with the strange memory." Brody had precious little interest in all of this—except for the part about Ellie.

"That's right."

"So who broke Ellie's heart?"

"Then Michelle found gold."

"What?"

"We could talk all night if I told you all that had gone on around here."

"Do you think the gold was MacKenzie's Treasure?"

Josh paused. His forehead furrowed. "That never occurred to me. It was nowhere near that green pool. In fact, there's no pool anywhere in those part." Then Josh must've decided to quit tormenting him. "As for Ellie's broken heart, she was engaged to a rich, influential man who kept a mistress . . . while he was betrothed to my sister. A cheat and a liar. She came home heartbroken and bitter, with a dim view of love."

Brody suddenly felt the need to find this fool who'd had someone as precious, brilliant, beautiful, and kind as Ellie Hart willing to marry him, and yet he'd wanted another woman. Brody wanted to thump the man.

"You treat my sister right," Josh added, "or you won't live to take your treasure home. I'll bury you somewhere on the Two Harts where no one will ever find you."

"Is that where the former fiancé is? Buried on your land somewhere?" Brody sincerely hoped so.

"No, but Zane pounded him into the dirt, and the fool's father cut him off and tossed him out of the house."

"That's not enough," Brody said, "but it's close."

"I missed my chance with Loyal Kelton. Well, I won't miss it with you."

Brody stuck out his hand and reached across Lock. "Fair enough."

Josh gave a wry smile as he shook Brody's hand firmly.

"As you know, I've a debt to repay back in Boston. I have no wish to hurt Ellie." Brody thought of his ma and how her own heart had been broken when Pa abandoned her. He'd finally come back, and she'd forgiven him enough that they'd had two more sons together. After that he went and abandoned her again.

"If I think I deserve it," said Brody, "I'll dig the hole myself before you bury me in it. Save you some work."

Josh nodded, and then the two of them went back to keeping Lock in the saddle while making their way slowly home.

TWENTY-THREE

Lock's injuries were many. He was a week out from his fall, and his knee was so hurt he'd've been using crutches to get around except that he had a shoulder that was wrenched so badly he couldn't handle the things.

Brody shook his head. "You have at least three cracked ribs. I don't think they're broken, but they're going to pain you something terrible for a while every time you move or even breathe."

"I'm well enough. We can go now."

"Not for another week, Lock." Brody thought it should be more like a month. "At least. You can't begin to ride a horse. And we're going to have to do a lot of hiking. You can't walk without help."

Lock slapped the journal on the table in their kitchen. "If we wait much longer, the cold is going to be a problem in those mountains."

The three of them had settled into the rooms over the doctor's office. The first flood of patients seemed to have ebbed to a less frantic pace, though Brody still had folks coming in several times a day. He's started charging each patient a dollar for a visit. Apparently, the hands at the Two Harts were well paid because they didn't balk at the fee.

When he wasn't doctoring, Brody joined Thayne and Lock in searching through the journal. "We need to be careful with this book," he said. "It's real old."

"What difference does it make how old it is?" Lock picked up the journal. "Besides, I pretty much have it memorized by now. So does Thayne."

"I've about committed it to memory myself," Brody said proudly. "And yet we haven't found anything to narrow our search beyond that mention of Loch Uaine."

"I could burn the stupid thing and it would make no difference." Lock whacked it hard against the table. Then, in a sudden fit of impatience, he grabbed it and threw it straight for the fireplace.

"Hey!" Brody scrambled to snatch it out of the fireplace. It hadn't gone into the fire, so no harm was done except it had landed facedown, open, its pages bent with the cover ripped partway down the spine.

He could see Lock was in pain and fretting over that as much as over the stingy directions in the journal. Brody picked it up and saw that the paper glued to the inside of the front cover had been torn. "You could have destroyed it, Lock." He was gentle with the old book as he closed it. "Even if we never find the treasure, this is something Grandpa left us. We should treat it with care."

Thayne scowled at his little brother. "That's what Pa tried to do. Burn it."

Lock's head dropped until his chin rested on his chest. "I'm sorry, Brody, Thayne—I know I'm acting like a stupid kid." He glanced at the journal. "How bad is it?"

Brody tried to smooth the endpaper back into place, but

the brittle page tore a bit more. Brody stopped touching it, hoping to do no more harm. The Hippocratic oath for books.

He froze, then moved to look closer. "What's this?" Brody set the book on the table with the front cover lying open. Gently, he tugged on the torn endpaper. He heard a gentle rip.

"Stop, you're making it worse." Lock made a frantic grab for the journal. Instead, he caught the front cover, and the paper attached to it tore almost completely away.

"No, stop," said Brody. "Don't—"

Something fell out of the journal.

All three MacKenzie men froze now, their eyes locked on the sheet of yellowed paper that had come free—folded and deeply creased. It'd been hidden behind the front endpaper.

Brody's hand trembled as he reached for the yellowed paper. He unfolded it. "It's a map." Using both hands, he carefully laid the fragile map on the table and smoothed it flat.

The three of them stared at it for a moment.

"Pretty sure that's Grandpa's handwriting." Brody recognized his grandpa's rough scrawl from reading the rest of the journal.

Lock leaned so close to the map, he blocked Brody's view of it. "Is that mark right there—" his breath caught as he jabbed a finger to the map—"is it an X?" He lifted his head and looked straight at Thayne.

Thayne rose from his chair, his eyes darting from Lock to the map and back to his brother. "As in X marks the spot?"

Both of the boys turned to look at Brody, their eyes flashing like a fireworks display on Independence Day.

"W-we found it." Thayne's voice cracked as it sometimes did at his age.

"We found MacKenzie's Treasure!" Lock pounded his fists on the table.

Both of them leapt at Brody and threw their arms around him, screaming for joy.

Tilda was finally in San Francisco. She'd have to find work right away if she wanted to eat. After asking a few questions, she had some idea of where to look for those who had knowledge about street children. She hoped she could find the boys and fast.

The answers to those questions had led her to a corner on one of the noisy, bustling streets of downtown. She listened to the clang of the trolly cars, watched the horses as they pulled the throngs of people along on the steep streets. She smelled the ocean and heard the shouts of men hawking their wares. They stood by carts overflowing with fresh food, flowers, bread, and vegetables. And they stood in the doorways of dance halls and gambling dens, promising wealth and pleasure to all who happened by.

A modest-looking door around the corner had a cross hanging above it and the words *Child of God Mission* painted on the single window in the door's center. So at odds with all the city's garishness surrounding it.

Tilda strode over to the door, eager but also a little afraid because she didn't know where to look next. She reached for the doorknob, twisted it and swung open the door, and stepped into the noise and commotion. It was a beehive of a room, full of dirty-faced children dressed in rags. She guessed there were at least twenty of them, each one devouring bread as if it were their last meal.

A disheveled woman in a dark blue calico dress and a

stained white apron stood at the front of the sweltering room. She clapped her hands loudly and demanded everyone quiet down at once. The children all looked at her with wary eyes as if ready to bolt at any minute.

The woman held an infant in her arms. A few seconds after the room turned silent, the infant burst into tears, and the children ran straight for Tilda.

The woman shouted, "Quick, shut the door!"

Tilda stepped all the way inside, closed the door, and was hit by a stampede of children who were . . . what, trying to escape? But why would they want to escape a room with food being offered, a roof over their heads? Unless this was an orphanage similar to the more dreadful ones she'd seen back in New York.

And now she was being a party to keeping the children imprisoned.

She reached behind her and grabbed the doorknob, thinking for one wild moment she should fling the door open and let the children escape. Then she twisted the knob and found it securely locked from the outside.

"Please don't leave . . ." The disheveled woman's voice broke. In a moment she'd be crying as loud as the child she held. "I'm begging you."

TWENTY-FOUR

Brody heard Lock yelp in pain. He bit the sound off quick, but Brody stopped hugging the poor battered kid and said, "Ease up now. Sit down and let's study this map."

"We need to go right now, Brody." Lock sat with a poorly stifled groan, even as he demanded action.

Brody's younger brother needed a bit more time to heal up. "Yes, we should go, but it's Thursday. I don't think we can go this weekend."

"Brody, c'mon!" Lock howled.

"We *have* to go," said Thayne, whose protest ran right over the top of Lock's.

Brody had to smile at them. "We will go, and soon. As soon as it's safe for Lock to sit in a saddle for hours on end. Cracked ribs often feel much better after two weeks. You're close, Lock, but not this weekend. The next one, though."

He urged Thayne to sit down at the small table. They were in the kitchen above the doctor's office. Brody had finished the day's work. The boys had gone to school and returned. They'd eaten a simple supper one of his patients had brought over instead of her dollar. Then, as they did most evenings, they'd started going over the journal again, looking for more clues.

Lock's frustration at seeing nothing new had erupted. He'd thrown the old book, and the map had come to light.

"Let's study it." Brody's heart sped up as he focused on the map. He rested one hand on each boy's shoulder, and that drew their attention. Brody might not have exactly *rested* a hand; he might've squeezed, a bit hard, in his excitement. He relaxed his grip, but he had his brothers' full attention now. "I promise you, I want to go just as badly as you do. But, Lock, you agree with me, don't you? You're not up to riding for hours, then hiking over rough ground. You want to feel strong when we go searching, don't you? You two won't run off again, right?"

Lock's cheeks turned pink, a smile curving his lips. "We won't run off again."

Thayne turned to the map laid out on the table. "We haven't sunk so low as to turn to horse thievin', and we know how far it is to that green pond." He jabbed a finger onto the old map. "He's written Loch Uaine. The map will lead us from there."

"I'm going to heal up just as fast as I can, and then we can finish this treasure hunt." Lock grinned. "I can't believe it—there really is a treasure. Grandpa's map proves that, doesn't it?"

Brody was struck by how young Lock was. He was fourteen and had done a fair amount of growing. He was gangly, not as tall as Brody and Thayne, but Brody had gotten to thinking of him as a man. Yet his smile, his cheeks pink with excitement, the glow of wonder in his eyes—all of it told Brody there was still a lot of kid in there.

This treasure hunt had to be about the most fun a kid could ever have.

A man too. He couldn't wait to tell Ellie.

The three of them bent over the map.

"Wait!" Brody said, his hand in the air. "I'm going to fetch some paper and try to copy this. We don't want to harm the original map."

"Good idea." Lock barely glanced up from the chicken scratches of Grandpa's handwriting.

Brody pounded down the stairs and was back up fast. When he returned, his brothers were leaning close to the map but kept their hands well away from it. Brody sat down and gently slid the map in front of him.

"Now," he began, "let's talk about what we're seeing here."

"Don't forget," Thayne said, "we may see something that'll help us better understand Grandpa's notes."

Brody looked up at his brother. "Good thinking. First thing I'll do is draw in Loch Uaine. That much we know."

"We can ride back to that very spot." Thayne pointed to the area on the map. "This looks like a trail or a path of some kind, don't you think?"

Brody nodded. "But it's hard to know if it's long or short. It could be a hundred feet long, or it could go for miles."

"Let's just do our best to follow the map as accurately as possible." Thayne's eyes were riveted on the map. "We'll have to take the trail once we're there. Hopefully some of these strange shapes Grandpa drew will make sense once we're back down there by the green pond."

"Does this look like an oddly shaped rock to you?" Brody stared at the paper, and his brothers debated what they were looking at.

The three of them continued to fuss over the map, with Brody sketching a replica of it. One that wasn't on the verge of crumbling. They spent all evening laboring over it. As Brody worked, he thought of Ellie and wished she were there. And it wasn't all about helping with the treasure hunt.

—— ✧ ——

The next morning, Ellie swung open the door to the doctor's office.

Brody needed to get the boys fed, and then he and Thayne had to work hard to get Lock to school. They'd built a special chair in which to carry him. Once they got Lock settled at his school desk, he had to stay there throughout the day—although Annie had told Ellie that Lock had been doing a bit of limping around. It seemed he was healing fast.

If Ellie came too early, she distracted them from what needed to be done in the morning. And unless there was an emergency, Brody wasn't working anyway. She forced herself each day to eat some breakfast before coming over. She often packed a loaf of bread, cheese, and a couple of apples and some cookies. Today it was gingersnaps. And she primped just a bit more than maybe was necessary. A few curls in her hair hurt no one. It was all because she didn't want to get there too early.

Today she'd put on a new everyday dress, pink calico with blue-and-white flowers scattered over it. There was lace at the neck and on the wrists. But not floppy lace. She was here to work, so she dressed accordingly. Still, the lace was white and delicate. She'd tatted it herself.

When she stepped inside, she saw she was alone in the doctor's office. Listening, she heard no sound overhead, so probably Brody wasn't back yet from the trip to school.

She set the basket of lunch fixings on the table and looked around. Brody was a good doctor and ran a fine office. He'd asked for supplies Ellie hadn't thought of stocking the doctor's office with, and she'd seen to it that things were as he'd requested. She enjoyed the quiet moment in the office where she worked with her handsome new friend.

The door opened behind her, and there he was. His eyes shone as if he was thrilled to see her. She thought he might be ready to say something about their growing feelings for each other. Tell her she'd become important to him. Tell her he'd decided not to leave her.

He rushed over to her and wrapped his arms around her waist, hoisted her off her feet, and spun her in a complete circle.

She was right. He was ready to tell her—

"We found something." Brody howled with pure joy and spun her around again. "There was a map stuck inside the front cover of Grandpa's journal."

So he was ready to tell her about . . . that stupid journal? Arms wrapped around his neck, she gritted her teeth and considered how she was in the perfect position to box his ears.

He plunked her back onto her feet, grabbed her hand, and dragged her up the stairs to his apartment. Which wasn't at all proper. She shouldn't be up there without the boys present. As they climbed the stairs together, she sighed, knowing full well she was safe from any impropriety because this was all about the journal, and because Brody was a half-wit.

He led her to the kitchen table, where she saw two sheets of paper along with the journal, one of them yellow from age and badly creased. It was torn along one of the creases. Beside it lay new paper and a pencil. And on that new paper she saw a copy of the old sheet of paper.

She decided right then that if Brody was a half-wit, then she was one as well. "This old map was in the journal?"

"Last night Lock was angry and frustrated, mainly because I'd told him he needed another week to heal up before we could go treasure hunting again." Brody reached for the journal and put it in front of her. "He was rough with the journal and tore it. That was when we found this map." He jabbed his finger at the brittle paper. "I made a replica so we wouldn't damage the original map further." Pointing to a spot on the replica, he went on, "Here's the green pond, or at least we're figuring that's what it is. Do you think—?"

The door squeaked open downstairs. "Doc? Are you here?" a woman called.

"That's Harriet," Ellie said. "I asked her to bring the baby in when it was a couple of weeks old."

He gave the map a longing look, then turned to Ellie and smiled that glowing smile of his.

"I can't wait to hear more, but we'll do it later." Ellie headed for the stairs.

Brody followed her. From behind, he said, "I shouldn't have dragged you upstairs. I'm sorry about that. I forgot myself."

He hadn't forgotten about the map, though. Yes, he definitely qualified as a half-wit.

TWENTY-FIVE

Brody rode beside Ellie with Thayne and Lock ahead of them. Josh led the way.

The sun wasn't quite up yet, but the sky was no longer black, and this first part of the trail was familiar. They were making good time.

"I hope when we get there," Brody said, "that the map makes more sense."

Ellie turned to give him an encouraging grin. "We'll figure it out. We've got the whole weekend, and the weather is warm."

"Down here it is. You said yourself it starts snowing in the highlands by September. And we're there."

It had been two weeks since they'd found the map. Lock had fussed plenty but had needed the time to heal, a fact he'd finally admitted. Even now the boy limped. His knee was slow to improve. But his ribs had quit hurting mostly, and his shoulder was functioning with only minimal pain. All the scrapes and bruises had faded to a sickly yellow.

"Josh hopes we'll get to the green pond before noon," Ellie said. "Now that we know where we're headed, he won't need to study the trail or second-guess himself. Then we'll have all day today and tomorrow to find what your grandpa wanted us to find."

"That journal dug into Pa like a thorn, and he couldn't get it out of his skin. He held off for three years or so. He tried to convince Ma he should go, search for Grandpa, but we all thought he must be dead or he'd've written again or sent for us."

"Did he consider taking you all west with him? The whole world was heading west on wagon trains by then."

"I don't remember that. I just remember Pa getting more and more fascinated by the journal. He read it over and over. Finally, one day he just up and left."

Brody saw his brothers glancing back at him. Had they heard all this before? They'd certainly heard a lot of it.

"I was seven by then, and Theresa was four. Just before Pa ran off, he told Ma he'd find Grandpa or MacKenzie's Treasure and come back for us. Five years later he came back. Theresa had died. Pa was a defeated, broken man. Skin and bones. His temper was . . . uncertain."

Brody thought that was a nice way of saying his pa had snapped, was shouting at everything, complaining and grumbling, and he'd started drinking.

"Even with his being a different man, things were better with him there. At least there was food and coal in the winter once he settled in and went back to work. He'd given up on the journal. Ma cared about him, and despite her anger at being abandoned and his short temper, things were better for a while. I reckon Ma and Pa were getting along well enough because Thayne and Lock were born. We got by for a few years, but then he started reading the journal again and muttering to himself about treasure. Before long, Pa rode off again. I was old enough to work by then. Ma found a better job than taking in washing. She cooked at a hotel. The boys were old enough for school, so she didn't have to leave them alone when she went to work. That was one of the reasons she'd taken in washing. Theresa and I were too young to leave, and no one would let her bring me or Theresa along. The rest you know—medical school, Ma dying, Pa kicking the boys out, the orphan train, Pa dying."

Josh called out, "I can see the trail that leads down to the green pond. We're almost there."

Lock grinned and wriggled in the saddle.

"And then I came hammering on your door, and you've been witness to all the rest of our MacKenzie madness," Brody finished.

Minutes later, they reached the bottom of the trail and rode straight to the green pond.

"Let's put up our horses, everyone." Josh dismounted, and the rest of them followed suit. "We can then spend some time with the map and figure out where to go next."

Lock laughed and rubbed his hands together. "We're gonna find that treasure—I can feel it!"

———— ✧ ————

"I really have to go, Rosa Linda."

Rosa Linda Rycoff's face turned an alarming shade of red. "Not now. Please, just a little longer."

"I can't stay much longer." But hadn't the Lord called her to care for orphans?

Maybe, but these weren't the *right* orphans.

She recognized the hypocrisy as it flitted through her mind.

"I've got the meal going now. I'll take over the babies. You tend to the lessons."

Tilda smelled cabbage soup, again. She hadn't figured out

if cabbage was all they had? Or was it all Rosa Linda knew how to prepare?

Tilda fought down the urge to offer to make the next meal. Already she was a nanny and a teacher. She did laundry and cleaned up after the meals. She wiped faces and mended clothes. Everything was badly needed. Honestly, she was bringing order to the Child of God Mission.

"How could your friend have abandoned you like this? I'm sure her mother needs her." In fact, Tilda had begun to doubt there was a mother. Rosa Linda's helper had run away, and Tilda couldn't blame her. At the same time, she'd've liked to hunt that faithless "helper" down and give her a sound thrashing.

"To leave you with twenty children, four of them babies? It's unconscionable." There were two equally fussy baby girls in Rosa Linda's room.

Rosa Linda's shoulders slumped. "I haven't been here that long. I think she knew I couldn't manage, but she was so desperate to get away."

"Do you think she's coming back? I mean, honestly?"

Rosa Linda's eyes darted to Tilda. "What? Of course Sister Agatha is coming back."

"Sister? She's a nun?" Tilda abandoned her plans to thrash a nun. For now. "And she abandoned you? Isn't this mission affiliated with a church? Nuns usually have a church that helps oversee missions. Can we check and see if they've got any spare nuns?"

"I suppose the church we're connected to sends over the food. I just walk out the back door each morning, and the food's waiting there. I never see who brings it."

"Well, I'm going to rise early tomorrow and keep watch. We need to get someone else in here."

"Miss Tilda, can you help me?" Little Bobby, who didn't know what his last name was but could spell his first, waved his pencil at her.

Rosa Linda called him Bobby Smith. Tilda hated the ordinariness of that, but she went along with it, having no idea what else to do.

"Let's see what you're working on, Bobby." There were two tables in the small room—eight girls around one table, eight boys around the other. None of the children was older than ten. And they were small and hungry looking and given to squabbling.

Which probably described Tilda and Rosa Linda, too.

Rosa Linda had thrown a blanket on the floor, and all four babies sat there or crawled under the tables. Two of them could pull themselves to their feet. A door led to the kitchen, which was kept firmly closed so that, except for maybe getting stepped on, the babies were reasonably safe.

Rosa Linda was after the babies while Tilda helped children she didn't know with education levels she had no idea about, while cabbage soup simmered in the kitchen. Tilda was hungry enough it smelled pretty good.

She'd learned during her hard, lean growing-up years that hunger made the finest seasoning.

While she helped Bobby, who was struggling to shape his letters correctly, Tilda watched Rosa Linda wrangle the babies and help the girls study and check the soup a few times in addition to everything else.

Tilda's hand crept up to her throat as she thought of all that could have happened to Lock and Thayne.

Twenty-Six

Lock was so giddy, so full of excitement, he was practically bouncing from one landmark to the next. Brody kept his eye on the kid for signs of pain but couldn't detect a single flinch. The kid had to be hurting, though. Brody still hurt, and he hadn't been nearly as battered as Lock.

They'd planned to camp out tonight and search all day tomorrow. Brody hoped Lock had energy to spare for a second day of hunting.

"This has to be the rock formation Grandpa drew," Lock said. He and Thayne rushed toward a strangely shaped stone about half as tall as them.

Ellie came up beside Brody, and they followed after the boys, all of them on foot. "Whether we find any treasure or not, the boys are enjoying every second of this." He held up the map he'd drawn. "Does that look like this picture? Is it a rock formation?"

Ellie studied it. "Things change with the passage of time out here. Rocks get broken up by ice freezing and thawing. There are avalanches and rockslides. Up this high, a heavy snow can move massive stones, break off trees."

Josh approached the rock the boys were dancing around.

"If this is right, then what's next? How far does the map take us?"

Brody shrugged a shoulder. "The dotted line winds north and then east from the green pond. This is the second picture Grandpa drew, and we've been walking and searching for a long time now."

Josh clapped him on the back. "Let's agree for now that this is the formation your grandpa saw and go on. If it doesn't lead us anywhere, we'll go back to the pond and try again. We've got two days. You're thinking too hard."

Brody arched a brow at Josh. "Thinking isn't a bad idea, Josh. You should try it sometime."

Josh laughed. Not an easy man to insult, it seemed. "Only as a last resort, MacKenzie. Now let's head on from here."

Lock pulled his own copy of the map out of his pocket. Brody had made two because he wanted to get the drawing more precise. In the end he decided to bring both copies along, even though they were very similar.

"Next we head along this stream."

"Didn't you say earthquakes could reroute the path of a stream?" He looked at Ellie.

"I did indeed. I've done some studying of dry creek beds. Lock has too for his cartography classes. We'll follow this for now. I think I'd recognize an old creek if I looked closely. With thirty years' worth of falling leaves and branches, it might be hidden."

"This lowland we're on is carved out by the San Joachin River, isn't it? This little creek must flow into it." Lock was thinking like a mapmaker.

Josh said, "The San Joachin is a little too far south for us. The Sacramento flows out of the state capital and heads to the ocean. It flows west and north, I think." He looked at Ellie. "Do you know?"

"The American River flows west of Sacramento." Ellie eyed the map. "It's more likely this is the American River drainage region. And this little stream is too small to be the American, so yes, it's a stream that drains into it or some other river. But nothing on this map looks like it leads to a big river. For now, let's not worry about which river we're dealing with."

Lock said, "There are hundreds of streams that flow all over these mountains. It would be a good idea to spend time mapping this whole area. Or we can search through the maps you've got back at the house. See if such maps already exist."

"We've got a lot of maps at the house," Ellie said, "but I'm not sure what we've got for this area. We should have looked around to see what all we've got."

"Too late for that now," said Lock. "C'mon, everyone. Let's follow the stream. If Grandpa drew the proportions true from one turning point to the next, we'll be following this stream for a while. We're searching for a clump of trees growing out of some boulders. We should be able to spot that."

Lock and Thayne were off again. Brody exchanged a look with Ellie, then Josh. "I'm half exasperated and half thrilled. Let's go."

———— ✦ ————

Cord smiled to think of how annoyed Grandpa Westbrook would be if he found out Cord wasn't rushing to track down information about that stupid fable of MacKenzie's Treasure.

He thought of that cranky old man and how alone he was and felt guilty. Whatever his temperament, the man loved

Cord. And Cord knew it and returned that love. He never let a day pass, not even an hour, without praying that Grandpa would find some kind of peace in life.

Cord knew peace came from God. That was what Grandpa needed. And no one near him even tried anymore to reach the old man.

No one except Cord. And right now, this task might bring the old man some happiness, and maybe that would ease his mind enough to think of bigger things. Eternal things. Yes, it was time to go.

Even so, even knowing he should hurry, he walked leisurely to the water trough and dunked his head, enjoying everything about life on the farm.

As he lifted his head and flung water away, he saw his ma at the backdoor with a furrowed brow.

"Cord, come in here. We've got a telegraph from Grandpa Westbrook. He wants you back in Sacramento. It sounds urgent."

TWENTY-SEVEN

"This has to be the trail marked on the map." Josh knew the wilderness better than all of them. "It looks like a draw between two bluffs, carved out by the same stream we've been following."

"I didn't expect it to be so far." Lock looked worn out.

The day was wearing down. Brody knew they shouldn't have gone out treasure hunting quite so soon. Lock was mostly healed, yet he was a long way from being at full strength.

Brody had tried to keep his brother on horseback, but Lock was eager to hike through the wilderness. They'd abandoned any hint of a trail hours ago. Josh had worked at keeping the horses with them, although leaving the critters behind on a patch of grazing land would've made more sense. But Josh said they might not end up going back the same way, so the horses needed to come with them. That had forced them from the path a few times, mainly just following the stream. They found that Grandpa's landmarks all led back to the water.

"I'm hoping we'll run across a game trail." Josh looked over his shoulder. His eyes met Brody's, then they slid to

Lock. Worry was evident on Josh's face. "It might be time to camp for the night."

Brody went to Lock and looked him over. His cheeks were flushed from the effort, and he'd taken to leaning hard on his horse while continuing to soldier on.

Josh was right in that there was no decent place to set up camp. The ground was so stony, they'd have a hard time finding a place where stretching out wasn't painful.

Thayne was ahead of Lock. Ellie had fallen in behind her brother, who was in the lead. Thayne glanced back, his forehead creased with worry. He had his copy of the map in hand. Glancing at it, he said, "If we find a downed tree ahead, Grandpa's map says we're to fork away from the water at that point. And it doesn't look like we will come back to it. Maybe we should set up camp by the stream. That way we have water for the night. We may regret taking that fork without a rest and a chance to fill our canteens."

Brody knew they were all trying to come up with an excuse to stop. There was still sunlight left in the day. Normally, they'd've kept searching until full dark.

"What's that?" Lock pointed at a clump of trees. "I don't think that was on the map."

"Is it a cave?" Brody stopped to stare at the dark shadow behind the trees. "There was no aspen grove in front of the cave on Grandpa's map, but then those aren't very old trees. Could they have grown that big in thirty years?

"I'll check to see if that's a cave or just an indent in the rocks." Ellie tied her horse off so it could graze on the bit of grass surrounding the scrub brush, fallen branches, and leaves.

"You're not hiking into a cave alone," Josh said. "It could be a grizzly den or full of rattlesnakes." He tied his horse, too. Brody and his brothers did the same. None of them wanted to be left behind in case there was something to find.

"Rattlesnakes?" Thayne gave Brody a nervous look, but he kept moving.

"Grizzly bears?" Brody wasn't sure which was worse. "A man's imagination can run away with him on the best of days. And on a treasure hunt, it can run wild."

"The map goes on . . . but this isn't where the X was marked."

"Maybe Grandpa marked the cave like he did that green pond. Just as a way to keep on the right path. But we'd better look in it." Brody rested a hand on Lock's shoulder. "I can imagine Grandpa finding a cave when he was out here wandering. Maybe he slept in it or took shelter from the rain."

"How do you suppose he came to be out here?" Thayne grabbed an oak sapling to drag himself onward and upward. "Something must've turned him aside from the rest of the gold rush."

Brody shrugged. "Maybe he heard a rumor of less competition out here. Or maybe his horse came up lame. Maybe he was looking for a piece of good land. Maybe he just wanted an adventure. He didn't seem to have the same gold fever as Pa. I got the feeling he was restless after Grandma died. Heading into the foothills of the Sierra Nevada Mountains might have appealed to him."

They continued up the rugged slope, and not a foot of progress came easily.

Ellie reached the aspens first. She held on to the closest tree, then turned to smile at the rest of them trudging up behind her. "It's definitely a cave. No idea how deep it goes. I want to see what's back there so badly I think I should wait. Let you MacKenzies go in first."

Josh reached her side, then turned to stand and face them. "I'll wait too. You're right that this can't be the treasure. We haven't gone far enough on the map. But it's a place your grandpa must've seen. We're following in his footsteps, and he probably explored this same cave. You brothers should go in first. Be mindful of snakes."

Brody decided Ellie and Josh were as fine a people as he'd ever met—the rattlesnake comment notwithstanding. Only when they said they'd wait did Brody realize how much he wanted to go in first.

Well, first along with his brothers. This was Lock and Thayne's adventure, after all. He wouldn't be here without their reckless fever for treasure. He waved a hand in an exaggerated gesture. "You two go first. Be careful."

Thayne and Lock both grinned and stepped forward.

Brody looked at Ellie and saw an almost foolish smile on her face. He suspected it matched his. She looked away from the boys, and their eyes met.

Quietly, she said, "They're having the time of their lives."

"I am too."

Josh added, "I think we all are."

"Treasure or not," Brody added, "we'll always have this grand adventure to look back on."

The boys went ahead, and Brody followed. He'd gone only a single step when Lock shouted, "Brody, everyone. Get in here!"

Sonny grabbed Loyal's arm when they heard shouting.

Loyal was ready to run toward the sound. Sonny's hand gripped like a vise, and he pulled Loyal low. As they crouched, Loyal focused on the direction the shouting had come from.

"I see someone." Sonny's voice was just above a breath. "Someone else is on MacKenzie's claim. Get lower so you can see what's going on."

Loyal dropped to his knees and looked through a thick barrier of scrub pines. He gasped and clapped a hand over his mouth.

"What is it?"

They were far enough back it was probably safe to talk quietly. Only when folks had started shouting had they heard anything.

Anger burned in Loyal's chest as he watched. "That's Beth Ellen Hart, my former fiancée. She's out here on the trail of that treasure."

Just like she'd found gold on the Two Harts Ranch, and Loyal had a chance to grab it until her big brother knocked him cold. Just like she'd abandoned him, which precipitated his father kicking him off the Kelton family's mother lode.

Now an already wealthy, pampered woman was going to find more when she already had plenty.

"Why did she come out here to this remote place?"

"I see only her and another man."

"That's Josh Hart, her big brother." A former sailor, now a rancher. He probably had the same iron fists as his big brother Zane.

"I saw someone else go in the cave ahead of her. I didn't get a good look, but that's who shouted. It echoed, which means it came from inside."

"They've found the treasure. They're in there right now, gathering it up." Loyal surged to his feet.

Sonny grabbed him and dragged him back down. "The weak part of our plan was always how to locate whatever treasure old man MacKenzie found out here. Sure, the land he claimed wasn't much, but if we have to dig up every acre, it'll take the rest of our lives. I'd've thought we weren't to the claim yet, not by my figuring. But if they found a gold mine or a treasure chest, then they just saved us a lot of work. We can't go charging in there until we're sure what they found. For all we know, the shout was about a rattlesnake or something. No, we wait and watch, and we let them do the toiling. Then when they've found our treasure, we rush in there and kill every one of them and take it."

Loyal hadn't quite descended to murder yet, but he knew Sonny had killed before. Loyal had been imagining a fight, but bullets flying balanced out the strength of two against three. Except one of them was Beth Ellen. Loyal swallowed hard. He bore a grudge, blaming her for most of his problems.

Yet to shoot that pretty woman, a woman he'd once held in his arms, even kissed a time or two, to shoot her . . . Loyal's stomach twisted. He wasn't at all sure he could do it. He wasn't sure either if he could step back and let Sonny do it.

Maybe waiting and watching was the better idea. Maybe he could find a way to avoid turning cold-blooded killer.

A noose seemed to be tightening around his neck as he considered the price a man had to pay for murder. Kill a woman and for certain he'd hang if caught. And when the judge passed the sentence, and the executioner walked him to the gallows, there'd be no one to utter a single word of protest.

Not even his mother.

"All right. Yes. We watch and wait."

Loyal sank to the ground, relieved to put off turning killer for a bit longer. Whatever twists there were in his soul, he wasn't stupid. If he was Sonny's partner, and Sonny went and killed someone, according to the law Loyal knew he'd be deemed just as guilty.

Relaxing, Loyal decided waiting was exactly what was called for.

———— ⟡ ————

"Grandpa, what is it? What happened?" Cord heaved a sigh of pure relief to see Grandpa sitting up, looking fine. "I was afraid you'd be in the hospital or—"

Grandpa cut him off. "Someone's out to steal MacKenzie's Treasure."

Cord didn't roll his eyes, but oh he wanted to. That stupid treasure again. "Grandpa, your wire made it sound like something terrible had happened."

"It has! Some no-account lied his way into meeting me and asked me questions about the treasure. He thought I was an old fool."

Cord didn't respond to that like he wanted to. "Who was it? He didn't harm you, did he?" After his initial relief, he wanted to know whether Grandpa had indeed been threatened. Maybe something terrible *had* happened.

"I first got suspicious when he mentioned the Two Harts Ranch."

"So he really is onto something."

"Yes, Cord, and I knew you'd stop and loiter at your grandparents' home." Grandpa slammed the side of his fist on his desktop. "I figured I would catch you."

"You did know. I was riding in that direction. I always stop for a visit whenever I can."

"My business was urgent. Not as urgent as now, but if this Loyal Kelton character beats me to the treasure, it'll be because you lingered."

"It's lucky I did stay for a while, so we can talk this over before I go to the Two Harts. If the MacKenzies are there like you think they are, then I'll need all the information I can get." Cord stumbled over his next words. "D-did you say Loyal Kelton?"

"That's right. He's the son of one of the richest men in San Francisco. His father is a banker like me. I'd heard his name, but I've never met him. I'd never heard of the son until recently."

"I have." Cord had heard enough to be very worried. "Loyal Kelton got fired from his father's bank for . . . well, the whole affair was hushed up, but word got out. Loyal was no good."

Grandpa paused from his grumbling and met Cord's gaze. All the fussing was set aside as Grandpa's keen mind worked over what Cord had said. "No good, huh? I wonder what that young pup is planning."

"So do I." For some reason, Cord was more upset about the treasure hunter going to the Two Harts than he was about possibly losing out on a treasure.

"Just how bad is Kelton?"

Cord searched his memory. "It's been a few years since he was run out of the bank. Only whispers, you understand."

Grandpa nodded. He knew how damaging rumors could be for a bank.

"Kelton always had too much money and was reckless with it. Being a rich man his whole life, it wasn't easy to raise eyebrows with rash spending." Cord shouldn't gossip. After all, they were just rumors. "There was a broken engagement, and it was said his father was very unhappy about that."

Grandpa waved him off with a grunt. "No father would fire his son over such a thing as a broken engagement."

Cord couldn't help but smile. "That agrees with the rumors. Even so, that was the story put forward by Old Man Kelton. Of course, the whispers always claimed it was more—lots of money missing, gambling, things like that."

Grandpa's brows shot up. "Gambling using bank funds? That's the kind of thing that can ruin a bank. His father wouldn't put up with that sort of behavior."

Cord nodded. He had no interest in being a banker, but even he knew that to be true. Taking good care of their funds was the most important function of any bank. And if a man with access to all that money had a problem with gambling, well, that couldn't be allowed to stand.

"Should I head out now?" Cord asked. "I was going to ride horseback to the Two Harts, but the train would get me there faster."

Grandpa opened the belly drawer of his desk and pulled out a small purse that jingled with coins.

"I can get myself to the ranch, Grandpa." Cord shook his head at the leather bag with the drawstring. "No need to pay for it."

Grandpa giving out money or withholding it, that was how he controlled folks. Cord had grown up watching it fail to work on his father and knew that such giving would have strings attached. Grandpa's money always did.

"I'm sending you on behalf of myself. I want you to go down there and find my treasure and bring my money back here. This isn't a bribe or charity. You're working for me. You'll need money to do that work." Grandpa tossed the leather bag at Cord, and he caught it.

"Grandpa—"

"Go on now, Cord. I know you're careful with money. You're trying to get ahead, and I respect that."

But he didn't know that Cord's plans to get ahead included buying a farm and leaving Sacramento for good. He looked down at the purse. "I don't need this, Grandpa. You pay me a fair wage at the bank, and I save up. One train ticket down and back isn't going to set me back."

Grandpa's eyes flashed then. "You're a good grandson, Cordell. Hearing about this Kelton boy possibly stealing from his father . . . well, it reminds me that I'm lucky to have you as my grandson. I don't say it often enough, but I'm proud of you, boy. Take the money, and if you don't spend it all, you can have it as a gift or give it back at the end of your journey. Sometimes a bit of money can smooth the way. I can't do much from here, but at least I can help by providing the funds."

Cord smiled and closed his hand around the leather bag. "Thank you, Grandpa. I'm not sure how long I'll be gone, but you should visit my church while I'm away. Tell the pastor what's become of me. I sent him a note that I wouldn't be there to play the organ for a while."

Maybe it was Cord understanding what had gone unsaid, but Grandpa managed a genuine smile in return. "I might just do that, my boy. Now, a train is heading south before nightfall, and it's getting late. Be on your way."

Cord nodded and headed for the door.

TWENTY-EIGHT

Ellie stumbled when she saw what had caused Lock to shout.

She was tempted to shout herself. "That's . . . that's a human skull," she said shakily.

Brody went to his brothers and held them back. Then Ellie decided that, no, he hadn't held them back. They weren't exactly charging toward the skeleton they'd found in the cave.

Ellie glanced at Josh, who had a cool look in his eyes he sometimes got when there was trouble. He had the ability to stay calm, thinking the situation through clearly whenever things turned bad. She liked to think she had that skill herself.

He took her arm and guided her behind him, then walked up to Lock. It was a surprisingly large cave, considering its small opening. Brody and his brothers were a few feet ahead of Ellie, and the cave stretched at least ten feet in front of them.

Josh stood to Brody's right. Thayne was on his left. Now Josh was in a line with the three MacKenzies, Ellie just a pace behind. She probably should have protested being left behind like some delicate little female critter who needed to be protected from unpleasantness. On the other hand, she

226

didn't want to get any closer to a skull. She could see plenty from where she was.

Moving behind Brody, she glimpsed the whole skeleton. There were clothes, but they'd worn away to mere rags. Around the waist, a leather belt with an old gun in its holster was still strapped on. The boots were mostly intact, leg bones sticking out of them. Scraps of a red kerchief were tied around the skeleton's neck.

Considering the clothes, it had likely been a man. At a glance there was no obvious signs of violence. The skull and bones were laid out in a way that seemed as if the man had simply lain down to sleep and not awakened . . . many years ago.

"What do you think happened here?" Brody looked over his shoulder at her, his eyes solemn. Then he looked back at the skeleton.

"I think we found our grandfather," said Brody.

"How can you know that?" Ellie asked.

"See that blanket he's lying on?"

Ellie didn't notice it at first, but sure enough, here and there, she saw the remains of a plaid blanket. "Yes. I see it."

Brody nodded grimly. "That's the tartan plaid of the MacKenzie clan. And Grandpa had such a hat as that one, with a little circle of plaid to match his blanket. I remember my ma creating the hatband with his tartan colors. They laughed over it. I suppose it's not the only hat like that in existence, but it's unusual."

"Brody, you really think that was Grandpa?" Lock had been the first of them to step into the cave, who then shouted for his big brother.

Brody, his arms across his brothers' shoulders, patted both of them. "I think it might be. He wrote in that journal and then mailed it off to us. I suppose he came back here to gather whatever he'd found, or maybe he wasn't done with his exploring."

"This cave wasn't where his trail led on the map. It was on the way, though. He drew the cave as one of his landmarks."

Josh pointed. "Look. He's got saddlebags. We should see what's in them."

Ellie hadn't noticed them, but there they sat. And they seemed to bulge. Her heart rate picked up. And since it was already racing from her coming upon a skeleton, that made it pound like mad.

"I'll check those saddlebags if you want," Josh said. "I mean, if you don't want to get too close to your grandpa's remains. But one of us is going to have to get close because I think . . ." He glanced uncertainly at Brody.

"You think what?" Brody seemed calm. Maybe he was faking it, putting on a brave front for his brothers. But Ellie decided if he could fake it, so could she.

Ellie turned to Brody. "Josh is asking if you'd prefer to go through your grandpa's things. We don't want to intrude."

Brody swallowed hard as he stared at the saddlebags, lying between the skeleton and the back wall of the cave. "Go ahead."

Josh looked at Brody for a long moment. Then his attention shifted to Thayne and Lock, who both nodded at him.

Walking over to the skeleton, Josh reached across it and snatched up the saddlebags. He brought them back to the group. The leather tore at one seam as he lowered them to the ground . . . where gold fell out.

Gold coins. Three of them. They bounced, and one rolled right back toward the skeleton until it stopped flat, gleaming at them. No tarnish after at least thirty years—ever since the day Graham MacKenzie had found them and tucked them into that saddlebag.

Only gold shone like that.

Lock reached as fast as a striking rattler and grabbed one of the gold coins from the ground. He held it up toward Brody. All three brothers leaned toward the coin as if it were a magnet and they a pile of iron filings.

Ellie watched as Josh plucked up the runaway coin that lay near the skeleton's rib cage. Then he got the other one and handed one each to Thayne and Brody.

That broke their feverish spell as they each had one to look at now.

"Let's see what else is in these saddlebags," Josh said.

Brody shook himself out of his little dream world and crouched down to where Josh had laid the bags. Looking up and behind him, he said, "Boys, come and search this bag with me. Ellie, you and Josh come as well. This may be the treasure Grandpa spoke of. We all searched, so we're all in on the discovery."

"The bag's heavy," said Josh, hefting it. "I don't think it's as heavy as a bagful of gold, but there's definitely something else in here."

Brody carefully untied a leather thong on one of the saddlebags and flipped it open. In it was a skillet, a tin cup, a pouch of coffee beans, and a small parcel. Brody set the rest aside and picked up the parcel. Whatever was in it had rotted nearly to dust. "Hardtack maybe or jerky. Which is what a man out here in wild country would bring with him."

They all nodded in agreement.

Again Brody reached into the saddlebag, this time pulling out a small piece of paper, badly stained. As he unfolded it slowly, Ellie could see writing of some kind.

"Looks like another map. See there, it says 'To Frasier' in the upper corner. That's Pa's name. Whatever decayed in that parcel leaked onto this map. I can't tell much about it without taking more time and getting better light on it." Brody set it all aside and reached for the second saddlebag, the one that had torn open.

Ellie wasn't sure how he could have resisted opening that bag first. She thought Brody showed remarkable maturity. Either that or he was scared. Or maybe saving the best for last.

Brody's hands trembled. He was dreading revealing whatever was in this saddlebag because there was a good chance it'd tear his family apart. It had ruined his father's life and his mother's along with it. It had killed his little sister and, it seemed, his grandpa.

No amount of gold was worth that. He knew it, but his brothers didn't.

He gripped the flap on the bag, his heart pounding. Before he opened it, he looked at Thayne, then Lock. "You both need to understand that coming upon a bag of gold is bound to make a mockery of Ma's life. She worked her heart out for years to feed us, to keep coal in the stove and a roof over our heads. Right now, with one flip of this saddlebag leather, we just might find more money than Ma had her whole life."

Lock, his attention riveted on the saddlebag, suddenly tore his gaze away, his brow furrowed. "What about that mocks her life?"

"Money means work, Lock, *hard* work. And there's pride in that—in caring for yourself and for those you love. Look at the Hart family. They work hard every day, and they've

230

done that to make the land they own provide them all a living. My years of study to become a doctor, that was work. That was me achieving something. You boys had to work too, didn't you? While I was gone? You ran errands and swept out stores and toted supplies for folks. Now, if this is a whole bagful of gold coins, what will you do? Will you sit on your backsides and eat fine food and wear silk suits for the rest of your lives? Because there's no meaning in that."

"And having lots of money can corrupt you," Ellie added. She crouched beside Brody and spoke as much to him as to the boys. "I was mighty close to marrying a rich man once. He worked in a bank owned by his father. He was rich from the day he was born. Whatever work he did or didn't do, it was never in doubt he'd be handed a fortune someday. Then he proved to be so worthless, his pa tossed him out of the bank. My former fiancé didn't know how to fend for himself. He was helpless and foolish. And while I've never paid much mind to what became of him, I know he's not welcome in the high-society world he once lived in. You boys need to know how to take care of yourselves regardless of what's in that saddlebag. It's hard to find your way when you've got things so well fixed, but you have to be able to."

Lock listened and nodded, then looked at Brody. "You're right." His eyes shifted to Ellie. "Both of you are right." He sighed, looking back at the saddlebags. "With all of my chasing around, all of my wild dreaming, it never seemed quite real that we might find a treasure."

Lock laughed quietly. "It was more the hunt that excited me." He looked at Thayne. "What do you say, brother? No matter what's in that saddlebag, shall we keep on studying? Shall I keep on with my plan to be a cartographer, and you to make something of yourself?"

Thayne nodded. "Living with Brody has given me an interest in being a doctor. I think I'll chase after that no matter how many gold coins are in this bag."

Both of them turned to Brody. Thayne said, "Sound all right to you, brother?"

"Both of you sound more sensible than I've ever heard you." Then a smile broke out across his face. "All right. Let's see what's in here."

Brody hesitated, more to gather excitement than anything else. Holding his breath, he flipped open the saddlebag and tipped it over . . . to see another journal fall onto the ground, along with five more gold coins and an old knife. An ornately carved knife with a strange etching on one side. He stared down at the knife, then pulled the first journal out of his shirt pocket where he carried it. He studied the barely visible engraving on the front cover—a square with an X in the middle. The symbol matched the one on the hilt of the knife. "What is that?" He looked at Ellie and pointed.

"I've seen it before." Josh looked at the knife, then the journal and back to the knife. "On a . . . a flag, I think. A Spanish ship maybe. Or a pirate ship? I can't remember exactly."

"It's hard to make out the engraving on the journal cover, but it sure does look like a match." Ellie reached into the saddlebag and pulled out a piece of paper as old as the one Brody had found inside the cover of the journal.

"Is that all the gold there is?" Lock sounded forlorn. A second later, he perked up and said, "But the cave wasn't where the map had an X marked on it. This place was just a landmark along the way." Lock and Thayne exchanged a look. "An X on the map," continued Lock, "another one on that knife handle, and a third one on the journal—does the

X mean something more than the location of a treasure? Josh, if you saw it on a flag, something to do with Spain, and the writing is in Spanish, could this gold be from . . . from Coronado's City of Gold? Could that be what we might still find?"

Brody eyed his brother, who was getting all worked up again. His words of encouragement to Lock and Thayne just a few minutes ago—with Ellie's added to it—had seemed to temper the brothers' fervor a bit. And maybe it would have stayed that way were there no more gold to find. Now, though, he wasn't so sure about this.

TWENTY-NINE

"Lock and Thayne, can we just hold on a minute before we go haring off after more treasure?" Brody gave an exasperated sigh. "I know you didn't know our grandpa, but I'd like to have a moment of silence and prayer, a moment to remember him."

Lock's eyes lost the feverish look. He nodded and sank to the floor of the cave. "It's not where I'd like to spend the night, but let's eat our supper here, and we can be quiet while we remember Grandpa. I never met him, but I've heard plenty of stories. Then we can go on for a time while we've still got the light."

Brody was worried about Lock with his wild dreams of treasure. Add to that, the kid was worn clean out. Sure, they could stay here, eat something, and remember Grandpa, yet Brody thought it might be best if instead they found a place nearby where they could set up camp for the night. Their adventuring needed to end, at least for today.

Brody took the leather packet of papers and handed it to Lock. "Look over these papers while we get a fire going and a meal ready. Thayne, you help. Be careful with the papers— they're as brittle as that map."

Ellie looked at the paper she'd found by itself in the saddlebag. She gave it the brothers. "This is fragile, too. Study it along with the papers."

Josh went outside but was back shortly with the packs on their horses. He then gathered up an armload of kindling.

Brody had to admit he'd've liked to go over those papers too, but then he figured their finding Grandpa would have been enough for him for this weekend. He'd rather they headed back to the ranch and planned another treasure hunt some other weekend—or next spring. Any treasure that had stayed hidden for thirty years could wait another week or two. But what about Boston? He certainly couldn't treasure-hunt from the far side of the continent.

"Brody, look at this." Lock thrust a paper at his brother. Written on the paper in an elaborate hand were the words, *Al norte de la Bahia de Los Piños con Capitan Cabrillo en una espesa niebla.* "Grandpa must've copied that in the journal." Lock handed it to Brody and went on to the next paper. "He must've found all this with the rest of whatever treasure there was. Maybe it's all he found, or maybe—"

"Brody, look." Ellie's tone drew everyone's attention. She pointed at a tattered spot on Grandpa's leg. The fabric of his pants was so old, Brody could see the bone.

"A broken leg." Brody knelt beside the skeleton and concealed how much this grieved him. He did his best to act as if this were a simple medical situation. But it was Grandpa, and how or why he'd met his demise and came to be lying here in this cave made Brody sad. "He must have visited a post office and sent the journal to Pa. On his way back, guided by his map to where he found these things, somehow he ended up with a broken leg."

"Not that hard to get hurt out in rugged land like this." Josh frowned as he stared at the bone.

"He couldn't go on." Brody sat back on his heels. "He might have hoped it was only a bad sprain. Hoped if he rested here for a while, he could recover."

Brody locked eyes with Ellie, and he saw that she understood what it was he'd been struggling with as he knelt by his grandpa's body. She stepped forward and rested a hand on his shoulder.

"Grandpa crawled in here for shelter and never left."

"He really did want us to share in the treasure, didn't he?" Lock sounded so young when he said it.

"I think he hoped we would join him out here," said Brody, nodding. "Just those few gold coins we found would've paid for the trip out here for Pa, Ma, Theresa, and me. Grandpa and Pa could have built a house and bought a few head of cattle. You boys would've been born out here, and then our whole family would've been together. That might've been enough for Grandpa to call it a treasure."

"But why mail the journal? Could it be he thought he was in danger?" Ellie couldn't help but wonder.

Brody shook his head slowly as he considered that. "We're just guessing about all this, I suppose. Grandpa was secretive in the journal, so he might—"

"Brody." Lock waved a paper, his eyes wide. "Look, it's a letter from Grandpa. He wrote it after he broke his leg, hoping we'd find it."

Brody took the letter and read it swiftly.

Frasier, me lad,

Your da broke his leg bad. I ain't gonna make it, I'm affeered. If ye found me here, it meens ye found my map in the book. Gotta tell you what I done . . .

Brody frowned. "He says he sent a second map and a letter to someone else. Someone he owed money to. A man named Mayhew Westbrook. He says the map he enclosed in his journal is only half of it. We need the other half to find his treasure. And he filed a claim on this land . . . no, on *some* land. He filed it in Cornerstone, California. We're to find that claim. Find Mayhew. Find the other half of the map. Mayhew's map is hidden from him just as ours was hidden from us."

Brody lowered his grandfather's note and looked from Lock to Thayne, then to Josh, finally to Ellie. Then he glanced down at his grandpa's remains. "What did he find? What was important enough that he needed to hide clues and maps and write in such a secretive way? A map in two halves? What does this Mayhew Westbrook have? Did Grandpa mail two journals?" So many questions still.

"Is there any point in going on?" Ellie asked. "It's very likely that X your grandpa marked on the map is just the end of your map and the beginning of the other half. I'd say the next step in your treasure hunt is to find Mayhew Westbrook. And find out if he'd like to join your hunt."

Brody looked at the letter in his hand, then the map. "What do you say, boys?"

"I say we need to find the other half of the map." Lock nodded to the one Brody held. "But we've got another day. Can we go to where Grandpa's map leads us? If he marked it with an X, maybe there's something to be found. We can at least discover the right trail."

"I agree," said Thayne. "We found the green pond after a long day of searching. This time we rode straight to it. It took another long day to find this cave. If we get to the end of our map, then go find this Westbrook partner of Grandpa's, we can all ride to the right starting spot."

237

Brody turned to Ellie and Josh. "That makes sense, I suppose."

Josh nodded. "We'd planned to be out another day. Let's keep following the map."

Brody considered the gold coins they'd found, eight in all. He had them in a little stack beside him. He picked up the coins and handed them around.

Josh waved him off. "That's MacKenzie's Treasure. It's yours. We're way off the Two Harts Ranch—we have no claim on this."

"We can talk about that later," Brody said. "I suppose half of this is owed to Mayhew Westbrook. Grandpa said he promised the man half of his treasure for funding the search. For now, let's split up our little treasure right here. If something happens to any of us, a hole in our pockets or something, we'll have a good chance of getting back to the ranch with most of the coins."

Ellie took her coin and held it up. "It's heavy. Probably two or three times the size of a twenty-dollar gold piece, and it's old. I suspect it's very valuable. The eight of them together may be worth a sizable fortune. Your grandpa was right that he could bring your whole family out west and buy land here with just these coins. This could be all the treasure he found. And that dagger is probably valuable, too."

Lock got that gold, feverish gleam in his eyes again. "There are more papers to go through," he said. "Maybe it's written down what else Grandpa found. Maybe he brought back these coins as a sample but left behind a larger hoard of them."

Ellie closed her fist around the coin. "We'll find your grandpa's X location tomorrow, then ride back to the ranch before sundown."

Brody nodded. "Then we'll go to work finding May-hew Westbrook, whoever he is. He could be long dead by now—or long gone."

"We should ask Michelle about Westbrook. She may have heard his name before." Josh dropped his coin into his pocket, then pulled the pocket open and looked into it. "No holes."

Brody divided the rest of the coins between his brothers and kept two for himself.

"Good idea. Michelle's family knows a lot of people, and they might have a better idea of where to search." Ellie opened her hand that held the coin. "I just wanted to hold it for a few seconds. I don't have a pocket. Brody, you carry my coin along with yours."

Brody took it from her, checked his own breast pocket for holes, and put the three coins inside it.

Lock pocketed his coins. "So we'll find Westbrook and bring him and his map with us next time. We'll ride to the end of our map and pick up where his map starts."

Something about the way Lock put the coins away gave Brody a notion, and he turned to Grandpa's skeleton. He reached for the pocket he could see on the shredded remains of a pair of pants. He drew out three more coins from the pocket. He checked Grandpa's other pants pocket and found three more.

Lock gasped as Brody handed the coins to his brothers. Their eyes shone with excitement.

"These have to be a part of MacKenzie's Treasure," said Thayne, "or Grandpa wouldn't have drawn two halves of a map."

"While we've been in the cave, the sun has sunk low in the sky," Josh said, gesturing toward the entrance. "Let's go. Get a little farther down the trail. The next landmark looks like . . ." Josh tilted his head at the map he held. "It's an arched rock, I think, or maybe a bent-over tree."

"Bring all the papers along," said Brody. "We'll head for home tomorrow in time to stop back here. I want to wrap up Grandpa's body and take him back to the ranch to bury in a proper grave." He paused and looked around the cave. "Or maybe we should leave him here where he's been for so long. But I like the idea of him being buried somewhere we can visit. Ma and Pa are together in New York with marked graves. Is that the right thing to do for Grandpa, to bring him to the Two Harts?"

Ellie patted Brody on the shoulder. "We'll talk it over, then you can decide what's best to be done. Now, let's follow that map for a while longer."

Tilda couldn't leave. The truth was that this place was going to fall apart if she left. And the missing helper was a nun. A wildly irresponsible nun, and that didn't seem right. Surely she'd come back, or they'd send someone else. But had something happened to Sister Agatha? It made no sense that she'd just walk away and leave Rosa Linda with all these children.

Could this be where God wanted her? Working with orphans was what Tilda had been called by Him to do. But what about her two missing boys?

Cooking, cleaning, teaching, tending children while they ate and studied and slept kept her busy every hour of every day—including a lot of the night hours. The two babies she cared for had a tendency to wake up in the night, needing food or a dry diaper.

Tilda set the last plate of boiled cabbage in front of Bobby, then poured him a scant cup of milk. The bottle of milk left every morning wasn't overly generous.

"Thank you, Miss Tilda." Bobby smiled his gapped-toothed smile, and her heart softened for the little boy, for all the children.

The children chattered on, utensils clinking on tin plates as they ate their beans and side pork for the evening meal. Occasionally, there were apples, and once they'd been left a sack of potatoes and meat from which to make a stew. There was flour and sourdough, which Rosa Linda used to make biscuits. But mostly it was beans, side pork, and milk. Not the best nutrition, but the children could probably grow up on them with an apple added in once in a while.

Bobby knocked over his tin cup of milk, and Tilda gave up on even considering making a break for it.

How long had she been here? She mopped up milk, wiped chins, earned a giggle or two, and just settled in because she saw no other choice.

And she prayed for Sister Agatha to return soon.

In the midst of her praying, the front door swung open, and a pretty dark-haired woman stepped inside. A red-headed woman right behind her. Next in was a blonde. All of them quickly entered and swung the door shut. Tilda had to wonder if they knew they'd be locked in here, possibly forever.

The three of them were a picture. As pretty as any women Tilda had ever seen. They wore beautiful dresses, and their hair was perfectly styled. They made Tilda conscious of her one-and-only dress, her disheveled hair. The length of time it had been since she'd bathed.

It irritated her because she was probably only judging herself, as none of these ladies seemed to look down their noses at her. Or if they did, it was all inside their heads because their expressions were more than friendly.

"I'm Michelle Hart, and these are my sisters. Jilly's the redhead, Laura the blonde. We're here to see if any of you children would like to come out to the Two Harts School. We've got plenty of children out there and have found a few from the Child of God Mission." The woman's eyes sparkled with intelligence and kindness as she looked at Tilda.

"We don't just let folks come in here and abscond with children." Back in New York, Tilda had known people who had terrible plans for children. She knew that knowledge rang in her voice. Rosa Linda was silent. She most certainly didn't jump in with a big welcome for these three ladies. A glance told Tilda that Rosa Linda was just as confused as she was.

The woman called Michelle Hart studied her. She seemed to look through Tilda as if she were thinking of what to say and wanted to say it just right.

Finally, the blond lady behind her asked, "Where's Sister Agatha?"

THIRTY

Ellie read for as long as the light held out. They'd split the packet of papers between them all.

The papers were old, as dated as the journal, and much of them were written in Spanish. Though she could understand the language a little, there was a lot she didn't understand. She did notice the word *cabrillo* in a number of places.

Lock had found one letter written in Graham MacKenzie's hand, or they all assumed it was his. It included a second reference to the deal he'd made with Mayhew Westbrook that needed to be honored. And vague references to a treasure. Deliberately vague, Ellie was sure of it.

Josh picked up his rifle as Thayne and Lock moved with their blankets away from the fire.

"What's wrong?" Brody asked.

All of the MacKenzie brothers turned to look at Josh.

"I think I'll stand watch," Josh answered quietly. "I don't like the feel of the night."

"What do you mean by that?" Brody shoved aside his blanket.

Josh looked away from the firelight. "If you stare into the fire, your night vision is no good." Josh grinned. "Just a little hint from someone who's used to camping out in the wilderness."

Ellie figured she'd done more camping than all of the MacKenzies. "I haven't noticed anything unusual." Then, after thinking on it further, she realized she *had* noticed something. She'd been on edge and had blamed it on the skeleton in the cave. But it was more than that. Ellie looked around where they'd set up camp. "Listen. There are no night sounds. No owls or crickets, no frogs chirping. It's too quiet. Sometimes when the wilderness sounds go quiet, it means there's something or someone scaring them back into their nests and holes."

Brody peered into the night in a direction that was opposite of where Josh was watching.

"We're on a treasure hunt," said Josh. "A thirty-year-old treasure hunt, but still . . . there's no reason really to think we won't face any trouble."

"I'll stand watch, too," Brody said, reaching for his boots.

Though he sounded calm and sensible, Ellie knew Brody lacked the temperament needed to stand sentry for the night.

Josh shook his head. "No need. Go on and get some rest. I'm going to take a look around. If I'm satisfied it's safe, I'll sleep. Trust my horse to warn me of trouble."

"Your horse?" Brody stared at the animals grazing nearby.

"Yep. There's lots I can teach all of you." Josh stepped to the edge of their camp, almost out of the light. Over his shoulder he said, "I reckon there's plenty you could teach me, too. We can all spend some time learning when we get home."

———— ✧ ————

Ellie settled by the fire, looking right square into it. She wasn't quite ready to sleep.

MARY CONNEALY

Thayne and Lock pulled their blankets up to their chins
and were soon snoring. The two brothers lay at the edge of
the small clearing. Josh was keeping watch, although she
couldn't see him at the moment. Brody had turned away
from the fire. She hadn't given much thought to danger, and
if she felt any uneasiness, she put it down to being around
a skeleton in a dark cave. That was enough to make anyone
nervous.

She knew she'd need a few minutes to think and pray
before trying to sleep.

Brody, staring into the woods, glanced over at her. She
had her back pressed up to a rock wall. The campfire had
warmed the rock's surface, which helped to soothe her sore
muscles. The day had been fine, but they'd been climbing,
and up this high, even in summer, it turned cool at night.

Brody stood and came to sit beside her. He was facing the
fire, but he wasn't looking at it. He was looking right at her.

"Do you . . . ?" he began, then swallowed hard.

Her heart lifted. Up until now they'd shared very few moments alone together. Now here they were . . . not exactly
alone, but close. The night was starlit, the air savory with
the scent of woodsmoke and pine. The fire crackled in a way
that could almost be described as romantic.

"Do you," he started again, "think we should—"

"Should what?" Oh, she had a few things she thought
they should do.

". . . should take my grandpa's body back to your ranch?"

Ellie let her head fall back, and if it rapped a bit hard
against the rock behind her, it was what she deserved for
hoping Brody would seize this private moment to speak of
better things than old bones. Honestly, did she have to do
all the work?

245

It would seem that she did.

With a sigh, she leaned forward and kissed him.

Brody pulled away, sat up straight, gave her a wide-eyed look, then got the notion fast enough. The second kiss was all his idea.

The moment stretched on as the fire warmed her. The kiss helped warm her as well.

Brody straightened away again and studied her carefully. "Ellie, finding my brothers was all I had on my mind for so long. And when I found them, I found you. It's almost impossible to believe such a beautiful woman could have come into my life." He stopped talking and kissed her again.

It was her turn to talk. "Since the day you arrived, Brody, it's been one thing after another all the time—reuniting with your brothers, searching for treasure, doctoring."

"And don't forget, I have to leave."

She couldn't forget that if she tried. "But in the midst of all that, well, I found you, too."

Another kiss. When it finally ended, Brody eased away and slid an arm around her, pulling her close to his side. Side by side, they sat there watching the blazing fire.

"We need to talk about the future, Ellie. I would like a future that included us being together forever. Would you consider coming with me to Boston?"

Ellie felt an odd turmoil stirring within her. *Forever* was something that had never felt real to her. Her parents had died suddenly. Her fiancé had betrayed her when she thought she'd found a man she'd spend *forever* with. Annie's husband had been shot and killed. She had little trust in *forever*. But with Brody, she very much wanted it to be true. And she wanted it to be true because, she realized with a sharp twist to her heart, she loved him.

"Brody, I—"

The crack of a cocking gun turned Ellie and Brody toward the darkened forest. Something moved among the shadows.

No, not something. Someone.

THIRTY-ONE

Brody saw Josh stagger out of the woods, a trickle of blood running down from his temple.

Brody lurched to his feet.

"Stay where you are."

He looked past Josh to a man holding a six-shooter, aimed right at Josh's head. The man had his arm wrapped around Josh's neck.

Ellie gasped. "Loyal, what are you doing?"

Loyal? Brody had heard that name before. Loyal Kelton. Josh told him that Zane had beaten Loyal into the ground. This man was Ellie's former fiancé, the one who'd cheated on her and lied to her and betrayed her. What *was* he doing here?

"Give me that map."

"The map?" Ellie clutched her throat.

Brody heard rather than saw the blankets at the edge of their camp shift silently. His brothers. Everything Brody cared about was right here. Ellie, Thayne, Lock . . . Was this man planning to kill them all?

"You've come here on a treasure hunt?" Ellie's voice rang with scorn. "Really, this is what you've come to, Loyal? A thief now? Assaulting an honorable man, threatening a woman?"

Loyal laughed as a second man stepped out of the forest, also with a gun raised. This one was aimed at Brody.

"Come over here, Ellie."

"No, stay back." Brody took a step forward.

The stranger fired, and the bullet struck right in front of Brody's feet and blasted dirt into his face. "Next bullet goes into her knee if you move again."

Loyal said, "If you all want to live through this, Beth Ellen, you get over here right now."

Ellie, her face washed white with terror in the firelight, gave Brody a look of such fear for his worthless hide, he had to fight not to throw himself between her and the gunmen. He'd've done it, gladly, if it would have saved her. But for right now, all it would do was get him killed. And with Josh being injured and barely conscious, and the boys . . . were they cowering under their blankets?

Brody decided he had to bide his time. Pick the right moment. He had no gun, and no real skill for using one if he did have one.

Ellie took one shaking step at a time. She reached Loyal, with Josh standing, unsteady and dazed, between them.

Then Loyal slashed his gun butt viciously across Josh's head. Brody watched the toughest of them collapse in an unconscious heap. Loyal leapt over Josh's body and grabbed Ellie's arm.

She shrieked as he twisted her arm behind her back. Now she stood facing Brody with a gun to *her* head. Loyal shifted his grip and wrapped an arm around her neck.

"Loyal, what are you doing?" Choking, Ellie grabbed at his forearm. "What's the matter with you?"

"You can have whatever you want." Brody saw the cruelty in Loyal's eyes. He'd loved hitting Josh. The man wanted an excuse to hurt Ellie. "The map, just take it and go."

Brody saw the map resting next to Lock's blanket. It was a copy, but would Kelton know that? The same glance picked up that both blankets were lying flat on the ground. His sneaky little brothers were gone. Relieved that they at least might have gotten themselves out of harm's way, he risked a bullet as he walked slowly over to the map and picked it up. He held the map out for Loyal.

"I promise you," Brody said, "on my grandfather Mac-Kenzie's grave"—and since Grandpa hadn't been buried, it wasn't much of a promise—"we won't do any more searching. Take the map and leave us. Please. If you find any treasure, it's all yours."

Brody hoped he sounded defeated when in truth he was boiling with anger at this brute and his partner. He had thought Loyal was a rich man. Hadn't Josh told him that when he'd talked about Ellie being hurt? What made a man who was already rich turn to thieving and threatening murder? And all for a mysterious treasure that might not amount to a thing. Maybe the very word *treasure* was enough. Clearly it had been in Loyal's case.

"Sonny, get the map." Kelton kept Ellie in his grasp.

"No! Stay back." Brody made a swift move and extended the map over the fire. "Let her go first. I'm not letting you touch this map while Ellie's in danger. I'll burn it. I can see in your eyes you want to drag her out of here, but you'll lose your chance at the treasure if you do that. Even if you shoot me, my last act will be to drop the map into the flames."

Loyal was dressed in a fine suit, although it was rumpled

and stained. Sonny, his partner, wore rugged-looking western clothes. Tattered and faded. The clothes of an outlaw.

What else had Josh told him about Loyal? Brody racked his brain. Josh said Loyal's father had cut ties with him. So maybe he wasn't so rich now. That might be excuse enough for a dangerous, greedy man to hurt Josh, put his foul hands on Ellie, and threaten Brody at gunpoint. All for treasure.

"We'll saddle up," Brody went on. "We'll head home and never search for the treasure again. Just let her go."

Brody saw Josh stir. He lay just behind the two outlaws. Brody prayed Josh wouldn't make any move that would set off gunfire.

"I won't hand over the map until you do." Brody saw Josh wobble and collapse again, too dazed to fight.

The outlaws' eyes were riveted on the map and the licking flames only a few feet below it.

"I said *let her go*. Then I'll give you what you want."

Loyal's eyes narrowed. He looked hungry with the need to hurt someone. Greedy with the need to get the map in his hands.

Sonny had a different look. A cold, calculating expression that told Brody he was more dangerous than Loyal. But if he killed them, he'd do it because he thought it would help him get away with his crimes, not out of a belly-deep pleasure in killing. Loyal was the one who'd take pleasure in doing harm to others.

Josh raised his head again, then dragged himself toward the edge of the clearing behind Kelton.

Brody, speaking louder to keep the men's attention on him, said, "The treasure map is what you came here for, isn't it? I'll trade it gladly for our lives."

Loyal exchanged a glance with Sonny. Brody trusted neither of them.

How could he protect Ellie? He prayed desperately for
God's divine intervention. And then Brody had an idea. A
divine one.

Loyal relaxed his hold on Ellie and said, "Take her then
and give me the map."

Brody lowered the map closer to the fire. "All the way loose
of her or the map burns."

Loyal released Ellie with a shove.

"Get into the woods, Ellie, and hide." Brody still held the
map over the fire.

Loyal reached for her again, which only proved he couldn't
be trusted.

"No!" Brody lowered the map again. "Not until she's in
the woods where you can't find her. Then you can have the
map."

Loyal didn't seem to have noticed the boys were gone. Or
maybe he hadn't been watching the camp for long. Maybe
he thought only Ellie, Josh, and Brody were here.

"I won't leave you, Brody. He'll kill you." Ellie didn't sound
like herself. She sounded overly frightened. And since she was
a level-headed woman who responded well in an emergency,
Brody thought she might be planning something or trying to
sound defeated to get Kelton to underestimate her.

"Ellie, go. Please just go. Hide in the woods. Let me do
this."

And by *this* he meant maybe die. He was asking her to
let him sacrifice his life for hers. He'd do so willingly. As he
thought it, and as his mind added the verse from the book
of John, "Greater love hath no man than this, that a man
lay down his life for his friends," he realized he loved her.

Their eyes met across the flames, and he saw the same kind of love coming from her.

They'd been drawn to each other from the first. He knew he respected and admired her. He had certainly loved her as a neighbor and a friend. He'd known he was growing increasingly fond of her.

But love?

He didn't even know what that meant. Not really. He'd've failed if he'd tried to define it. But what he felt right now, as he offered his life for hers, was love. A feeling that bloomed in his heart as bright and true as the flames that danced between them. It was unlike anything he'd ever felt before.

"Please, Ellie."

Tears welled in her eyes, and she nodded, then quickly turned as if she had to tear herself away to leave him. She vanished into the woods. He heard the crunch of her footsteps for a few seconds, then nothing. His Ellie knew her way around in the woods.

"Give us that map right now or we shoot you dead."

Brody didn't so much as glance at Josh, but he was aware Josh was moving. He was much quieter than Ellie, and within seconds he was gone into the woods behind the two men.

Brody lifted his hand away from the fire and moved around it slowly. He gave everyone a chance to hide. Finally, not getting one step closer than necessary, he handed the map to Loyal and stepped back to put the fire between them again.

"Stand still." Sonny lifted his gun, and Brody froze.

Loyal studied the map. "It looks real to me."

Sonny took a second to study the paper. "Me too. We've got what we need."

Sonny aimed his gun and shot Brody in the chest.

Brody slammed backward into the rock wall behind him

and slid to the ground, only distantly aware of Sonny saying, "Let's hunt down the woman. Hey, where'd the other man go?"

Kelton said, "We aren't taking the time to hunt anyone down. Let's get out of here."

That was the last Brody heard as he tipped to his side and faded into darkness, wishing only that he'd told Ellie how much he loved her before he died.

THIRTY-TWO

Ellie surged to her feet, and a hand slapped over her mouth.

She swung a fist as a voice hissed in her ear, "Shut up."

Josh. She sagged against him. The terror that somehow Loyal had circled around and found her and grabbed her rushed away, but not her terror for Brody.

Another hiss. "I'm going in there and dragging Brody into the trees." He thrust cold iron into her hands, and she recognized it was a gun.

Where had he gotten a gun? Surely they'd disarmed him. "Cover me."

He let her go and silently slipped past her. She followed but stayed in the darkness. She heard rustling behind her and spun around to have the gun jerked out of her hand.

"It's us, Miss Ellie. But we couldn't let you shoot us." Lock gave her the gun back, and the boys went after Josh. Ellie went back to standing guard, pretty sure if someone wanted her gun, they'd be able to get it. She was proving to be worthless at defending the men.

Josh came back. He had Brody in his arms. Lock and Thayne were across from Josh, helping to carry their brother.

They laid Brody down. Josh snatched the gun away from

her. "You're a better doctor than I am. He's alive still. It looked like a hard hit with that bullet."

Ellie dropped to her knees beside Brody and fumbled to find the wound. "It's too dark. I can't see anything."

"He got hit in the chest. We'll get into the firelight if we have to, but that one, Sonny, he's slick. I never heard him coming. I hate making it easy for them to see us in the light."

And then Ellie found it. "There's a tear in his shirt, a bullet-sized tear, but no blood." Feeling for what had to be a terrible wound, she found only . . . "A coin." She didn't use the word *gold*. She pulled it out of Brody's pocket. There were three coins. He'd dropped them all in there. One of them had a deep dent in it.

"He had coins in his shirt pocket. The bullet didn't go in—"

"Ellie! Get into the woods! Get away, Ellie, my Ellie . . ." Brody was waking up.

Ellie threw her arms around him. "Brody . . ." Her voice broke, and she burst into tears.

"Wait, you boys—" Josh called out softly before running away, leaving Ellie there, only distantly aware that she'd just been abandoned. No, not abandoned, but left alone in Brody's arms.

Brody blinked quickly several times. "What's going on? Ellie, are you safe? Are they gone? Did they—?" Suddenly he was kissing her. Or maybe she was kissing him; she thought maybe she'd started it.

"You got shot, Brody. But the bullet hit the gold coins you were carrying."

"I had three of them. I put them in my shirt pocket, along with some papers I wanted to read."

"The bullet hit you and knocked you down, knocked you

out. But it didn't penetrate. Your grandpa's treasure saved your life."

A gun clicked in the darkness. "Let's see that treasure."

Ellie gasped and twisted around, still clinging to Brody, to see Loyal barely visible in the shadows.

"I've never shot anyone, Ellie. So perfect that I'd start with you, the woman who brought me low. And with the man you chose over me." Loyal raised his gun.

Sonny was a pace behind him. "Just get it over with, Kelton. There's no time for gloating."

Why had Josh and the boys run off? They were probably searching for these two and accidentally left Ellie defenseless.

The gun rose, a barely visible glint of black iron in the night.

A bloodcurdling scream made Loyal jump. The gun went off into the night sky just as something slammed into him and then into Sonny. The grunting and the thrashing around were all a muddle Ellie couldn't quite make out. But she heard no more gunfire.

Then a blow to Ellie's leg had her crying out. She shoved at whatever had hit her and found a gun. She pointed it away from her and Brody and the fighting because she didn't know who was out there in the dark.

A dull thud put an end to half the noise, then came another thud. This one harder, louder. A cry of pain, another thud.

"I've got rope," Josh called out. "Let's tie them up, boys, and haul them back to the ranch and into town. These two are going to spend long years in jail."

Ellie felt Brody's arms wrap around her. She collapsed on top of him. Brody cried out in pain. A bullet hitting at close range probably left a terrible injury just from the impact, even if it didn't break the skin. With a gasp of regret, she wrenched herself out of his arms.

"We got them both, Thayne." A shriek of victory. Lock and Thayne had come to save the day, or rather, save the night.

Josh said, "Thayne, you grab Kelton, I'll get Sonny. Lock, help Ellie get your brother back to the campfire."

Ellie was glad to have someone else take charge. She was so badly shaken now that it seemed to be over, it took everything in her to help a wobbly Brody to his feet. She slid an arm around him from his left while Lock did the same from his right.

She heard dragging and stumbling ahead of her, and when they reached the clearing where they'd camped, she saw Josh drop Loyal hard to the ground. Thayne dragged Sonny along on his back.

"I found where they left their horses, Josh." Lock eased Brody to the ground. "We should saddle up and head back. It'll be light in a couple of hours, but I don't want to wait."

"Good plan. We'll leave camp while these two are out cold. Bring the horses and let's start packing up. I remember our back trail well enough we can reach the cave by sunlight."

Brody said, "I'm sorry we can't go on treasure hunting now, but we have no choice."

"There'll be plenty of time later for hunting treasure," Lock said before rushing after the horses.

In the flickering firelight, Thayne dropped by Brody's side. "We were trying to get behind them. We'd hoped to gain the element of surprise."

"It was smart of you to slip away from camp. Josh slipped away too, and those two"—he gave their prisoners a look of disgust—"were so stupid they didn't even notice."

Brody launched himself at Thayne and hugged him. "You

gave me the chance to fight for Ellie's life. If they'd had all of us, they could have started shooting and I'd've had no choice but to hand over the map." He coughed and let go of Thayne, then rubbed his chest. "I might have a cracked rib." Then he rubbed the back of his head. "And another concussion."

Thayne beamed at Brody. "This treasure hunt has taken a toll on all of us."

Brody turned to Ellie. "When we get back to the ranch, we need to concentrate on finding Mayhew Westbrook. If he's still alive, we can talk with him. If not, we'll talk with his heirs. We'll read Grandpa's notes more carefully first, but if we understand it correctly, our map isn't going to lead us all the way to the treasure anyway." He glanced at Thayne and Josh. "Can I talk to Ellie in private for a minute?"

Thayne grinned, and he and Josh went to check the tightly bound, unconscious prisoners. "Let's go saddle our horses now, Thayne," said Josh. "We want to be ready to ride when Lock returns with their horses."

As soon as they were gone, Brody said to Ellie, "Finding this Westbrook fellow, well, it might be the kind of thing we could do together. We might need to travel a bit. Look at old newspapers and maybe census records . . ." He hesitated, taking her hand in his. "Well, it might be the kind of thing a married couple could do together."

Ellie's grip tightened.

Brody went on, "When I thought Loyal was going to kill you, Ellie, I realized how much I love you." He leaned forward to where she knelt at his side. "I've loved you almost from the first, or at least it was the beginning of love. As I've spent time with you and gotten to know you better, my love for you has only grown. And the thought I could lose you . . ." His voice broke.

She kissed him to stop him from having to say more. Easing back just enough to see his eyes in the firelight, she said, "It was the same for me, Brody. When that bullet hit you, all I could think was that I've lost the love of my life. Josh jumped on me to stop me from charging right back into that circle of light."

"Um . . . is that a yes? Will you marry me, Ellie? The search for treasure, well, there can be no greater treasure than to find a woman as special as you. I know the boys want more, but I've found the finest possible MacKenzie's Treasure right here in my arms."

It was his turn to kiss her.

Ellie said against his lips, "That's a yes. I can't wait to start a life with you. If you have to go to Boston, then I'll go with you. I'll go anywhere, as long as it's with you."

The warmth of the fire and the cool night breeze surrounded them in something so perfect, Brody was glad his mouth was busy or he might've broken into song or started spouting love sonnets.

They spent a few moments together talking, and a few moments not talking, until Josh and Thayne led the horses into the clearing. Then Lock returned with the outlaws' horses.

As they mounted up, Brody groaned, his chest hurting more with each passing moment. His head throbbed every time he moved. Barely able to sit on his horse, with Ellie riding at his side, they headed for home.

They rode into the Two Harts Ranch in time for an early supper.

"Lock the prisoners in the icehouse and post a guard." Josh planned to ride to town first thing in the morning—for the arrest and then a wedding.

Brody and his brothers were invited to eat at the ranch house. Every one of them was exhausted after not sleeping last night, though Thayne and Lock had managed an hour.

When Ellie told Annie she was getting married, the squealing was enough to keep Brody awake long enough to eat.

They planned to ride into Dorada Rio tomorrow for the wedding. With Thayne and Lock to lean on, Brody got home before he passed out.

THIRTY-THREE

The next morning, Ellie wore her Sunday-best dress, a lemon-yellow silk she hadn't worn since she came home from San Francisco, her heart broken from the betrayal of Loyal Kelton, that low-down vermin.

San Francisco, where she'd lived with Annie's husband's family, had been a dreadful time in her life, considering how it ended. But she'd dressed well.

Brody looked fine in his clean city suit. He hadn't worn it since the first couple of days after he arrived at the ranch. He usually wore black trousers and a white shirt with a black vest, which was his doctoring outfit. But today he'd broken out the suit. Annie had gone after him last night, gotten the suit away from Brody, and brought it back to the house to wash and iron.

Ellie had gone directly to sleep. She had no idea how long her big sister had stayed up, cleaning and pressing Brody's suit to shine him up fit for a wedding. And she'd done a wonderful job of it.

Ellie emerged the next morning to find the family's buggy waiting outside the back door, hitched to a pair of black geldings. The buggy had two seats in the back and could hold four passengers. Josh was sitting up front, the reins firmly in hand.

Annie and Caroline would join them in the buggy. Thayne and Lock were on horseback. A half-dozen cowhands rode along with them to take charge of Loyal and Sonny, who were cold and sullen and well-guarded.

They headed for town with Ellie sitting next to Brody facing the horses, across from Annie and Caroline.

"How are you this morning?" Ellie watched Brody climb into the buggy. He was clutching his chest.

"I've got a bruise on my chest the size of the saucer you use under your coffee cup." He gingerly rubbed the spot. "And I've a lump on the back of my head from when that bullet slammed me into the rock wall."

Ellie's heart turned over with love. When she thought of the bullet hitting him right in the heart, it made her tremble.

"It's swollen and red and so tender it hurts to breathe, but the rib is cracked, not broken." He turned and smiled at her. "Nothing serious enough to stop me from marrying you, Miss Hart."

She returned the smile. Caroline giggled across the seat from them. Whatever Annie did was unknown because Ellie couldn't take her eyes off her soon-to-be husband.

They were nearly an hour riding to Dorada Rio. They could have made it there faster on horseback, and Ellie wanted to gallop straight for her future with Brody, but considering his wounds, traveling by buggy had been best.

The sound of the train pulling into town barely penetrated her happiness.

Josh drove them straight to the church, where he tied the

team to the hitching post. "I'll be back as soon as I get our prisoners behind bars. Brody, you get yourself in the church and sit down. Lock and Thayne, the house next door is where the parson lives. Get him to the church." With that, Josh rode off with his men.

Brody smiled at Ellie. "Your big brother likes to be in charge."

Ellie laughed and held on to Brody's arm with both hands. She wanted to be as close to him as she could, and yet holding him up was also a consideration. She probably should have let him heal for a few days before getting married.

She quickly shook that thought off and headed into the church with Brody. Annie and Caroline followed close behind. They'd barely reached the front of the small church when the door slammed open. Ellie turned to see who it was. "Zane!" She whispered to Brody, "You'd better sit down. I'll bring my brother and his wife and . . . uh, maybe ten young children? I guess they took in more students." She looked again. "And another teacher?"

Brody sank gratefully onto the front pew.

Ellie rushed back to greet her brother. "You're not supposed to be here for a few more weeks."

Zane looked confused. "You're getting married?"

Michelle, very round with child, caught Ellie in a tight hug as the new teacher—Ellie heard the name "Miss Tilda"— shooed the children into their seats with the promise of a hot meal after the wedding. Ellie certainly hadn't expected this big a crowd.

Ellie linked arms with Michelle. "Come and meet Brody."

"Is this the doctor you wrote me about hiring?"

"Yes, and he's a fine man. But be gentle with him—he got shot last night."

Michelle gasped. "We saw Josh going into the sheriff's office, and he told us a little bit about what happened. That's how we knew you were here at the church. But he didn't mention anything about someone getting shot."

Brody turned in his seat. "I apologize for not getting up. I've only got a bit of strength left, and I'm saving it to stand at the altar with Ellie."

Michelle wanted to hear the whole story. Zane was right behind her and had a few questions of his own.

After learning about the gold coin and how it'd saved Brody's life, Michelle wanted to see the bruise on his chest.

"I'm not unbuttoning my shirt in front of my wife's family, especially not in church."

"Now, Brody, I was pretty much the doctor at the Two Harts before we hired you. I think—"

Zane caught her by the arm and dragged her to the pew across the aisle from Brody, whispering to her. She settled in just as the parson arrived with Thayne and Lock.

Tilda, the teacher, cried, "Thayne, Lochlan! Michelle told me you were here, but I . . ." Her voice faltered. "I-I've been searching for you." She rushed out of the pew and threw her arms around both boys.

Ellie had no idea what was going on.

"Ellie, introduce me to your young man." The parson smiled and clasped his hands together as if in prayer.

And it looked as though Ellie wasn't going to find out what was going on. Tilda and the boys were talking fast, but the parson was here, and Ellie wanted to get married.

But more introductions were necessary. The parson wanted to visit for a while. By the time that was finished, Josh was back, and he'd brought the cowhands with him. Between his crew and the orphans, the church was half full now. She wouldn't have gotten a bigger crowd if she'd planned it for a month.

"All right. Let's get on with the wedding now," the parson said to everyone, finally. As he moved to the front of the church, Ellie helped Brody to his feet. They stood arm in arm before God and man to take their vows.

"Dearly beloved . . ."

Toward the end of a very short ceremony, Ellie felt like she was keeping Brody on his feet by sheer force. After the parson blessed their union, Josh came up front and held a hand against Brody's spine to keep it straight.

Brody whispered, "Can I go sit in the buggy while you finish up here?"

"Are you up to sitting through a meal?" Ellie thought his face looked a little pale. "Have you eaten anything today?"

"Sitting somewhere for a bit might be good before we take the trip home, except . . ." He snuck a peak behind them without twisting hardly at all. "Are those orphans all ours?"

Ellie nodded. "Michelle brings children home now and then. Including your brothers. Let's go. The teacher with them seems to know Thayne and Lock."

"Maybe she was in San Francisco before the boys were brought here." Brody looked at all the people milling around. "Is there a restaurant in this town that can feed this many folks?"

Ellie turned to Zane, who was listening. "Is there?"

"We already sent someone with a note to warn Fatty's we're coming with a crowd. Told him to start frying chicken as fast as he could."

"That's only three blocks from the church," Ellie said, helping to guide Brody toward the door. "But let's use the buggy that's waiting out front."

Brody gave her a rueful smile. "Yes, otherwise I just might collapse."

She'd been trying to save his pride, but he seemed to have the wisdom to know his limits.

The cowhands all smiled and nodded at the newlyweds. Josh and Zane strode down the aisle behind them. Ellie thought it was probably to catch Brody if he fell.

They reached the buggy and climbed slowly into it. Everyone else would walk to the restaurant except Josh, who was driving the buggy and team of horses.

"Hold up, Josh." Thayne approached the buggy. Ellie wondered if they wanted a ride.

"Brody, Lock and I have been talking." Thayne reached into the buggy and rested his hand on Brody's forearm.

It struck Ellie then that Lock was an adult now. Brody had wanted to take his brothers home with him to Boston, but an adult man could do as he pleased. She knew Brody would be devastated if his brothers stayed out here, but he might have to accept that fact.

"What is it?" Brody asked.

Lock cleared his throat and gave him a sheepish smile. "We've decided we want to go back east with you. Someday we'd like to follow our map to the end, and we hope to find Westbrook and follow his half of the map, but more than that we want to stay with you, Brody. The treasure we found is enough—especially if the rest proves so hard to find. Thayne wonders if Grandpa didn't take all the gold he found and then draw a map to where he found it. What we did find, though, will set us up for a long time. It'll provide for the whole family."

"We know you have to go back." Thayne squeezed Brody's shoulder before pulling back. "We're going with you."

Brody nodded his head silently for a moment. Ellie saw him swallow hard, choked up by his brothers' supportive words.

"Thank you, boys. Here I am planning to take Ellie far from her family, all while not wanting to be separated from my own."

Very gently, Ellie leaned against his shoulder and said, "'Whither thou goest, I will go. Whither thou lodgest, I will lodge.'"

Brody kissed her on the forehead. "Thank you. All of you."

Thayne and Lock stepped away from the buggy.

Josh slapped the reins on the team's backs, and the buggy set off again. A terrible racket sounded as they began rolling. Brody jerked upright, then groaned.

After the solemn moment between her, Brody, and his brothers, Ellie laughed and patted his hand. "Someone with some spare pots and pans has adorned our buggy, as if we need more attention."

Everyone on the busy street turned to watch them ride by, the full wedding party following on foot. It was midmorning, so hopefully they'd have enough space in the diner for all those with the wedding.

As they rolled on, Brody said, "We've spent our time together searching for treasure. Even though God tells us not to lay up treasures on earth."

Ellie shook her head. "At the rate we're finding treasure, we won't have to worry about 'laying it up.' I suppose there's a pirate's hoard out there somewhere, but I wonder if your grandpa didn't take every single gold coin he found. There could be more, but maybe not treasure the way your brothers think of it. Maybe instead it's more journals or knives."

"Whether it's there or not—" Brody turned and kissed her softly—"we'll use the money for the orphans, and I won't charge my patients anything, at least until it's all gone. I don't need gold." He took her hand and wove his fingers through hers. "I've found my treasure right here, Ellie, in you."

EPILOGUE

"Thank you for the meal." Tilda spoke to Josh, but probably just because he was closest. "I should find out when the next train is heading for New York."

Tilda's shoulders slumped as she turned toward the train station. She carried a satchel that Josh thought looked mostly empty.

Michelle grabbed her by the arm. "You're not leaving yet."

Tilda said, "I've done what I came here to do, which was to make sure Thayne and Lock were all right. I need to get back now." She tugged against Michelle's grip.

But Michelle refused to let go of her. "We want you to come out to the ranch. We need another teacher." Michelle nodded at the happy couple. Well, happy except that Brody looked near collapse. "Ellie is working with Brody now as his nurse. She did a lot of teaching, so we can use the help."

"I'm not a teacher." Tilda shook her head.

Michelle grinned. "Neither was Ellie. And I'm not a doctor. But that hasn't stopped either of us. Now Brody is our doctor."

"I can't be a doctor at the ranch, though. I'm going back to Boston." Brody wobbled, and Ellie guided him to sit on the edge of the sidewalk.

Ellie said, "I'm not a nurse either."

Tilda's brow furrowed, almost as if she didn't approve of people being things they had no training for.

Josh noticed a rather long scar across her forehead. Old and well-healed, but it was there regardless. He wondered what had happened. Her hair was a bunch of coiled-up springs of dark brown. He could imagine her trying to bind it into a tidy bun every morning—and failing at it. Her eyes were so big, a man had trouble looking away, and so dark he couldn't tell where the color ended and the pupils began. And they had a way of looking at the world as if she expected life to always be hard. He wondered what had put that look in her eyes. Chasing after the MacKenzie brothers maybe. Yet the look was such a part of her that he suspected she'd had trouble for a long time.

She was five and a half feet tall, more than six inches shorter than him, and so thin he had to fight the urge to get her another piece of chicken and fuss at her until she'd eaten every bite.

Josh respected her worrying about being asked to teach when she'd never done it, but sometimes necessity intervened. Sometimes someone was better than no one at all.

"Ellie's been teaching, and I've been the ranch doctor." Michelle patted her round belly. "But I can go back to my inventing if we can persuade Brody to stay."

"You can't." Brody leaned against a post near the sidewalk.

"We'll see." Michelle gave Brody a concerned look before turning back to Tilda. "Like I said, we need more help."

Michelle—who had a knack for organizing everything she

touched to suit herself, which was usually the right way—leaned close to Tilda and applied her powers of persuasion. "Come with us, Tilda. You can send a wire home to tell the orphanage that Thayne and Lock are safe here. Tell them your return has been delayed. For now, try being a teacher. We'll start you out with the youngsters, so as long as you know more than them, you should manage nicely."

Josh had seen Ellie attempt to teach and knew there was more to teaching than that, but he didn't say so.

Tilda still looked hesitant.

Michelle continued, "At least ride home with us and stay a few days. You can better report about us if you've seen how the children are cared for." She nodded while speaking, and it seemed the force of her will took charge because Tilda began nodded along. "Good. Now let's talk about what you can expect as a teacher."

"But first," Zane cut in, "I want to know what happened to make you lock up Loyal Kelton. So he attacked Ellie and shot Brody?"

"No," said Josh. "Sonny, the one with Kelton, shot Brody." Josh rubbed his temple. It had a lump and a small cut, yet it didn't hurt as much after a good night's sleep. "Loyal hit me over the head and near to scrambled my brain, then held a gun to my head. And when he got Brody in his sights, he knocked me out cold."

Even sitting, Brody looked wobbly. Ellie slid her arm around his waist to hold him upright.

"Let's go to the sheriff's office so we only have to tell what happened once," Josh said. "And so Brody can get this over with so he can lie down."

They all headed for the jail to tell the story to the sheriff and make sure Kelton stayed locked up for good. Since Zane had once beaten Kelton into the ground, Josh enjoyed watching Kelton refuse to meet Zane's eyes.

Kelton had requested a wire be sent to his father in San Francisco the first minute he'd been brought in. The sheriff said the man had asked his father for a lawyer and for money.

As they entered the jail, a boy came running up with a return wire that refused those requests.

Loyal sat seething in his cell. Sonny was in his own cell, napping. Josh thought Sonny acted like a man who'd spent time in jail before.

Ellie guided Brody to the sheriff's chair and got him settled.

The sheriff looked grim. "Show me where you got shot, Brody."

Brody unbuttoned his shirt and showed the sheriff where Loyal's bullet had hit him.

Josh strode to Brody's side and peeled the shirt wide open. "That's ugly, Brody. You really do need to lie down."

The bruise was red, the size of a coffee saucer just like Brody had said. Near the middle, the wound was turning black. It was swollen and looked hot to the touch. Josh could see the outline of where the gold coin had been rammed into Brody's chest when the bullet struck it.

"You'd be dead, Brody, if that—" Josh hesitated and decided not to talk of gold—"if you hadn't had something in your pocket to stop that slug."

"I have at least two cracked ribs, probably more. One of them could be broken. Getting hit with a bullet at close range has about the same effect as being hit with a stout club. I've also got a huge lump on the back of my head, after the gunshot slammed me against the rocks." Brody tugged his shirt closed. "You're right. I do need to lie down. But first I want to answer the sheriff's questions. I don't want there to be any chance that Kelton walks free from jail." He turned to the sheriff. "Kelton had planned to kidnap Ellie. He knocked Josh out with the butt of his gun. Sonny stood there gloating over how they were going to steal from us. They wanted me to hand over a map we had with us. When I did so, Sonny shot me. And Kelton stood by and smirked."

Josh thought the doctor was fortunate he'd been training his wife to be a nurse. Brody needed professional care. There was a doctor here in Dorada Rio. Josh would urge Brody to go see him.

"That's attempted murder," the sheriff said. "And three counts because it sounds like they'd planned to kill you all. But shooting you like he did, that's cold-blooded attempted murder, pure and simple. A man who'd do that isn't a man who should be allowed to walk around free. And standing by smirking is aiding and abetting in the attempted murder. A man can be charged just as severely for that as he can for pulling the trigger. Add to that assault on Josh. Dragging Josh around against his will is kidnapping. That's a hanging offense right there. I already put out word for a jury. The trial's in one hour. You folks need to stay in town to testify."

Ellie nodded and said, "Brody, I think we should stay here overnight. We need to figure out how to find Mayhew Westbrook, and I'd think that starts in town."

"What do you want with him?" Michelle asked.

Josh turned to look at his very smart sister-in-law. "You know who that is?"

Michelle shrugged. "Sure. My family does business with his bank in Sacramento."

A low growl from the jail cell turned them to look at Kelton.

Josh saw clear recognition. "You know who Mayhew Westbrook is, too?"

"This search isn't going to be that hard." Ellie stepped forward and rested a hand on Brody's back. "It looks like we're the only ones who don't know who he is." Ellie steadied Brody as if the poor man needed someone to hold him upright. And he probably did.

Kelton narrowed his eyes and clamped his mouth shut, but there was something there.

Josh said, "Somehow Kelton knows Westbrook. We just read a name in a note left by—"

"Josh, stop."

Josh turned to stare at Ellie.

"We'll talk about this, but away from Loyal," she said. "He's not going to tell us anything, so let's leave and talk about it with Michelle and Zane. I don't want Loyal to know any more than he already does."

"I can tell you things that'll make a difference," Kelton said, his eyes lighting up. "I can speed things up for you—that is, if we can get this nonsense about a trial stopped. I didn't hurt anyone."

"Brody's plenty hurt, and you fully intended to kill him or stand by while your partner did." Josh crossed his arms and glared at Kelton.

"No, you and this whole family misjudged things. No real harm was done. We can just all go on our way, and with what I have to tell you, you'll have a lot more information than you have now."

Josh studied Kelton for about five seconds, then said, "Nope. I want you locked up. San Quentin is going to be your home for a long time."

All the color drained from Kelton's face at the mention of the notorious prison near San Francisco.

With a nod of satisfaction, Josh added, "I'd rather do this

the slow way rather than speed things up with your help." He turned and led the way out of the sheriff's office, his family trailing behind him.

The town was bustling. The sound of a train pulling in from the north underpinned the rattling of wagons and the jingling of traces. They walked down the steps to the boardwalk and away from the jailhouse, where Josh turned to Michelle and said, "Brody's grandpa sent a journal to Brody back in New York City, telling about a treasure he found out here."

"A treasure?" Zane groaned. He'd had a lot of trouble when gold was found on the Two Harts a few years ago. Of course, he'd had a lot of gold, too. Josh had trouble feeling too sorry for him.

Tilda stood next to Thayne and Lock, which made sense as they were the only people here she really knew.

"Then," Josh went on, "they never heard from him again. Brody's pa spent a good chunk of his life in a fruitless search for that treasure. That's what brought Brody's little brothers out here." Josh nodded at Thayne and Lock.

Ellie said, "Brody and I are going to get a room at the hotel so he can lie down. Josh, with Thayne and Lock help-ing, knows the whole story. If the sheriff needs us, someone come and get us. We'll rest until it's time for the trial."

The two of them walked away, not looking like they were heading for a wedding night, but rather like Brody needed somewhere to pass out. Josh felt sorry for them, but then he didn't like thinking about his sister and the wedding night, so he couldn't say he was that sorry.

"We've been following clues in the journal, and yesterday we found Grandpa MacKenzie's body lying in a cave."

"You found your grandpa's body?" Tilda rested a hand

on each of the boy's shoulders. Thayne was taller than her. Lock was just as tall, yet she acted as though they were still children and in need of comfort.

Since they'd never met their grandpa and were viewing all of this as the best kind of adventure, they'd handled finding a skeleton without much trouble.

"We also found more notes. They talked of owing money to Mayhew Westbrook and sending Westbrook half a map at the same time he sent the journal with the other half to Brody's family back east. Yesterday was the first we heard of any partner in the treasure."

"You've got a treasure map?" Michelle's eyes lit up. "This'll be fun."

Zane shook his head and pulled his rather round wife against him. They were due to have a baby anytime.

"Maybe." Josh watched his sister and Brody climb the steps to the hotel entrance. Brody wasn't going to be doing much doctoring for a while. "Ellie and Brody will talk to Westbrook and try to figure out if he has that map, then get back here with it so we can find the treasure."

"What kind of treasure?"

"We don't know," Josh admitted. "We've found about a dozen gold doubloons, very old. Maybe the map will lead to a pirate hoard."

"That's my guess," Lock said, nearly bouncing. "And it was fourteen doubloons. Pirates' treasure. There's probably a fortune buried somewhere."

"Yep, the map has some strange foreign words written on it—most likely Spanish, although a lot of them don't make any sense."

"I'm fluent in Spanish," Michelle offered.

Of course she was.

Thayne watched as Brody slowly entered the hotel. Lock might be obsessed with the treasure hunt, but Thayne had the sense to worry about his injured big brother.

"I'll tell you exactly where to find Mayhew Westbrook. You can find him with no trouble. But why do you want to find my grandpa?"

A new voice turned them around to face a tall, well-dressed stranger, leading his horse down the street from the direction of the train station.

"Mayhew Westbrook is your grandfather?" Josh asked.

Michelle reached out a hand. "You're Cordell Westbrook. I'm Michelle Hart, formerly Michelle Stiles. We've met, though it was a few years ago."

"Call me Cord. You're one of Liam Stiles's daughters? I think your family owns shares in several companies my grandfather has invested in."

Josh remembered that Michelle's family knew the governor as well as the man who owned Wells Fargo Bank. And probably everyone else in the state.

Michelle introduced everyone, including Tilda, whom she said was a teacher at the Two Harts School.

Tilda arched a brow but didn't comment beyond saying hello.

"Now, what's all this about my grandpa?"

All Josh could think was that their treasure hunt wasn't even close to being over.

Read on
for a sneak peek at

Legends of Gold

BY MARY CONNEALY

BOOK 2 OF
✦ GOLDEN STATE TREASURE ✦

Available in the summer of 2025

ONE

August 1874

"I was surprised the sheriff didn't find an excuse to hang that blackhearted varmint," Josh Hart said as he rode beside Tilda Muirhead on their way to the Two Harts Ranch near the town of Dorada Rio, California.

Josh's big brother, Zane, and his wife, Michelle, who was near to having her first child, led the way home. Brothers Thayne and Lochlan MacKenzie came next, with Josh and Tilda bringing up the rear.

Brody MacKenzie and his brand-new bride, Josh's sister, Ellie, had stayed in town after the wedding because Brody had needed to attend the trial of the man who'd shot him, breaking his ribs and knocking him insensible.

True, a gold coin had stopped the bullet, saving Brody's life, but Sonny Dykes hadn't killed him for lack of trying. He and his outlaw partner, Loyal Kelton, Ellie's one-time fiancé, were both lucky to be spending the rest of their lives in jail instead of being hanged when cold-blooded murder had been their intent.

"I don't like the idea of hanging anyone." Tilda raised a

hand to her throat as if she could feel a noose there. "But locking those two outlaws away for the rest of their lives is just good sense. He shot your brother-in-law right through the heart. A life sentence with hard labor should keep your family safe now."

They trotted for a time, Tilda on Josh's right. When they reached a rugged stretch, they slowed to let the horses walk. The clopping of hooves was a friendly sound that reminded Josh he'd been away at sea for too long before coming home to stay a little over a year ago. He once thought the sea was in his blood, but now he knew this was the life he'd always wanted. "Have you thought more about being a teacher?" he asked her.

Tilda had shown up with Zane, Michelle, and a few dozen orphans to live on the ranch. Originally from New York, she'd come west searching for Thayne and Lock MacKenzie, who'd ridden out here on an orphan train, then vanished into the wilderness after running away from the train and Tilda.

Tilda looked sideways at him. She was not a skilled rider, but then sitting astride a well-trained horse was no great trick. Under careful observation, she'd even handled trotting with just a few pointers from him.

The trail curved ahead, and Josh hadn't noticed that they'd lagged behind until the MacKenzie boys were out of sight. For the first time since he'd returned home, he rode alongside a woman who wasn't his sister or married to his brother. He found himself wanting to talk with Tilda, but not about work and not about orphans. But he had a tongue tied in knots and a brain stuffed full of cotton wool.

Searching desperately for something to say, he returned to the subject of her working at the ranch. "You know, Tilda, if you work for us, you'll be required to sleep with me."

She gasped and whirled around to face him, her hair snapping free from its pins. A long, dark braid whipped across her face. "What did you say?" Her eyes flashed with fury.

That's when what he'd just said echoed through his brain. "I-I mean at the school—you and I will both sleep at the school."

Tilda reined in her horse. "I'll do no such thing." She tugged at one rein as if to turn the horse back to town. Except her horse wanted to go home, and she wasn't handling it right. The stubborn horse refused to let her guide it.

"I'm going back to town. No, I'll get the children first. What kind of place do you run out there anyway?"

"I'm sorry," said Josh. "What I meant was you'll sleep with the orphan girls, who live at our school. I'll bed down in the dormitory we have for the boys. There'll be no sleeping together. I have no interest in you at all."

As her eyes widened, he quick reviewed his words again, not sure what he'd babbled out. Whatever it was, it was clearly wrong. Maybe he should just head out to sea again.

She pulled the reins with more force, and her horse skittered sideways. Josh reached out to grab the reins before the horse got its dander up, but Tilda slapped his hand and shrieked as if he were attacking her. He snatched his hand away just in time for her to miss him and slapped the horse on the neck. Instantly, the horse kicked with its back legs, sending Tilda flying.

Josh netted her as if she were a saltwater fish on the line, and she landed with a thud right on his lap, nose to nose with him. Startled, she quit fighting and shrieking. Their eyes met. He only distantly saw her horse, running for home.

"Tilda, I didn't mean to insult you. I was only . . . what I meant was . . ."

"What?" She sounded breathless. Maybe it was because

she'd just been tossed off a horse's back. But it didn't sound like that. Instead, it sounded like . . .

He leaned forward, an inch at a time. She didn't fight or shriek or demand to be set down on the ground. In fact, she leaned distractingly forward.

"Josh, what happened?" Zane's voice broke in.

Josh jerked away, which wasn't far considering she was sitting in his lap. There was only so far a man could go in those circumstances.

"Tilda got bucked off her horse when she swatted a . . . a fly." Right now, Josh felt as low as a bug, so it wasn't far from the truth.

Michelle came next around the curve in the trail, then Thayne.

"Are you all right, Miss Tilda? Seeing your horse come running without a rider scared me."

Thayne looked at Tilda in a way that struck Josh as a bit too mature for his age. Thayne was in many ways a man grown. It struck Josh that Thayne might have ideas about his pretty teacher. One who'd worried enough about them to travel clear across the country.

"Mr. Hart caught me before I fell." Tilda's eyes glowed as if a knight on a valiant steed had saved her life.

Josh probably shouldn't enjoy that so much. "Where's her horse?"

Lock rode around the bend, leading it.

Tilda clutched at Josh's shirt and whispered, "Please, I don't want to go back on that horse. Not alone. I'm afraid."

Josh kept his horse moving forward, even though her hand held the front of his shirt so tight he was in danger of being strangled. "Since we're almost home, Tilda will ride double with me the rest of the way."

Really it wasn't far at all. Holding this pretty little woman in his saddle made him wish the ride were a bit longer.

Michelle approached and rode at Josh's side. "We can't ride fast with Josh carrying double, so we may as well talk. Josh and you MacKenzie boys, tell me more about this treasure hunt of Graham MacKenzie's."

Their treasure-hunting party had found fourteen gold coins in a saddlebag when they'd come upon Grandpa MacKenzie's body. There were old papers too, but they hadn't had time to go over them yet.

"Did you say there's some Spanish involved?"

Lock, who probably had his grandfather's whole journal memorized, said, "Yes, several sentences. One we found in the journal, and later in the papers with Grandpa's body, read, '*Al norte de la Bahia de Los Piños con Capitan Cabrillo en una espesa niebla.*'"

Michelle frowned. "All right. 'North of Los Piños Bay with Captain Cabrillo in a thick fog.'"

"I've heard of Los Piños Bay," Josh said. "It's called Monterey Bay now. It's south of San Francisco Bay. Considering the fog that surrounds that area, maybe he was writing about seeing fog around San Francisco, not the bay."

Lock's jaw sagged open. "Why didn't you tell us this before?"

"Why didn't you ask? You know I was a sailor. If you'd asked about a bay, I'd've answered you. Where did you say you found this?"

"Grandpa's journal."

Josh shrugged. "I've never read it. Never even talked with you about that old book."

"But you went on the treasure hunt with us."

"You had a map—or half of one anyway. That's what I was paying attention to."

Quietly, Tilda said, "I've heard of Captain Cabrillo."

Josh's head pivoted hard to stare down at the woman in his arms. The whole group was looking at her.

"Who is he?" Michelle asked. Michelle liked to know more than everyone, and here she was not knowing two whole facts about what she'd no doubt flawlessly just translated.

"Juan Cabrillo was with Fernando Cortes, the Spanish conquistador whose expedition led to the fall of Mexico's Aztec Empire. That was over three hundred years ago. Captain Cabrillo was sent by Cortes to explore the California coastline with a small armada of ships. Some say he went as far north as the Columbia River in Washington State. He took very thorough notes, but most things had different names back then. Cabrillo gave places names, although not all of them stuck. There's a record of all the places he found. But he never found San Francisco Bay. Historians claim he missed the bay because it was shrouded in a thick fog."

"'*En una espesa niebla*,'" Michelle said. "In a thick fog."

"The first European explorer to find San Francisco was Don Gaspar de Portola in 1769," Tilda went on. "And he came over land, not by sea."

"How is it you know so much about California history?" Josh asked.

Tilda's cheeks pinked up. "My adoptive father was a history teacher in New York City. He had a library, and I love to read. I've always had a fascination with California history and the stories about Spanish explorers."

Josh studied her. Dark hair, dark eyes. Could she be Spanish maybe?

Michelle's eyes narrowed. "Might one of the ships in his

armada somehow become separated from the fleet in the fog? Could they have been left behind in California? Run aground, followed a river into the interior and been stranded? Maybe they set out to explore, planning to rejoin Captain Cabrillo later, but then their ship sank and they were trapped here." She looked up, her eyes gleaming.

"Or maybe they jumped ship and swam to shore." Josh knew of sailors who'd done such things. "They could've run off from Cabrillo, hoping no one would ever find them."

"Cabrillo was the first to travel up the California coast." Tilda sure spoke like someone who'd memorized a history book. "But San Francisco Bay wasn't charted for hundreds of years. The men who left that journal and those coins may have been driven into the fog by a storm. Maybe their ships were wrecked and they were left to wait for help, which never came. Maybe they set out to hike back to Mexico where Cortes was, then looked around at this lush, beautiful land and decided to stay."

"You do know a lot about California history," Michelle said.

Tilda shrugged. "My father inspired me with his love of American history. I've read a number of history books on the subject."

Michelle's eyes sparked. "We need a history teacher at the school."

Zane shook his head. "We're training most of those kids to be cowhands."

Michelle, riding at his side, smiled at Zane like she'd noticed a caveman in her presence and found him amusing. "Tilda, you can teach history to the older students. Zane's library in the ranch house has quite a few history books. I wonder if Captain Cabrillo is listed in any of them." Michelle patted Zane on the shoulder. "If we can prove a bunch of Spanish conquistadors were inland in California in . . ." She looked at Tilda. "When was all this?"

"Cabrillo explored the coast in 1542."

Josh tightened his arms around Tilda. She probably needed support if she was going to deal with Michelle. Not that Michelle didn't have some good ideas. They just usually had the relentlessness of an incoming tidal wave about them.

"I want to see that journal." Michelle's eyes lit up—not with the fever to find treasure, but with an interest in history.

"I want to see that journal, too," echoed Josh. He knew Michelle thought she knew everything, but surely he could do a better job of recognizing anything that dealt with seafaring.

Tilda said, "I, too, would love a chance to study something connected with Captain Cabrillo and the conquistadors."

The woman really did love history, it seemed. An odd preference to Josh's way of thinking. Better to pay attention to the present, such as if the cows had enough grass and water.

"The journal itself is old," Lock said, "but the *writing* in it was done by Grandpa. He must've found it included in what he called a treasure and used it to take notes. He then mailed the journal to us. Later, he went back to his treasure and died before he could tell us more. The notes, including the Spanish about Los Piños and Captain Cabrillo, don't seem to be from Grandpa. We think he copied them from somewhere else. For one, he wasn't much of a speller. He had no schooling. And Grandpa didn't speak a lick of any foreign language, except maybe a few words from his Scottish ancestors."

"Brody called it Gaelic," Thayne said, guiding his horse alongside Josh's. "What about the papers we found with

Grandpa's body, Lock? Were those written by Grandpa, or were they written hundreds of years ago?"

Thayne scratched his chin. "Let's get back to the ranch and look at that journal again."

Zane said, "I need to check how things are running at the ranch."

Josh sensed a spirit of annoyance. "They're running fine, Zane. We know what we're doing."

Zane gave him a sharp look, and Josh wondered what he'd sounded like. He had spent a lot of time running around the last few days, but it had been the weekend when they'd gone on the treasure hunt, and they usually worked lighter days on weekends, especially Sunday. Today was Monday, and Josh had talked to the men before they'd headed with their prisoners to town. It wasn't time to drive the cattle to market yet, so even though Josh had brought plenty of hands along to handle the prisoners, he'd left a crew to keep up with the chores on the ranch.

Zane shifted his horse around so he was riding on Josh's left. Thayne was riding close on the right, probably so he could keep an eye on Tilda.

Zane clapped Josh on the shoulder. "I haven't got a worry in the world about you keeping things running, Josh. I'm just curious. I've been gone for nearly two months. I can't wait to see how the spring calves have grown."

Josh nodded. "I know. I'm anxious to have you around again. You ran things alone for a long time while I was at sea. But I'm back now. And I'm a full partner, not a junior partner, not anymore."

"Agreed."

Josh heard the words, but he knew Zane and knew his big brother had a bossy streak in him.

"Let's pick up the pace for home. Josh, if it's too much for your horse, do you mind if we ride on ahead? It's only a few minutes more."

Josh looked down to see the alarm on Tilda's face. She needed riding lessons, and Josh was just the one to teach her. "Go on. I think we'll keep things to a slower pace."

Zane smiled, then urged his horse along faster.

Michelle and Lock kept up, Lock leading Tilda's horse. Thayne looked torn. He wanted in on studying the journal with Michelle, but maybe he also wanted to ride alongside Tilda. Finally, his treasure-hunting enthusiasm won out, and he kicked his horse into a ground-eating trot. He soon caught up with the others. Before long they were all galloping.

Josh glanced down at the woman in his saddle and remembered his fumbling words of her staying in the school dormitory with the girls while he stayed with the boys. He clamped his mouth shut so that nothing stupid would come out again.

Tilda said quietly, "Do you think I'd be doing the right thing to stay out here? I felt like I had a true calling from God to ride on the orphan trains. He put it in my heart to care for orphans after I became one."

Josh stopped losing himself in the pleasure of carrying a woman around and focused on her words. "You're an orphan?"

"Yes, didn't anyone mention that to you? I'm sure Michelle knows." Tilda's brow furrowed. "I did tell her, didn't I?"

"She didn't say a word to me about it."

"And Thayne and Lock know. I talked about it with the orphans." Tilda frowned. "Although those two were such scamps. They might well have not been paying attention."

"That sounds like them. Did your parents die? Do you remember them?"

"No, my earliest memories are of being alone on the streets in New York. I heard much later that there was an outbreak of fever, and a lot of people died from it. The orphanage I went to live in speculated my parents might've died in that outbreak. I was left on the streets with so many other children."

"My parents died, too."

Tilda's hand clutched his shirtfront. "Josh, I didn't know you'd been orphaned, too."

"Well, I was a grown man who'd gone to sea. I came home for a visit and found out they'd died. That's not the same as being an orphan. I wasn't left fighting for my life with no food and no roof over my head. But it's mighty sad nonetheless."

Tilda's eyes shone with tears. "I was so busy trying to survive it, I wasn't given much chance to think of how sad it was. I don't remember my parents. I don't even know their names. That all got lost in the cold and hunger." She blinked back her tears, suddenly interested in smoothing out the wrinkles she'd made in his shirt.

"Not Muirhead?"

She shook her head. "I was adopted by a couple named Muirhead."

Josh rounded the corner toward home. "Look, that's our ranch. See the big white building, just past the barn and bunkhouse?"

Tilda twisted in the saddle to look. "The white building is where the orphans live?"

"Yep, the north side is the girls' living quarters—Michelle calls it a dormitory—and the south side is for the boys. There is no door connecting the two sides on the second floor. The first floor is where the classrooms are. Most of the time I sleep on the boys' side. There's a small bedroom for each adult who stays with them. Ellie used to do most of the turns on the girls' side, though Annie, my big sister, would do it on occasion. Her daughter—you met them at the wedding, remember?"

"Yes, I sat next to Caroline when we ate. Someone said her pa died?"

Josh nodded, trying desperately to think of a new topic. "Caroline is school age now. Annie does a lot of teaching now that Caroline goes to classes. Some nights, when Ellie's forced to be away, especially now that she's been a nurse to Brody, Annie would put Caroline to bed in the ranch house, then go sleep at the dorm. But that wasn't usual. It was Ellie's job for the most part. Now Ellie's going to want to stay with Brody, I reckon. It'd be a big help if you joined us. You could write to the orphanage in New York and tell them to hire someone else. Lots of folks looking for work in a big city like that. Out here teachers are scarce."

Tilda smiled. "I do feel a calling to help orphans. God opened the door for me to help with the orphan trains, but now a new door is open." She shifted again to take in the ranch and surrounding area. "It really is a beautiful place. So many houses."

"Yep, when one of our cowhands gets married, we build them a house. We've got a blacksmith shop and farrier, too. Of course, that's mainly for keeping up with ironwork at the ranch—shoeing horses, repairing wheels and tools and such. We've got a doctor's office, too. Michelle even got a telegraph wire out here. It was a modest ranch before Zane married Michelle. And Michelle's sister Jilly loves to build."

"I met Jilly and Laura, her other sister, in San Fransisco.

They came to the mission where I was helping with the children. So Jilly loves to build?"

"She doesn't do all the building herself, but she's the boss. She also built a railroad."

Tilda quit looking around and stared at him. "A woman built a railroad?"

"A line up a mountainside. And Michelle is an inventor. She's got several patents. And their sister Laura is a chemist with training in dynamite. Michelle and Jilly did a lot of the work organizing our little village. The cabins welcome family men rather than footloose cowpokes. It's helped to give us a steady work crew. We have single cowhands as well who live in the bunkhouse."

"You call it a village, but I can't help but compare it to New York City. That's the only town I've ever really known." Tilda spoke with quiet wonder. "I think this is a big improvement."

"Then you'll stay?" Josh tried to act like it was all about needing her help and not about how nice Tilda felt in his arms.

"I'll pray about it, but this place seems to be calling to me. I find it very appealing, Josh."

She glanced at him briefly when she said that, her cheeks flushed, before quickly turning away to look around the ranch again.

Mary Connealy writes romantic comedies about cowboys. She's the author of the BROTHERS IN ARMS, BRIDES OF HOPE MOUNTAIN, HIGH SIERRA SWEETHEARTS, KINCAID BRIDES, TROUBLE IN TEXAS, WILD AT HEART, and CIMARRON LEGACY series, as well as several other acclaimed series. Mary has been nominated for a Christy Award, was a finalist for a RITA Award, and is a two-time winner of the Carol Award. She lives in eastern Nebraska with her very own romantic cowboy hero. They have four grown daughters—Joslyn, married to Matt; Wendy; Shelly, married to Aaron; and Katy, married to Max—and seven precious grandchildren. Learn more about Mary and her books at

MaryConnealy.com
facebook.com/maryconnealy
petticoatsandpistols.com

Sign Up for Mary's Newsletter

Keep up to date with Mary's latest news on book releases and events by signing up for her email list at the link below.

MaryConnealy.com

FOLLOW MARY ON SOCIAL MEDIA

Mary Connealy   @MaryConnealy   @MaryConnealy

More from Mary Connealy

Beth Rutledge and her mother's one chance to escape Beth's tyrannical father is a wagon train heading west. Wagon train scout Jake Holt senses the secretive Beth is running from something and finds a new hope for his future in protecting her. Can they risk trusting each other with their lives—and their hearts—with danger threatening their every step?

Chasing the Horizon
A WESTERN LIGHT #1

After living in hiding for six months, Kat Wadsworth and Sebastian Jones are desperate to start a new life in the west—and marrying each other may be the only way to freedom. But will the dangers from their pasts tear apart their hopes for a better future and a chance at love?

Toward the Dawn
A WESTERN LIGHT #2

To escape her controlling husband and the threat of an asylum, Ginny Rutledge embarks on a perilous journey to prove her sanity with the help of her friends. Amidst confronting dangers, Maeve and Dakota grapple with their pasts as they navigate a dangerous mission, and Dakota fights for the woman who has captured his heart.

Into the Sunset
A WESTERN LIGHT #3

BETHANYHOUSE